SPACEWORLDS

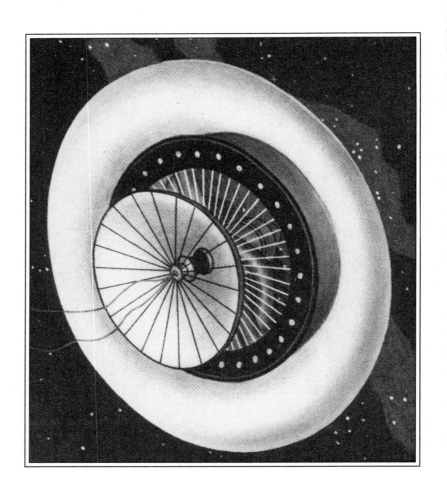

SPACEWORLDS

Stories of Life in the Void

edited by

MIKE ASHLEY

This collection first published in 2021 by
The British Library
96 Euston Road
London NW1 2DB

Cataloguing in Publication Data
A catalogue record for this publication is available from the British Library

ISBN 978 0 7123 5309 0
e-ISBN 978 0 7123 6718 9

The frontispiece illustration and the illustration on p316 are two 1929 technical drawings of an imagined space station by Herman Potočnic, who wrote as Hermann Noordung. The frontispiece shows the *Wohnrad*, or habitat wheel, whilst the other illustration shows the accompanying observatory and the machine room, with an 'umbilical' connecting the three components.

Cover image: 'Pittsburgh at L2', or 'Mining an Asteroid' by Chesley Bonestell, 1976. Cover design by Jason Anscomb.

Text design and typesetting by Tetragon, London
Printed in England by TJ Books Limited, Padstow, Cornwall, UK

CONTENTS

INTRODUCTION

Imagine having to live in a space environment, on board a space habitat, such as a space station, a spaceship or a generation starship.

The Apollo 11 mission which saw the first manned lunar landing took four days to reach the moon, a period of time I'm sure we could all cope with, depending upon our companions. The longest time any individual has spent in space was 438 days, endured by Valeri Polyakov on the Mir space station from January 1994 to March 1995. It is anticipated that the first manned journey to Mars will take at least that amount of time for the round trip. If we want to go beyond Mars, the journeys will take years and, if we want to visit another star system, we're talking lifetimes.

Space exploration is going to take its toll on both our physical and mental health and science-fiction writers have explored this problem for decades. This anthology brings together nine stories written during the latter part of the classic period of science fiction, from 1940 to 1967. They consider the problems of people working together in space, or being isolated on a wrecked ship or lost in space, or trying to cope with being launched to another star system knowing it will only be your children or grandchildren who make it. Two authors consider different types of spaceships, one being a light-ship colloquially known as a "sunjammer", and one being a brain-ship, under the control of a human being integrated into the ship itself.

These are just a few examples of how writers have considered the problems we might encounter when venturing into space. There are many more, and to provide a more complete picture I shall look further at how space habitats developed in classic science fiction. By all means jump to the stories themselves, if you wish, and I'll wait patiently here until you return—whether that's hours, months, years or generations.

Safe journey…

LIVING IN SPACE

Early writers gave little thought to what it would be like travelling in space, even though it was demonstrated as far back as 1646, by Blaise Pascal, that there was no atmosphere beyond the Earth. At least in "Hans Phaall" (1835), Edgar Allan Poe took notice and provided his adventurer with a "condensing apparatus" to ensure a breathable atmosphere in his lunar balloon trip but, aside from food, there were few other creature comforts. Jules Verne, in *Autour de la Lune* (serial 1869; usually translated as "Around the Moon"), ensured his capsule was airtight and comfortable with "thickly padded walls" and even a circular divan, something the *Apollo* astronauts would have welcomed.

Yet, the idea of creating a real space habitat came surprisingly early, even if I discount the avian constructed city of Cloud-cuckoo-land or *Nephelokokkygia*, built in the sky in Aristophanes's play *The Birds*, first performed in 414 BC. Whilst Verne's serial was running in the French weekly *Journal de Débates*, Edward Everett Hale's short novel, *The Brick Moon* appeared in *The Atlantic Monthly*. Hale was a clergyman and historian and had been something of a child prodigy. The depth of his scientific knowledge is evident from the details he provides about the Brick Moon. The idea was to launch an artificial satellite that will stay in synchronous orbit and serve as a navigational aid. It was to be 200 feet in diameter and built of bricks because all known metals at that time would melt or distort under the pressure of the launch. The satellite was coated with a material that would melt during the launch and plug any gaps in the brickwork thus making it airtight. A series of internal spheres, braces and arches helped strengthen and stabilize it. When it was launched it was discovered that thirty-seven men and women were still inside and in a short sequel, "Life in the Brick Moon" (1870), Hale describes how the inhabitants managed to grow food and survive, using the sleeping quarters built by the original workmen. Unfortunately, the two stories make tedious reading today because of the wealth of technological and contemporary detail, but for its day the work was extraordinarily advanced.

Towards the end of the nineteenth century there was a growth in interplanetary fiction, much of which is discussed in my introductions to the anthologies *Moonrise* and *Lost Mars*, but only gradually did authors give thought to how their spaceship should be designed to protect and support them on their journey, especially the longer journey to Mars. One example of particular interest was *Across the Zodiac* (1880) by the historian and journalist Percy Greg. His spaceship is powered by "apergy", a form of antigravity, and his adventurer anticipates his journey to Mars will take at least forty days and possibly longer. Allowing for his time on Mars and the return journey, the narrator ensures the spacecraft is suitably provisioned. Greg goes into considerable detail about the construction of the craft and the journey. The main compartment was carpeted with alternate layers of cork and cloth and furnished with a couch, table, bookshelves and other items. Then Greg adds, surprisingly:

I made a garden with soil three feet deep and five feet in width, divided into two parts so as to permit access to the windows. I filled each garden closely with shrubs and flowering plants of the greatest possible variety, partly to absorb animal waste, partly in the hope of naturalizing them elsewhere. Covering both with wire netting extending from the roof to the floor, I filled the cages thus formed with a variety of birds.

Greg was the first, to my knowledge, to consider how to install a toilet in a spaceship! Greg's work was an influence on H. G. Wells whose space-sphere in *The First Men in the Moon* (1901) is also powered by antigravity—*cavorite*, but even Wells sidestepped the matter of a toilet, simply noting:

> …we had to discuss and decide what provisions we were to take—compressed foods, concentrated essences, steel cylinders containing reserve oxygen, an arrangement for removing carbonic acid and waste from the air and restoring oxygen by means of sodium peroxide, water condensers, and so forth.

No one in Britain seemed to be giving much thought to creating permanent space habitats or even developing spacecraft. The German writer Kurd Lasswitz has Martians visit Earth in *Auf Zwei Planeten* (1897; usually known as *On Two Planets*), which has yet to be fully translated into English. The Martians establish two space stations above the Earth's North and South Poles from which they shuttle to and from Earth. Two explorers at the North Pole encounter the Martians and travel to the space station. We don't learn much about the living facilities on the station, though it is full of large halls and communal areas, but we do know that the station itself was in the form of a giant spoked wheel, rotating on its axis to create artificial gravity. This became the iconic image for generations including in the film *2001: A Space Odyssey*.

At the same time as Lasswitz was writing, the Russian scientist Konstantin Tsiolkovsky, inspired by reading Jules Verne, was exploring the precise technical requirements to explore space, his notes appearing in both detailed articles and fanciful stories. It was Tsiolkovsky who foresaw the multi-stage rocket as the most effective way of leaving the Earth's gravity, and he also foresaw the construction of orbiting satellites. In *Grezy o Zemle i nebe* ("Dreams of Earth and Sky") (1895) he places an artificial satellite in orbit 300 kilometres from the Earth's surface. When the Russian space station Mir was launched in 1986, its orbit was 358 kilometres. In *Vne Zemli* ("Outside the Earth"), which he began writing in 1895 with only part publication in 1916 and a full appearance in 1920, Tsiolkovsky describes the construction of a spacecraft by a team of international scientists, its launch into space and the construction of a space station. His description of the latter, with its lack of gravity and the cosmonauts "flying" from one compartment to another or strapped in chairs, is not far removed from the pictures we see from the International Space Station.

The works of both Lasswitz and Tsiolkovsky were immensely influential in continental Europe, but little known in Britain. German scientists used both works as a basis for exploring rocketry and the manned exploration of space. Hermann Oberth, for one, was working on practical experiments with rockets as early as 1917, and it was he with Wernher von Braun, who developed the V1 and V2 rockets in the Second World War. Oberth's work inspired fellow scientists and with the initiative taken by Max Valier and Willy Ley the German Rocket Society was formed in June 1927. The American Interplanetary Society came into being in April 1930, and the British Interplanetary Society in January 1933.

American writers were becoming more aware of German research and experimentation because of material reprinted by

Hugo Gernsback in his science-fiction magazines. One such was "The Problems of Space Flying" by a young Austrian army officer Herman Potočnic writing as Hermann Noordung. Published in Germany at the end of 1928 it was translated by Francis Currier and serialized in *Science Wonder Stories* from July to September 1929. Barely had the last part appeared in print than Potočnic died of pneumonia aged only 36. He probably never saw the American printing, and may not even have known of it, but the August 1929 issue carried a full colour painting of his proposed "Space House" as it was called. This is almost certainly the first colour portrayal of a space station (see frontispiece).

Currier also translated two novels by the German author Otto Willi Gail of which *Der Stein vom Mond* (1925) ran in *Science Wonder Quarterly* as "The Stone from the Moon" (1930) with a detailed description of the satellite *Astropol*. This had been constructed like an Earth-Moon system with a large and small sphere connected sixteen hundred metres apart. Revolving around each other creates artificial gravity. The primary sphere is coated with a giant reflecting mirror which absorbs solar energy which can be used to warm parts of the Earth as necessary or as a weapon—the original Death Star!

Gernsback was so taken with the technical detail that in commenting on the story he said "…there is no reason why, with the funds available, it could not be built within the next decade." Not one of his most accurate predictions, but a clear sign of what could be achieved.

It was through Noordung, Gail and other works translated from the German that most American readers became aware of developments in concepts of space travel and which encouraged more speculation in the sf magazines. David Lasser, Gernsback's editor and one of the founders of the American Rocket Society, compiled what was the first popular book on space travel in English, *The Conquest of Space* (1931).

Space stations now began to feature regularly in American science fiction. Murray Leinster's "The Power Planet" (1931) has a satellite orbiting the Sun from which it draws power to supply electricity to Earth. It operates for all nations and is unarmed, so that when a war erupts on Earth, the satellite is vulnerable to attack. Likewise, in Manly Wade Wellman's "Space Station No. 1" (1936), this refuelling station in orbit near the asteroid belt is attacked by pirates but is saved by the ingenuity of a Martian.

Starting with "QRM—Interplanetary" (1942) George O. Smith began a series of stories collected as *Venus Equilateral* (1947), each of which posed a new problem that might arise on the vast eponymous relay station which orbits the Sun in the same plane of Venus. The station is three miles long and a mile wide. Housing nearly three thousand employees, it operates much like a city. Arthur C. Clarke, who read these stories as they appeared during the 1940s, later admitted that they may have played a part in his own thoughts for his essay "Extra-Terrestrial Relays" (1945) which suggested the geostationary communication satellite.

In "Asylum Satellite" (1951), Fletcher Pratt showed how satellites could be used as weapons of mass destruction but all the time the Soviet Union and the United States had one each there was a political stalemate. Jack Vance, whose story in this anthology deals with another form of space transport, saw artificial satellites as pleasure worlds in "Abercrombie Station" (1952) where the weightlessness in space creates different ideals of beauty. In 1957 James White began his Sector General series featuring what was the biggest space station envisaged at that time serving as a hospital for all alien species. One of those stories is reprinted here.

Just days before that first Sector General story appeared the Russians launched the first Sputnik satellite into space on 4 October 1957, and the Space Age truly began. It was not long before science fiction morphed into science fact—at least as far as satellites and space stations.

In order to travel to the stars, science-fiction writers tried all manner of gimmicks, notably faster-than-light ships or space-warps and worm-holes, but to follow the laws of physics it was known that it was impossible to travel faster than the speed of light, roughly 300,000 kilometres per second. The fastest space probe yet is NASA's Parker Solar Probe which has reached speeds of over 466,000 kilometres per hour or 130 kilometres per second. At that rate the journey to the nearest star, Proxima Centauri, which is 4.25 light years away would take over 9,800 years or about four hundred generations. Even if it were possible to travel at one-tenth the speed of light it would take over 42 years, meaning anyone leaving the Earth in the prime of life would be old upon arrival.

One proposal to increase speed was to use the power of the Sun—the solar wind. Tsiolkovsky had considered this in *Extension of Man into Outer Space*, written in 1921, where he remarked that we may be able to "harness the pressure of sunlight to attain cosmic velocities". The idea was further considered by J. D. Bernal in *The World, the Flesh and the Devil* (1929).

The idea was to build an enormous but extremely light sail which, once unfurled, would react to the photons emitted by the Sun. The velocity of the craft would depend upon the size of the sail. The solar wind itself accelerates as it leaves the Sun and can reach up to 750 kilometres per second. Even if the light-ship reached 500km/second, which is 0.16% the speed of light, the voyage to Proxima Centauri would still take around 2,600 years.

Nevertheless, the solar sail was taken up by various writers including Cordwainer Smith in "The Lady Who Sailed the Soul" (1960) and Jack Vance in "Gateway to Strangeness" (1962) reprinted here with the revised title "Sail 25". By a bizarre coincidence both Arthur C. Clarke and Poul Anderson wrote stories about light-ships and entitled them "Sunjammer" and both stories appeared within a month of each other, in March and April 1964, though Clarke's is better known now as "The Wind from the Sun".

The first actual solar sail to be launched was the Japanese *Ikaros* in May 2010 and continues to orbit the Sun. Other plans for such ships have been limited and even the latest, called *LightSail 2*, launched by the Planetary Society in June 2019, has served only as a moderate experiment.

Perhaps some time in the next century or two humans will take up the challenge and create a ship that will take families out to explore the exoplanets that are being discovered around distant stars. They will travel in what has been called a generation ship, an idea that has fascinated writers because it allows them to explore the conflicts of an enclosed society. The American rocket scientist Robert H. Goddard had considered this possibility in an early paper he wrote in 1918, "The Last Migration", though here he was talking about humans leaving the Earth when the Sun is dying. Even earlier, the British mechanical engineer John Munro had suggested the idea in *A Trip to Venus* in 1897 almost as a throwaway point during a discussion at the start of the book.

> "...with a vessel large enough to contain the necessaries of life, a select party of ladies and gentlemen might start for the Milky Way, and if all went right, their descendants would arrive there in the course of a few million years."

"Rather a long journey, I'm afraid."

"What would you have? A million years quotha! nay,
not so much. It depends on the speed and the direction
taken. If they were able to cover, say, the distance from
Liverpool to New York in a tenth of a second, they would
get to Alpha in the constellation Centaur, perhaps the
nearest of the fixed stars, in twenty or thirty years—a mere
bagatelle. But why should we stop there?" went on Gazen.
"Why should we not build large vessels for the navigation of
the ether—artificial planets in fact—and go cruising about
in space, from universe to universe, on a celestial Cook's
excursion—"

Murray Leinster considered this idea in his story "Proxima
Centauri" (1935). A giant space sphere, *Adastra*, almost a mile in
diameter, has taken seven years to reach Earth's nearest star and
in that time unrest has already broken out amongst the occupants
and crew of several hundred. The ship is a self-sufficient biosphere
with everything recycled and four-hundred acres of land for plants
and vegetables. At one point a member of the crew notes that
the ship could continue ad infinitum, sustaining generation after
generation.

Laurence Manning followed it to the extreme. "The Living
Galaxy" (1934) is set millions of years in the future when astronomers realize that our galaxy, now fully inhabited by humans, is
being threatened by some menace from another galaxy. Hollowing
out a small planet, the chief scientist and a select band undertake
a voyage to this other galaxy which may take a million years.
However, in this far future, immortality has been perfected, meaning the crew will all survive the journey, so whilst it might be a
voyage on a galactic scale, it's not a generation ship!

There was another precursor to the generation starship concept, "The Strange Flight of Richard Clayton" (1939) by Robert
Bloch. Clayton is sealed in his spaceship prepared for a voyage to
Mars which he believes will take ten years. Unfortunately, when
the door is sealed the instrument panel is shattered and Clayton
has no idea of the passage of time or of where he is in space. At
the end, when Clayton is released after only a week, he is an old
man. J. G. Ballard developed that idea in "Thirteen to Centaurus"
(1962) where a crew believe they are on a starship heading to Alpha
Centauri with no idea that really they are part of a government
experiment to see how people will survive on long journeys.

The first writer to take the plunge and produce a full-blown
generation starship story was Don Wilcox in "The Voyage That
Lasted 600 Years" (1940), which is reprinted here. Wilcox explores
all the ideas that typify the starship adventure—suspended animation, monitoring, guardianship, unrest and disbelief over the
years and a final, perhaps inevitable but nevertheless unexpected
surprise ending.

There have been many subsequent starship stories, two of
which are included here, "Survival Ship" by Judith Merril from
1951 and "Lungfish" by John Brunner from 1957, each of which
introduces further surprises. Amongst other works perhaps the best
known, and written soon after Wilcox's, was Robert A. Heinlein's
"Universe" and its sequel "Common Sense" (both 1941), later com-
bined as the novel *Orphans of the Sky* (1963). Heinlein develops the
idea of an onboard mutiny to the point where the survivors have
no idea that they are on a ship or of its purpose. At the start of the
story those on Earth suspect the project failed as nothing more
was heard from the ship, but the story explains what became of
the expedition. Brian W. Aldiss would later take Heinlein's basic
idea and rework it with a twist ending in *Non-Stop* (1958), whilst

in "Spacebred Generations" (1953) Clifford D. Simak revealed that those who planned the multi-generation journey would take the "great forgetting" into account.

Other novels on this theme worth tracking down from the classic period of sf are *The Space-Born* (1956) by E. C. Tubb, *200 Years to Christmas* (1961) by J. T. McIntosh, *Rogue Ship* (1965) by A. E. van Vogt, *The Watch Below* (1966) by James White and *Captive Universe* (1969) by Harry Harrison.

It is worth mentioning one further novel which deals with one of the biggest space habitats ever conceived, *Ringworld* (1970) by Larry Niven. The Ringworld is a vast space station in the form of a ring that revolves about its star. The construct itself has a width of about a 1.6 million kilometres, a circumference of 940 million kilometres and the entire ring is 300 million kilometres across. Niven later estimated that the Ringworld had an area three million times that of the Earth. There are no constructs quite that size in this anthology, but there are many that when considered as a whole pose questions about our future in space.

The idea that an individual may be born, raised and die on an extra-terrestrial man-made space habitat, whether a space station or generation ship is mind-blowing, especially when considering that the individual may have no idea that they are on a ship. This is what makes the idea of spaceworlds so fascinating and which this anthology explores.

MIKE ASHLEY

UMBRELLA IN THE SKY

E. C. Tubb

For our first story we do not go far from Earth but rather than visit a space station, which seems barely science fiction anymore, we're heading for a space shield. How do we protect the Earth if the Sun threatens to go nova? And what would life be like amongst the construction gangs building a protective shield. It's the kind of environment that delighted E. C. Tubb who enjoyed depicting the harshness and unpredictability of space.

Edwin Charles Tubb (1919–2010) was one of Britain's most prolific writers and one of the most talented. Although he could write formulaic work if necessary, he could turn his hand to inventiveness and originality when needed and he was at his best when pitting men against insurmountable problems. He is probably best remembered for his 32-volume series about Earl Dumarest's search to find his home planet, Earth, that began with The Winds of Gath *in 1967, but his work goes back to 1951 with his first novel* Saturn Patrol *under the pseudonym King Lang. Amongst his many books is the generation starship novel* The Space-Born *(1956).*

WHEN IT GOT TO THE POINT WHERE THEY WERE MAKING book on who went next they sent for me. General Thorne, Officer in Charge of Shield Construction, nodded from behind an acre of desk, flipped a package of cigarettes in my general direction, waited until I had lit up and made myself comfortable.

"Mike Levine," he said. "How would you like to save the world?"

"Thinking of retiring, General?"

He didn't like that and I couldn't blame him. He wasn't an old man, nearer to forty than fifty, but he'd aged twenty years since I'd seen him last and something other than time had dug those lines in his cheeks. The responsibility, perhaps, of three billion lives?

"I'm serious, Levine." His hand shook a little as he flipped ash into a dispenser. "The Shield's in trouble. You can help."

"I pay my taxes and vote the party ticket. What more can I do?"

"You can co-operate."

I didn't like that word. Too many policemen had flung it at me, too many politicians had used it as an excuse. In my book it meant do as you're told, or else. I was stubborn enough to accept the alternative. Thorne must have read my mind.

"Relax," he said. "No one's riding you. All I'm doing is asking a favour."

"Which means you can't do whatever it is you want to do any other way. Right?"

"Close enough." He looked at the butt in his hand, tossed it aside and immediately lit a fresh cigarette. For a general he was a mass of nerves. I gave him three months before cracking up, six at the outside. Sunburst must have been a lot closer than the newsfax had let on.

"I'll be straight with you, Levine," he said. "I'm in trouble and I need your help."

"Now wait a minute, General. I'm a Professional Quarry, not a Professional Assassin."

"I know what you are, what you've done and what you've been. I know all about you, Levine, how you live and all the rest of it. That isn't important."

"It is to me."

"Isn't the world important to you?"

Put like that what could I say?

I didn't need the training but I got it anyway. Long hours on the seabed learning how not to fall. Longer hours suspended in the water learning how to control an apparently weightless body. Days cooped up in space suits and weeks of assorted maintenance, survival drill, all the rest of it. I'd been through it all before and the hardest part was to keep that fact a secret. Thorne wanted me to appear as a new boy and what Thorne wanted I was willing to do.

Don't ask me why. He'd been President of the Court Martial which had kicked me out of the Service and I had no reason to love him. Still, in a way, he'd done me a favour at that. Luna Station was no place for any man with a yen for living and, looking back, I suppose I shouldn't have done what I did. Taking a swing at a superior officer could have got me ten years, no matter what the provocation, so, in a way, he'd been on my side. Anyway, all that was five years in the past. Now was the time to safeguard the future. There were a dozen of us in the class and all but two made the grade. We shipped out as a team, stopped off at Luna Station and had five hours to see the sights. I pleaded sick and called at the dispensary. The medic was expecting me. He checked his file and led me to an inner room. Thorne was waiting.

"Any regrets, Levine?"

"You kidding?"

He didn't comment and I was grateful. A Professional Quarry lives dangerously but he lives well and, with my reputation for eluding the Hunters I'd been able to demand high fees. I wondered if, in a way, I wasn't putting myself out of work. Sunburst hysteria would last only until the Shield was completed. Now, if ever, was the time for a man to cash in.

Certainly it was time for more information. Thorne gave it to me, reluctantly, seemingly afraid of his own shadow. I wondered when he'd last had a good night's rest.

"You've passed the training," he said. "You're on your way. If you wanted to sell out you can't do it."

"If you can't trust me maybe we'd better call the whole thing off."

"I've got out of the habit of trusting anyone." His voice was thick, heavy, suspicious. I began to get an inkling of what was wrong with him. Paranoia. He was beginning to believe that everyone was against him as well as the universe. I'd seen Quarrys get like that. When they did they didn't last long.

"Take it easy." I lit a cigarette in defiance of the warning notice. "Calm down a little. Blowing your top won't help."

"Nothing will help but the Shield. Nothing!"

His hands began to tremble and he rose and paced the floor. I didn't like to see the expression on his face. It reminded me too much of the days immediately following the Sunburst announcement. Society had never been quite the same since.

"Snap out of it." I blew a smoke ring towards the notice. "We're all in this together, remember. If one goes we all go. Now, how about getting on with the briefing?"

"All right." He slumped in a chair and wiped the sweat from his face with a handkerchief. He caught the lighted cigarette I tossed towards him and gave himself a lungful of smoke. After a little while even his hands stopped their shaking.

"From here on you'll be on your own," he said. "The rest of your class will be held here for further training. There's no point in sending them to the Shield until we can clear up what's wrong out there."

"What is wrong?"

"We're falling behind on construction." He said it as if he were announcing the end of the world. In a sense he was. I felt my heart begin to accelerate.

"How far?"

"Too far. We're way behind schedule and falling back all the time. Unless something is done we aren't going to make it." He took a deep breath. "Now you know why I can't trust anyone."

It was an understatement. Thorne had the kind of knowledge which no man should ever be burdened with. I could understand the way he felt. One word, one hint to the newsfax agencies and the world would go crazy. Things were wild enough now when everyone believed that there was nothing to worry about; tell them the truth and the following hysteria would make the Sunburst panic a kiddies' tea party.

And the agencies wouldn't be censored, not if they guessed. After all, the end of the world wasn't everyday news.

In the shuttle heading for the Shield I had plenty of time to go over the rest of Thorne's briefing. Boiled down it was simple.

The Shield was behind schedule. Find out why and fix it. Just like that.

Sitting alone in the shuttle, the drive humming behind me, supplies stacked all about me, the automatic pilot clicking as it rode the beam, I should have felt proud. It was a big responsibility Thorne had given me, too big. So big that I wasn't fooled for a minute. Thorne had sent for me because he was desperate and for no other reason. And, if I had entertained any thoughts that I was something special, the view beyond the vision plates would have reduced me to size.

A man can't feel big in space. The stars are too overwhelming, the distances between them too vast, the entire universe so damn big that conceit hasn't a chance of survival. I'd forgotten that back on Earth. I'd forgotten a lot of things in the rush and frenzy of civilization. The training, the trip to Luna and the sight and touch of familiar things had worked their magic. Maybe I was a fool to throw up a soft life, soft between working hours, that is, for what I was doing. But I didn't regret it.

The Shield began to grow in the vision screens. A mass of cable, foil, squat vessels, cylinders with spouting nozzles, strange fabrications turning in the void and, above all, the Shield itself.

You couldn't miss the Shield. Edge-on to the sun it was a gigantic snowflake of shining metal drifting in nothingness. Ten thousand miles in diameter it would be, when finished, the largest man-made construction history had ever recorded. And, if it didn't get finished in time, there would be no more history.

Seven years ago a probe ship had exploded in a manner which startled the astronomers and, when they had found the cause, the world had gone a little insane. Sunburst hysteria we called it now and the effects were still with us. The Hunts, the Addicts, the Lobojags, the Sensors, all the wild, vicious, selfish amusements the threat of imminent death had raked from the bottom and floated on the surface of society. For the probe ship had met a meteor shower of seetee which was heading directly towards the sun.

It would be, so they told us, like tossing a can of petrol on a coal fire. When the anti-matter hit there would be eruptions not seen since the birth of the world. There would be heat, colossal heat and Earth would be seared to ash. Unless that heat could be baffled. Unless we could duck behind something until it was over. And so the Shield.

And, according to Thorne, the Shield wouldn't be finished in time.

He didn't know what was wrong, if he had he would have fixed it. It wasn't sabotage and it wasn't supply. No one in their right mind would deliberately wreck the Shield and the entire world was behind the flow of supplies. It reduced itself to the human element. The construction workers weren't working hard enough. The men were dying too fast.

So fast that they even made a book on who was to go next.

Moody was waiting for me when the shuttle finally connected with the Beehive. An aide led me to his office, routine procedure for all new arrivals, and I sat patiently while he tested me and charted my psycho-stability and emotional index. The psychologist, like Thorne, was a man old before his time. A little, stooped runt of a man who looked as if he wanted to cry.

"Did Thorne tell you about me?"

"Yes."

"How? I thought all this cloak and dagger stuff was secret?"

"I've a private scrambled line," he explained. "Direct communication." He anticipated my next question. "Thorne trusts me. He has to."

I could have argued that but there was no point. Moody was the man on the job, he should be able to tell me what I wanted to know. He should also have been able to tell Thorne the same thing. He was a good psychologist.

"Each man to his trade," he said quietly. "I can tell you the facts as I see them."

"Am I arguing?"

"No, but you have your doubts about me. Forget them. I've been with this thing since the beginning. Maybe that's why I feel so helpless. If there's something wrong out here then I'm a part of it." He lit a cigarette without offering me one.

"Why does Thorne have to trust you?"

"Because there is no one else. Because I've known him almost all my life. Because everyone needs some other person. Take your choice."

He was aggressive and I could guess the reason. Thorne meant a lot to him and now Thorne had decided to lean on someone else. Or perhaps it wasn't that. Perhaps it was just nerves too highly strung for too long a period. I lit a cigarette and relaxed and tried to forget the passing of time. Something which Moody, obviously, couldn't do.

"All right," I said. "Tell me the facts."

"We're behind in construction."

"I know that. Why?"

"Because the men aren't working hard enough." He lifted a hand as if to stop my breaking in. "And getting more workers won't cure it. We don't want more workers—we want men who will work. Can you appreciate the difference?"

I could. On any construction job there is a limit to the amount of men who are able to work effectively. More men reduce progress, not increase it. It boiled down to a matter of logistics and on the Shield, logistics were quite a problem.

Men had to be fed, housed, entertained. The construction programme had to be integrated in terms of air-capacity, time in suits, time for relaxation, time for sleep, for sickness, for transportation. It took, I knew, an average of four hours for each hour's actual work. A man can only stand so much cooped up in a suit alone in the void.

More men, if they didn't want to work, couldn't cure the problem. A thousand shirkers can't equal the output of a hundred dedicated men. Thorne knew that as well as I did.

"You must have some ideas of your own," I said. "It would help if I knew them."

"Rule out sabotage," he said. "Rule out supply and sickness, physical sickness, that is. Rule out union trouble, strikes, dissatisfaction at forced labour. Rule out engineering inadequacy and rule out environmental hazards."

"Can we?"

"Can we what?"

"Rule out environmental hazards. From what I hear plenty of men are dying on the job."

"Too many." He shook his head. "A damn sight too many. That's the frightening thing about it. There's no reason why they should die at all."

He was wrong, of course, but there was no point in telling him so. Men do not die without cause. Moody simply did not know the cause. I sat and listened to his explanations and justifications and negative findings and all it added to was a great big question mark. When I had sucked him dry I went and reported to administration.

An officer checked my file, looked at me as if I should be familiar to him, then studied the papers.

"From what these tell me," he said, "you're a top-man. Are you?"

"Can't you believe what you read?"

"Not always." He looked at me again. "Nor always what I see. For example, you look like a serviceman I once met on Luna Station five years ago. I'm wrong, naturally."

"You're wrong." He wasn't but I'd hoped his memory wasn't as good as mine. "But for your information I'm what the papers say. I can stand heights, can handle a suit and work in vacuum with tools. There's no point in my getting acclimatized. Just send me to wherever the big money is to be earned."

"That would be out on the perimeter." He frowned as he checked his mental files. "Hive nineteen's short of men. Get kitted and report to A lock for the shuttle."

Getting kitted meant drawing a suit, signing a mass of papers and collecting a wad of closely printed instructions. I donned the suit, went through the routine tests and headed for the lock. The shuttle was an open platform, powered by a weak reaction. I climbed aboard, the magnetic grapnels were released and the centrifugal force of the spinning Beehive flung us into nothingness.

It was an odd experience.

No matter what they tell you there's nothing nice about free fall. I was standing on a thin metal platform, gripping a thin metal rail while all about me was just a great emptiness. To one side the sun flamed like a furnace and I knew, I just knew, I was falling directly towards it.

Quite a lot of men broke at that point. It was the biggest factor in determining the fitness of workers on the Shield. Inside, yes, they had no trouble; the Beehive, the huge administration depot, together with all the smaller, living Hives, had the artificial gravity of centrifugal force. But outside, where it counted, it was just a man alone with his terror.

The officer had known, of course, otherwise he would never have sent a greenhorn out without due indoctrination. I wondered what other surprises were in store for me. I didn't have to wait long.

The shuttle clicked on to Hive 19, a lock gaped open in the hub and I climbed inside. A man met me beyond the lock. He wore a suit, sealed but for the open faceplate, and he looked sick.

"New arrival?"

"That's right." I began to unseal my suit. He looked horrified.

"Don't do that! Keep it on and just leave the face plate open."

"Why?"

"If anything should happen you can slam it shut and be safe."

It made sense but a suit isn't noted for comfort. True, there was always the chance that a meteor would puncture the walls but a man crossing a street stands a greater risk of being run over. I stepped out of the suit, hung it on a numbered peg close to the airlock and smiled at my reception committee.

He led me to the Commander of Hive 19.

Recognition was mutual. Major Stanton, he'd been a captain then, leaned back and thoughtfully touched the spot where, five years earlier, I'd landed my fist.

"Levine! Well, well! This is a pleasure."

I didn't like Stanton and he didn't like me and five years had made no difference. The officer back in the Beehive must have had a peculiar sense of humour.

"Mike Levine reporting for duty, sir." My voice was neutral. "May I congratulate the Major on his promotion and suggest that we both forget the past?"

His voice matched my own. "Why not?" Then he got down to business. Hive 19, he told me, was a happy hive. The men had a good team spirit and he wanted to keep it that way. The work was hard, arduous and sometimes dangerous, but it had to be done. It was his job to see that it was done. "You understand me, Levine?"

"I'm sure I do."

"You call me 'sir'," he said gently. "The courtesy of rank, you know. I'm sure that you won't forget it." He pressed a button on his desk. "Glendale will show you around."

Glendale was the reception committee. He led me to a cell which I would share with five others, showed me the mess hall and other essentials then pushed open the door of the recreation room. A dozen men stopped playing poker as we entered. A big, squat gorilla of a man threw down his hand and rose to his feet.

"New guy?"

"Fresh in," said Glendale. Then, to me: "Jake Wilner. Your shift boss."

I nodded and looked around the room. The poker players seemed to have forgotten their cards. They were looking at me with a kind of hungry expectation. Wilner stepped forward.

"Your name?"

I told him.

"Welcome to shift two," he said, and held out his hand. I took it, felt his grip suddenly clamp down and knew what all the expectation was about. I was being tested, hazed, given the treatment. What Wilner had in mind I didn't know; what happened was that he found himself on the floor nursing an arm which I could have broken as easily as not. He swore, climbed to his feet and braced himself for a rush.

"I shouldn't," I said. "The next time I might not be so gentle."

For a moment it hung in the balance then one of the watching men let out a yell.

"Ten to one he tops you, Jake. Is it a bet?"

The tension snapped like a rubber band. Wilner scowled, then grinned and held out his hand. Gingerly I took it, this time there were no tricks.

"Just having fun," he said by way of apology. "Where did you learn judo?"

"Protecting my wallet from predatory females." I nodded towards the others. "Do I get introduced?"

"Why not?" He yelled at the others. "Hey, you guys, this is Mike Levine. Mike, meet Sam Galway, Joe Fisher, Bob Shaw, Fred Evans…" We went the rounds. Aside from their names there was little to choose between any of them, just the usual bunch of men to be found anywhere on a construction project. We halted by a studious looking man, pale-faced and with calculating eyes. "Sid Royston," said Wilner. "If you want a bet he's the man."

"Bet?"

"Sure he runs the book." He spoke to Sid. "Who's the favourite?"

"Glesgier. Shift three. A mill will get you even money he goes next. Want on?"

"I'll think about it." Wilner hesitated. "What odds do I carry?"

"Twenties."

Wilner drew a deep breath and a shadow seemed to lift from his shoulders. He caught me by the arm and tried to steer me towards the poker players. I resisted.

"I'm new here," I said to the bookie. "Can I bet on credit?"

"Uh, uh."

"Okay. Look, what odds do I carry?"

"None as yet." His eyes probed mine. "You're a long shot, a rank outsider. Why?"

"Just testing my life expectancy." I turned to Wilner. "Look, Jake, I'm safe not to go next. How about lending me a mill to payday?"

He hesitated, then dug a crumpled note from a heap in his pocket. I waved it aside.

"Give it to Sid. On the favourite, right?"

"It's a bet."

The next morning, before we went out to work, he paid me off. It was the easiest thousand I'd ever made in my life. I could have done without it.

The work, as Stanton had said, was hard, arduous and, as I could see, easily dangerous. The Shield was a web of cables covered with foil, the whole thing a flimsy, delicate looking structure which could never have resisted the smallest of planetary forces. Our job was to stretch the cables and spread the foil.

I rode a low-powered reaction engine, a titanic drum of fine cable unreeling behind me, aiming my mount towards a winking flare of light which was connection-point. I arrived, slowed my mount and braked the drum. A suited shape moved towards me and together we drew in the slack. An atomic torch flared, metal fused, parted, and another strand of the web had been completed. I studied my schedule and spider-like, laid another cable in the void.

I was alone and yet not alone. All around me I could see the winking spots of light from welders, signals, the helmet-lights of suited workers. All around and yet impossible distances away. The tiny figures of suited men seemed like ants against the tremendous expanse of the Shield. Some, like myself, rode hot-eyed engine spinning cable. Others unfolded wide sheets of foil like sparkling wings while men welded the thin sheets to the stretched cables. Still others controlled sprayers which cast molten metal against electromagnetic fields so that, from nothingness, a barrier grew.

And, always, impossible to ignore, the gigantic ball of the sun waiting to swallow my falling shape.

You couldn't help but look at the sun. Compared to it the Shield was nothing, a pitiful thing with which to save a world. Come Sunburst and tugs would swing it to face the solar furnace. Other tugs would strain to hold it in position against the fury of radiation which would beat against the flimsy metal. That radiation would have enough pressure to drive it like a sail before the wind. It would buckle and whip, strain and curve backwards in a gigantic convexity while, in the centre orifice, the tugs would fight against the pressure.

That was the reason for the cables, the bracing, the spiderweb design. The answer to those who claimed that a cloud of dust would answer as well, forgetting that Sunburst would last months and that, to do the job properly, a barrier had to be both mobile and quickly reducible.

There was no point in staving off heat-death in order to freeze.

I was glad when the shift was over. Three hours in a suit is enough for anyone and we were fully exposed to the sunlight most of the time. Back in the Hive I unsealed my suit, flung it towards its peg, then made for the showers. Wilner grabbed my arm.

"Not so fast," he growled. "You want to become first favourite?"

"I want a shower."

"Maybe, but first you check your suit. Check it good."

"I'll do it later."

"You'll do it now." He blocked my path. I could see that he meant it. Too tired to argue I checked my suit, found everything as it should be, hung it back on its peg. "Can I go now, teacher?"

He grunted at me and I went to the showers. A couple of men, I noticed, carried their suits with them, maybe they were so fond of them they liked to sleep in them, but I hated the sight of mine. I hated it still more when I had to queue for a shower and found the water tepid from overuse.

I learned. I learned the reason for the constant suit-check which Wilner insisted on each man of his shift making both before and after use. I learned of the dreadful fascination of the sun which seemed to draw a man towards its flaming brilliance. I learned to live like a cog in a machine. I discovered why the Shield was way behind schedule.

Way back in the time of the cold war unions got a power complex and struck for the least thing. After a time governments got tired of being held to continuous ransom and passed anti-strike legislation. The unions, after they found the new laws had teeth, fell back on a trick which the labourers must have used in the time of Cheops. They worked to the rules.

They didn't strike—but the results were as chaotic as if they had done. Each little regulation, every safety rule, every fiddling bit of routine procedure was adhered to with loving care. Production, transportation, industrial life as a whole slowed down to an uneasy stasis. And there was nothing anyone could do about it.

The unions won, of course, they had to. When a man can detain a train because, in his opinion, something seems wrong or a mechanic ground an airplane because some inspector hadn't signed his work sheet, or a driver refuse to take out his truck because his brakes aren't what he thinks they should be, management doesn't stand a chance. And working procedure on the Shield was loaded with safety regulations.

It wasn't deliberate, of course. The men weren't on a 'work to rule' strike or anything like that. It was that too many men had died and the rest didn't want to follow their example. So they were careful, ultra-careful, checking and double checking their equipment a dozen times a shift. They were more concerned about staying alive than building the Shield.

I faked sick and spoke to Moody about it. He heard me with mounting impatience.

"Really, Levine, you aren't telling me anything I am not aware of."

"So? Then why aren't you doing something about it?"

"I haven't been idle." He didn't meet my eyes. "The trouble is psychological, that goes without question."

"Agreed. And?"

"The difficulty is to find out just what is the trouble, an essential if we hope to cure it." He lit a cigarette. I waited, and, when he didn't offer me one, I lit one of my own. I had the impression he was uneasy, that he didn't want me around. "I told you all this the last time we met."

"You told me that you suspected it might be due to the General Adaption Syndrome," I said. "The men are spooky because they are living in an alien environment and can't fully adapt. Sure, they seem to, but way down inside tensions build up until something breaks. I think you're wrong."

"You are, of course, fully qualified to give an opinion?"

"I think I am. The men here are working, basically, for money. Out on the perimeter they earn a mill a day, five times what they could back home, and everything is found. With pay like that it doesn't take long to rack up a small fortune."

"You forget something," said Moody coldly. "They are also working to save the Earth."

"Maybe they are, but I wonder how many of them think of that? The money they think of all the time. It's human nature to want to stay alive long enough to spend it." I tossed aside my butt. "All that the men are suffering from is a simple anxiety neurosis."

"Ridiculous!"

"You think so?" I stared into his eyes. "Tell me, Moody, what odds do you carry?"

"Odds?" He looked blank. "What are you talking about?"

"You mean to say that you've never had a bet?" I shook my head. "You don't know what you're missing, it beats the ponies hollow. A little gruesome, perhaps, but it's a real man's sport—especially if you're the favourite."

He didn't seem to know what I was talking about and I had no time to waste. I caught the shuttle back to Hive 19. Wilner met me inside the airlock. I thought he looked odd. "Mike!" He grabbed my arm. "You okay?"

"Sure." I went to hang up my suit, wondering at his sudden concern. He stopped me putting it on the peg.

"Keep it with you," he urged. "Wear it all the time, sleep in it even."

"Like Glendale? Why?"

"No sense in taking chances."

I looked at him, knowing what he was going to say next.

"It's the book," he said. "You've jumped to odds on favourite. They're betting on you all over the Shield."

Tell a man he's going to die and you do something to him. You strike at the roots of his survival; just how hard depends on who you are and how much importance he places on what you say. A doctor wins all the time, a judge nearly as often, on the Shield the bookie was the voice of fate.

A man became a favourite because a lot of people had decided that he was the one due to go next. They were so sure of it that they placed big money on the fact. Human nature being what it is all those people wanted to win—they wanted me to die. It wasn't a pleasant feeling.

"Have you bet on me, Jake?"

"No, Mike."

"How come?"

He tried to joke about it. "Hell, the odds are way out. Me? I'm a sucker for the long shots." He punched my arm. "Anyway, there's no such thing as a sure bet."

Maybe there wasn't but he was about the only one who thought so. There was a silence as we entered the recreation room and a couple of men heading towards Sid Royston changed their minds and sat down instead. I crossed to the bookie.

"What odds on Moody, Sid?"

"Moody?"

"The chief head shrinker."

"Not listed." His voice, like his eyes, held no expression. "Stanton?"

"Not listed."

"Put me a mill on the second favourite." I threw him the note and moved away. Wilner joined me. Glendale, still wearing his suit, passed us on his way out. I'd seen the expression on his face. Jake cleared his throat.

"How about a game of poker, Mike?"

"Later." I pulled him to one side, kept my voice low. "Look, Jake, I want you to do something for me. Put ten mill each on Glendale and Royston. Can do?"

"Are you crazy?"

"Can you do it?"

"Sure, but why?" He seemed to think he knew the answer. "Don't let Glendale's habit of wearing his suit all the time fool you. He's a long shot. He works inside all the time. Royston too. Betting on either of them is throwing away money."

"It's my money." I pushed it into his hand. "Place the bets for me before next shift. Okay."

"Okay." He made as if to step towards Royston. I caught his arm.

"Not now, lunkhead. And don't let him know the money, comes from me." I laughed as if Jake had told me a risqué story then let him steer me towards a poker group. Sitting down I looked towards the bookie and caught his eyes on me before the two men who had sat down when I'd entered the room moved forward to place their bets. Another couple of men who wished me dead. I was learning what it was like to be popular in the wrong sort of way.

An hour of poker was enough. Maybe, because I didn't care one way or the other, I won hands down. No one was really sorry when I yawned, made as if I was tired and announced that I was ready for bed.

I didn't go straight to the cell. Instead I went to the airlock and collected my suit. Inside the cell I picked it inside and out, everything appeared as it should be. I was asleep when the other five men came in to hit the sack.

Wilner was worried when shift time came. He glowered at me through the open faceplate of his helmet.

"You're late, Mike. Suit checked?"

"I checked it."

"Maybe you'd better check it again?"

"I said I'd checked it. You place those bets?"

He nodded, glanced at the wall clock and passed out the work schedules. Together we passed through the lock into space. As usual I was on cable-laying detail, my equipment ready for immediate action. I wasted fifteen minutes checking it as far as possible, and then another ten until all the others had gone. Alone I headed towards the operations area.

For a man due to die I was in pretty good spirits but that could have been because, unlike the others, I knew how I was going. Not the exact manner of it, naturally, but the logic behind it. And, of course, I was confident that I wasn't going to die at all.

Some of that confidence evaporated as I drove my mount from the Hive. Death, in space, could come in so many ways. A puncture in the suit, a whipping cable, a smashed faceplate, a dozen ways all easily explained and expected. The only thing I was certain about was that it would come soon.

It came on my third run. Ahead of me the winking signal light showed my next connection-point and, as I grew closer, so did the old, familiar feeling inside of me grow stronger. I can't describe that feeling, no one can; it's something from the primitive, the instinct of warning which kept our ancestors alive. Having it had enabled me to become a Professional Quarry, men without it never became professionals; they rarely lasted beyond their first Hunt.

The light grew close and a suited figure became visible against the glare of the sun, painful despite the filters. I braked, braked again and slipped from the saddle as the mount came to a halt. The man glided forward, welding torch in hand, aimed, apparently by accident, in my general direction.

I kicked against the mount just in time.

The flame from the torch wasn't very big and not very long but it was hot enough to have stabbed through my suit like a hot needle through butter. If I hadn't kicked myself sideways that is just what would have happened. As it was we were drifting rapidly apart in opposite directions and no pretence between us.

The suits weren't fitted with general purpose radio, there was no point in encouraging a lot of men to fill the ether with a lot of idle chatter. Instead we had Hive-to-suit sets fitted with an emergency circuit for reverse transmission. I pressed the button on my belt, heard the hum of the carrier wave building then the peculiar snap as the set went dead. A gimmicked part, perhaps, one which looked genuine enough to pass examination but which couldn't stand the load.

My initial glide had carried me away from the cable-carrier and towards the sun. I looked towards the Shield, the edge was to one side of me, the side towards the sun a glare of brilliance. Against it I would be invisible, my helmet-light a glow-worm against a searchlight. Safety lay back from where I had come.

The suit carried the regulation reaction pistol, I used it to kill my momentum, praying that it hadn't been fixed like the radio. The Shield stopped moving away from me, the mount came closer. Twin points of flame advertised the whereabouts of my adversary. He was using the atomic torch as well as his pistol but it didn't give him much advantage. That torch had plenty of mass, it took all the reaction it produced to move itself.

Together we headed towards the cable-carrier. I reached it first.

There was no time to mount the saddle and get moving. No time to do anything but duck behind the cable spool and flatten myself against it, the tips of my gloved fingers hard against the metal. I felt the vibration as something heavy hit the other side, located the point of impact and jerked myself towards it.

The torch swung towards me but I was too close. The orifice hit my thigh, the flame missing the suit by a fraction, then I kicked at the torch and, at the same time, flung my arm around his helmet. For a moment we were together, staring at each other's filters, then I smashed my reaction pistol against the faceplate.

Glendale died in the suit he had loved so much to wear.

Thorne looked even older than I remembered but that could have been due to imagination or bad transmission. There was plenty of interference this close to the Shield and the scrambled synchronization could have been a little out of kilter. Moody leaned forward and adjusted the set but it made no difference. Thorne's features wavered as he stared from the screen.

"Well?"

"Mission accomplished," I said, and lit a cigarette. I heard Moody suck in his breath and moved back so that I could keep him visible in the corner of my eye. Thorne's voice rasped from the speaker.

"Stay in scanning focus, damn you!" Then: "You've licked it?"

"I think so. Better get some men out here right away. Service men, the kind you can trust."

"As bad as that, Mike?" It was the first time he had ever called me by my first name. I nodded, then grabbed at Moody as he lunged towards the screen.

"Don't listen to him," yelled the psychologist. "I tell you the man's insane! He came in here with some wild story and insisted that I contact you. I'm terrified of him. Terrified! He's..."

Moody was only a little man but it doesn't take much strength to ruin a set. I yanked him back from the screen, remembered not to hit him too hard, and let him fall gently to the floor. Thorne looked sick.

"Him too?"

"Him, Stanton, quite a few others. I don't know how many or how deep but they're the cause of your trouble." I picked up the cigarette I had lost in the scuffle, looked at it, lit another.

"Moody had to be in on it because it's something no psychologist could have missed. Stanton because he was responsible for the work schedules and, anyway, he kept a hatchet man in Hive 19. Maybe the bookies are in on it too, some of them must be, and the pay corps can't all be clean."

"I can't understand it." Thorne shook his head. "They know how essential it is to build the Shield. Why, Mike? Why?"

"Greed," I said. "Plain, ordinary greed. You can't beat it." I began to grow impatient at his lack of understanding of human nature. "Look, Thorne, you bribed men to come out here to work, right?"

"Wrong. I offered them high wages but that was all. We could have had volunteers for nothing."

"No you couldn't, and you know it. Cranks, yes, fanatics and a few, very few dedicated men but that is all. And how many of them would have been acceptable?" I shrugged. "You know the answer to that as well as I do. No, Thorne, you offered high wages to lure the men you wanted to work on the Shield. You got them—and you got what went with them."

Thorne had forgotten Sunburst hysteria. The whole world suffered from it and the men on the Shield were no exception. In a way they suffered even more, the constant sight of the naked sun, the sense of falling, the knowledge that, soon, a mass of contraterrene matter was going to blast the inner planets with flame, all had its effect.

And the Shield had to be built in a hurry. Safety precautions were overlooked, the death role mounted and, with grim gallows humour, the betting commenced. Relatively harmless at first it didn't stay that way. Men began to measure their lives by the quoted odds and began to think more of their own skins than the Shield. When that happened the slow-down was progressive.

"It became a racket," I said. "One of the biggest. You've a lot of men working out here and most of them draw a mill a day. My guess is that most of them bet, why not, what else is there to do out here except gamble? And when there's a lot of money to be collected things soon get organized."

He found it hard to believe and I didn't blame him. Men had to sink pretty low to bet on the death of their fellows.

"You can see the logic of it," I continued. "In order to work fast men have to take chances but, if they do, they become favourites. Favourites, Thorne, usually win; in this case it means they die. No one wants to be a favourite so no one takes risks so the work slows way down. But those running the book want a quick turnover. So they 'fix' a favourite so everyone gets even more cautious and the work slows down even more." I blew smoke towards Thorne's image. "It's what I think radio men call a negative feedback."

"You're sure about all this?"

"I killed a man to prove it." I forestalled his next question. "It was self-defence, he wanted to kill me, Stanton sent him."

I explained how Glendale had aroused suspicion. For a man with such long odds he had no reason to be so scared. He had an inside job too so what had made him constantly wear a suit? And I had seen his expression that time in the recreation room. Hunters looked like that when they saw their Quarry.

"His suit was an alibi," I said. "He could enter the Hive at any time and no one who saw him would even think that he'd been outside. Why should they? The guy always wore a suit. My guess is that you'll find someone like him in every Hive on the project. Moody, of course, signalled to Stanton to set me up. He must have grown a little scared that I knew too much."

"I trusted Moody," said Thorne, "I really trusted him."

"He couldn't withstand temptation," I said. "But, in this day and age, who can? And don't ask me what good they thought their money would be if the Earth got burned up. Greed is notoriously short-sighted." I sighed and shook my head. "One thing you've got to admit, they certainly knew an opportunity when they saw one."

Thorne looked grim and I knew what he was thinking. Service troops would be sent out, the records checked and quite a lot of people would have to do a lot of explaining. There would be cashiering, executions and confiscations. Law-suits and criminal charges, a new broom would sweep the Shield clean of corruption so that it could be finished in time.

But I wasn't thinking of that at all. I was reminding myself to get Wilner to collect on the bet he had placed for me with Royston. It wasn't often that I picked the long-shots.

THE END

Jack Vance

The solar sail, as already explored in my introduction, was proposed as a concept as far back as 1921, but only truly emerged in fiction in the early sixties with stories by Cordwainer Smith, Arthur C. Clarke and this one by Jack Vance. Whereas Smith and Clarke looked at the potential of the solar sail for space exploration or for sport, Vance considered the more basic aspect of how these vast sails can be constructed and how people can be trained to operate them.

John Holbrook Vance (1916–2013), who almost always wrote as Jack, is one of the towering giants of science fiction and fantasy who has left an indelible influence on the field. He began writing after the Second World War in which he had served in the merchant navy (which helped with some background for this story). His first story, "The World Thinker" (1945), showed us how his imagination could work on a vast scale, which he rapidly developed in such stories as his series about the interplanetary rogue Magnus Ridolph, eventually collected in 1966, and his tales set aeons in the future exploring the machinations of individuals coping with unimaginable science and magic, collected in The Dying Earth *(1950). If these did not already demonstrate his ability for setting adventures on a massive stage, then* Big Planet *(magazine, 1952) did. He experimented with several shorter works during the 1950s but then set himself the task of chronicling planetary romances on a vast scale, most notably in his* Demon Princes *series that began with* The Star King *(1964)—think* Game of Thrones *but on a galactic scale. In comparison with these epics the challenge of sailing a light-ship must have seemed straightforward.*

I

HENRY BELT CAME LIMPING INTO THE CONFERENCE ROOM, mounted the dais, settled himself at the desk. He looked once around the room: a swift bright glance which, focusing nowhere, treated the eight young men who faced him to an almost insulting disinterest. He reached in his pocket, brought forth a pencil and a flat red book, which he placed on the desk. The eight young men watched in absolute silence. They were much alike: healthy, clean, smart, their expressions identically alert and wary. Each had heard legends of Henry Belt, each had formed his private plans and private determinations.

Henry Belt seemed a man of a different species. His face was broad, flat, roped with cartilage and muscle, with skin the colour and texture of bacon rind. Coarse white grizzle covered his scalp, his eyes were crafty slits, his nose a misshapen lump. His shoulders were massive, his legs short and gnarled: as he sat before the eight young men he seemed like a horned toad among a group of dapper young frogs.

"First of all," said Henry Belt, with a gap-toothed grin, "I'll make it clear that I don't expect you to like me. If you do I'll be surprised and displeased. It will mean that I haven't pushed you hard enough."

He leaned back in his chair, surveyed the silent group. "You've heard stories about me. Why haven't they kicked me out of the service? Incorrigible, arrogant, dangerous Henry Belt. Drunken Henry Belt. (This last of course is slander. Henry Belt has never been drunk in his life.) Why do they tolerate me? For one simple reason: out of necessity. No one wants to take on this kind of job. Only a man like Henry Belt can stand up to it: year after year in space, with nothing to look at but a half-dozen round-faced young scrubs. He takes them out, he brings them back. Not all of them, and not all of those who come back are space-men today. But they'll all cross the street when they see him coming. Henry Belt? you say. They'll turn pale or go red. None of them will smile. Some of them are high-placed now. They could kick me loose if they chose. Ask them why they don't. Henry Belt is a terror, they'll tell you. He's wicked, he's a tyrant. Cruel as an axe, fickle as a woman. But a voyage with Henry Belt blows the foam off the beer. He's ruined many a man, he's killed a few, but those that come out of it are proud to say, I trained with Henry Belt!

"Another thing you may hear: Henry Belt has luck. But don't pay any heed. Luck runs out. You'll be my thirteenth class, and that's unlucky. I've taken out seventy-two young sprats no different from yourselves; I've come back twelve times: which is partly Henry Belt and partly luck. The voyages average about two years long: how can a man stand it? There's only one who could: Henry Belt. I've got more space-time than any man alive, and now I'll tell you a secret: this is my last time out. I'm starting to wake up at night to strange visions. After this class I'll quit. I hope you lads aren't superstitious. A white-eyed woman told me that I'd die in space. She told me other things and they've all come true. Who knows? If I survive this last trip I figure to buy a cottage in the country and grow roses." Henry Belt pushed himself back in the chair and surveyed the group with sardonic placidity. The man sitting closest to him caught a whiff of alcohol; he peered more closely at Henry Belt. Was it possible that even now the man was drunk?

Henry Belt continued. "We'll get to know each other well. And you'll be wondering on what basis I make my recommendations.

Am I objective and fair? Do I put aside personal animosity? Naturally there won't be any friendship. Well, here's my system. I keep a red book. Here it is. I'll put your names down right now. You, sir?"

"I'm Cadet Lewis Lynch, sir."

"You?"

"Edward Culpepper, sir."

"Marcus Verona, sir."

"Vidal Weske, sir."

"Marvin McGrath, sir."

"Barry Ostrander, sir."

"Clyde von Gluck, sir."

"Joseph Sutton, sir."

Henry Belt wrote the names in the red book. "This is the system. When you do something to annoy me, I mark you down demerits. At the end of the voyage I total these demerits, add a few here and there for luck, and am so guided. I'm sure nothing could be clearer than this. What annoys me? Ah, that's a question which is hard to answer. If you talk too much: demerits. If you're surly and taciturn: demerits. If you slouch and laze and dog the dirty work: demerits. If you're over-zealous and forever scuttling about: demerits. Obsequiousness: demerits. Truculence: demerits. If you sing and whistle: demerits. If you're a stolid bloody bore: demerits. You can see that the line is hard to draw. There's a hint which can save you many marks: no gossip. I've seen ships where the backbiting ran so thick it could have been jetted astern for thrust. I'm an eavesdropper. I hear everything. I don't like gossip, especially when it concerns myself. I'm a sensitive man, and I open my red book fast when I think I'm being insulted." Henry Belt once more leaned back in his chair. "Any questions?"

No one spoke.

Henry Belt nodded. "Wise. Best not to flaunt your ignorance so early in the game. Here's some miscellaneous information. First, wear what you like. Personally I dislike uniforms. I never wear a uniform. I never have worn a uniform. Secondly, if you have a religion, keep it to yourself. I dislike religions. I have always disliked religions. In response to the thought passing through each of your skulls, I do not think of myself as God. But you may do so, if you choose. And this—" he held up the red book "—you may regard as the Syncretic Compendium. Very well: Any questions?"

"Yes sir," said Culpepper.

"Speak, sir."

"Any objection to alcoholic beverages aboard ship, sir?"

"For the cadets, yes indeed. I concede that the water must be carried in any event, that the organic compounds present may be reconstituted, but unluckily the bottles weigh far too much."

"I understand, sir."

Henry Belt rose to his feet. "One last word. Have I mentioned that I run a tight ship? When I say jump, you must jump. When I say hop, you must hop. When I say stand on your head, I hope instantly to see twelve feet. Perhaps you will think me arbitrary— others have done so. After my tenth voyage several of the cadets urged that I had been unreasonable. I don't know where you'd go to question them; all were discharged from the hospital long ago. But now we understand each other. Rather, you understand me, because it is unnecessary that I understand you. This is dangerous work, of course. I don't guarantee your safety. Far from it, especially since we are assigned to old 25, which should have been broken up long ago. There are eight of you present. Only six cadets will make the voyage. Before the week is over I will make the appropriate notifications. Any more questions?... Very well, then. Cheerio." He stepped down from the dais, swaying just a trifle, and Culpepper once again caught the odour of alcohol. Limping on his thin legs as if his feet hurt Henry Belt departed into the back passage.

For a moment or two there was silence. Then von Gluck said in a soft voice, "My gracious."

"He's a tyrannical lunatic," grumbled Weske. "I've never heard anything like it! Megalomania!"

"Easy," said Culpepper. "Remember, no gossiping."

"Bah!" muttered McGrath. "This is a free country. I'll damn well say what I like."

"Mr. Belt admits it's a free country," said Culpepper. "He'll grade you as he likes, too."

Weske rose to his feet. "A wonder somebody hasn't killed him."

"I wouldn't want to try it," said Culpepper. "He looks tough." He made a gesture, stood up, brow furrowed in thought. Then he went to look along the passageway into which Henry Belt had made his departure. There, pressed to the wall, stood Henry Belt. "Yes, sir," said Culpepper suavely. "I forgot to inquire when you wanted us to convene again."

Henry Belt returned to the rostrum. "Now is as good a time as any." He took his seat, opened his red book. "You, Mr. von Gluck, made the remark, 'My gracious' in an offensive tone of voice. One demerit. You, Mr. Weske, employed the terms 'tyrannical lunatic' and 'megalomania', in reference to myself. Three demerits. Mr. McGrath, you observed that freedom of speech is the official doctrine of this country. It is a theory which presently we have no time to explore, but I believe that the statement in its present context carries an overtone of insubordination. One demerit. Mr. Culpepper, your imperturbable complacence irritates me. I prefer that you display more uncertainty, or even uneasiness."

"Sorry, sir."

"However, you took occasion to remind your colleagues of my rule, and so I will not mark you down."

"Thank you, sir."

Henry Belt leaned back in the chair, stared at the ceiling. "Listen closely, as I do not care to repeat myself. Take notes if you wish. Topic: Solar Sails, Theory and Practice thereof. Material with which you should already be familiar, but which I will repeat in order to avoid ambiguity.

"First, why bother with the sail, when nuclear jet-ships are faster, more dependable, more direct, safer and easier to navigate? The answer is three-fold. First, a sail is not a bad way to move heavy cargo slowly but cheaply through space. Secondly, the range of the sail is unlimited, since we employ the mechanical pressure of light for thrust, and therefore need carry neither propulsive machinery, material to be ejected, nor energy source. The solar sail is much lighter than its nuclear-powered counterpart, and may carry a larger complement of men in a larger hull. Thirdly, to train a man for space there is no better instrument than the handling of a sail. The computer naturally calculates sail cant and plots the course; in fact, without the computer we'd be dead ducks. Nevertheless the control of a sail provides working familiarity with the cosmic elementals: light, gravity, mass, space.

"There are two types of sail: pure and composite. The first relies on solar energy exclusively, the second carries a secondary power source. We have been assigned Number 25, which is the first sort. It consists of a hull, a large parabolic reflector which serves as radar and radio antenna as well as reflector for the power generator, and the sail itself. The pressure of radiation, of course, is extremely slight—on the order of an ounce per acre at this distance from the sun. Necessarily the sail must be extremely large and extremely light. We use a fluoro-siliconic film a tenth of a mil in gauge, fogged with lithium to the state of opacity. I believe the layer of lithium is about a thousand two hundred molecules thick. Such a foil weighs about four tons to the square mile. It is fitted to a hoop of thin-walled tubing, from which mono-crystalline iron cords lead to the hull.

"We try to achieve a weight factor of six tons to the square mile, which produces an acceleration of between $g/100$ and $g/1000$ depending on proximity to the sun, angle of cant, circumsolar orbital speed, reflectivity of surface. These accelerations seem minute, but calculation shows them to be cumulatively enormous. $g/100$ yields a velocity increment of 800 miles per hour every hour, 18,000 miles per hour each day, or five miles per second each day. At this rate interplanetary distances are readily negotiable—with proper manipulation of the sail, I need hardly say.

"The virtues of the sail I've mentioned. It is cheap to build and cheap to operate. It requires neither fuel nor ejectant. As it travels through space, the great area captures various ions, which may be expelled in the plasma jet powered by the parabolic reflector, which adds another increment to the acceleration.

"The disadvantages of the sail are those of the glider or sailing ship, in that we must use natural forces with great precision and delicacy.

"There is no particular limit to the size of the sail. On 25 we use about four square miles of sail. For the present voyage we will install a new sail, as the old is well-worn and eroded.

"That will be all for today." Once more Henry Belt limped down from the dais and out into the passage. On this occasion there were no comments after his departure.

II

The eight cadets shared a dormitory, attended classes together, ate at the same table in the mess-hall. "You think you know each other well," said Henry Belt. "Wait till we are alone in space. The similarities, the areas of agreement become invisible, only the distinctions and differences remain."

In various shops and laboratories the cadets assembled, disassembled and reassembled computers, pumps, generators, gyroplatforms, star-trackers, communication gear. "It's not enough to be clever with your hands," said Henry Belt. "Dexterity is not enough. Resourcefulness, creativity, the ability to make successful improvisations—these are more important. We'll test you out." And presently each of the cadets was introduced into a room on the floor of which lay a great heap of mingled housings, wires, flexes, gears, components of a dozen varieties of mechanism. "This is a twenty-six-hour test," said Henry Belt. "Each of you has an identical set of components and supplies. There shall be no exchange of parts or information between you. Those whom I suspect of this fault will be dropped from the class, without recommendation. What I want you to build is, first, one standard Aminex Mark 9 Computer. Second, a servo-mechanism to orient a mass of ten kilograms toward Mu Hercules. Why do I specify Mu Hercules?"

"Because, sir, the solar system moves in the direction of Mu Hercules, and we thereby avoid parallax error. Negligible though it may be, sir."

"The final comment smacks of frivolity, Mr. McGrath, which serves only to distract the attention of those who are trying to take careful note of my instructions. One demerit."

"Sorry, sir. I merely intended to express my awareness that for many practical purposes such a degree of accuracy is unnecessary."

"That idea, cadet, is sufficiently elemental that it need not be laboured. I appreciate brevity and precision."

"Yes, sir."

"Thirdly, from these materials, assemble a communication system, operating on one hundred watts, which will permit two-way conversation between Tycho Base and Phobos, at whatever frequency you deem suitable."

The cadets started in identical fashion, by sorting the material into various piles, then calibrating and checking the test instruments. Achievement thereafter was disparate. Culpepper and von Gluck, diagnosing the test as partly one of mechanical ingenuity and partly ordeal by frustration, failed to become excited when several indispensable components proved either to be missing or inoperative, and carried each project as far as immediately feasible. McGrath and Weske, beginning with the computer, were reduced to rage and random action. Lynch and Sutton worked doggedly at the computer, Verona at the communication system.

Culpepper alone managed to complete one of the instruments, by the process of sawing, polishing and cementing together sections of two broken crystals into a crude, inefficient but operative maser unit.

The day after this test McGrath and Weske disappeared from the dormitory, whether by their own volition or notification from Henry Belt, no one ever knew.

The test was followed by weekend leave. Cadet Lynch, attending a cocktail party, found himself in conversation with a Lieutenant-Colonel Trenchard, who shook his head pityingly to hear that Lynch was training with Henry Belt.

"I was up with Old Horrors myself. I tell you it's a miracle we ever got back. Belt was drunk two-thirds of the voyage."

"How does he escape court-martial?" asked Lynch with an involuntary glance over his shoulder, for fear that Henry Belt might be standing near by with his red book.

"Very simple. All the top men seem to have trained under Henry Belt. Naturally they hate his guts but they all take a perverse pride in the fact. And maybe they hope that someday a cadet will take him apart."

"Have any ever tried?"

"Oh yes. I took a swing at Henry once. I was lucky to escape with a broken collarbone and two sprained ankles. And he wasn't even angry. Good old Henry, the son of a bitch. If you come back alive—and that's no idle remark—you'll stand a good chance of reaching the top."

Lynch winced. "Is it worth two years with Henry Belt?"

"I don't regret it. Not now," said Trenchard. "What's your ship?"

"Old 25."

Trenchard shook his head. "An antique. It's tied together with bits of string."

"So I've heard," said Lynch glumly. "If I didn't have so much vanity I'd quit tomorrow. Learn to sell insurance, or work in an office…"

The next evening Henry Belt passed the word. "Next Tuesday morning we go up. Have your gear packed; take a last look at the scenes of your childhood. We'll be gone several months."

On Tuesday morning the cadets took their places in the angel-wagon. Henry Belt presently appeared. "Last chance to play it safe. Anyone decide they're really not space people after all?"

The pilot of the angel-wagon was disposed to be facetious. "Now, Henry, behave yourself. You're not scaring anybody but yourself."

Henry Belt swung his flat dark face around. "Is that the case, mister? I'll pay you ten thousand dollars to make the trip in the place of one of the cads."

The pilot shook his head. "Not for a hundred thousand, Henry. One of these days your luck is going to run out, and there'll be a sad quiet hulk drifting in orbit forever."

"I expect it, mister. If I wanted to die of fatbelly I'd take your job."

"If you'd stay sober, Henry, there might be an opening for you."

Henry Belt gave him his wolfish smile. "I'm a better man drunk than you are sober, except for mouth. Any way you can think of, from dancing the fandango to Calcutta roughhouse."

"I'd be ashamed to thrash an old man, Henry. You're safe."

"Thank you, mister. If you are quite ready, we are."

"Hold your hats. On the count…" The projectile thrust against the earth, strained, rose, went streaking up into the sky. An hour later the pilot pointed. "There's your boat. Old 25. And 39 right beside it, just in from space."

Henry Belt stared aghast from the port. "What's been done to the ship? The decoration? The red? the white? the yellow? The chequerboard."

"Thank some idiot of a landlubber," said the pilot. "The word came to pretty the old boats for a junket of congressmen. This is what transpired."

Henry Belt turned to the cadets. "Observe this foolishness. It is the result of vanity and ignorance. We will be occupied several days removing the paint."

They drifted close below the two sails: No. 39 just down from space, spare and polished beside the bedizened structure of No. 25. In 39's exit port a group of men waited, their gear floating at the end of cords.

"Observe those men," said Henry Belt. "They are jaunty. They have been on a pleasant outing around the planet Mars. They are poorly trained. When you gentlemen return you will be haggard and desperate. You will be well trained."

"If you live," said the pilot.

"That is something which cannot be foretold," said Henry Belt. "Now, gentlemen, clamp your helmets, and we will proceed."

The helmets were secured. Henry Belt's voice came by radio. "Lynch, Ostrander, will remain here to discharge cargo. Verona, Culpepper, von Gluck, Sutton, leap with cords to the ship; ferry across the cargo, stow it in the proper hatches."

Henry Belt took charge of his personal cargo, which consisted of several large cases. He eased them out into space, clipped on lines, thrust them toward 25, leapt after. Pulling himself and the cases to the entrance port he disappeared within.

Discharge of cargo was effected. The crew from 39 transferred to the carrier, which thereupon swung down and away, thrust itself dwindling back toward Earth.

When the cargo had been stowed, the cadets gathered in the wardroom. Henry Belt appeared from the master's cubicle. He wore a black T shirt which was ridged and lumped to the configuration of his chest, black shorts from which his thin legs extended, and sandals with magnetic filaments in the soles.

"Gentlemen," said Henry Belt in a soft voice. "At last we are alone. How do you like the surroundings? Eh, Mr. Culpepper?"

"The hull is commodious, sir. The view is superb."

Henry Belt nodded. "Mr. Lynch? Your impressions?"

"I'm afraid I haven't sorted them out yet, sir."

"I see. You, Mr. Sutton?"

"Space is larger than I imagined it, sir."

"True. Space is unimaginable. A good space-man must either

be larger than space, or he must ignore it. Both difficult. Well, gentlemen, I will make a few comments, then I will retire and enjoy the voyage. Since this is my last time out, I intend to do nothing whatever. The operation of the ship will be completely in your hands. I will merely appear from time to time to beam benevolently about or alas! to make marks in my red book. Nominally I shall be in command, but you six will enjoy complete control over the ship. If you return us safely to Earth I will make an approving entry in my red book. If you wreck us or fling us into the sun, you will be more unhappy than I, since it is my destiny to die in space. Mr. von Gluck, do I perceive a smirk on your face?"

"No, sir, it is a thoughtful half-smile."

"What is humorous in the concept of my demise, may I ask?"

"It will be a great tragedy, sir. I merely was reflecting upon the contemporary persistence of, well, not exactly superstition, but, let us say, the conviction of a subjective cosmos."

Henry Belt made a notation in the red book. "Whatever is meant by this barbaric jargon I'm sure I don't know, Mr. von Gluck. It is clear that you fancy yourself a philosopher and dialectician. I will not fault this, so long as your remarks conceal no overtones of malice and insolence, to which I am extremely sensitive. Now as to the persistence of superstition, only an impoverished mind considers itself the repository of absolute knowledge. Hamlet spoke on this subject to Horatio, as I recall, in the well-known work by William Shakespeare. I myself have seen strange and terrifying sights. Were they hallucinations? Were they the manipulation of the cosmos by my mind or the mind of someone—or something—other than myself? I do not know. I therefore counsel a flexible attitude toward matters where the truth is still unknown. For this reason: the impact of an inexplicable experience may well destroy a mind which is too brittle. Do I make myself clear?"

"Perfectly, sir."

"Very good. To return, then. We shall set a system of watches whereby each man works in turn with each of the other five. I thereby hope to discourage the formation of special friendships, or cliques. Such arrangements irritate me, and I shall mark accordingly.

"You have inspected the ship. The hull is a sandwich of lithium–beryllium, insulating foam, fibre and an interior skin. Very light, held rigid by air pressure rather than by any innate strength of the material. We can therefore afford enough space to stretch our legs and provide all of us with privacy.

"The master's cubicle is to the left; under no circumstances is anyone permitted in my quarters. If you wish to speak to me, knock on my door. If I appear, good. If I do not appear, go away. To the right are six cubicles which you may now distribute among yourselves by lot. Each of you has the right to demand the same privacy I do myself. Keep your personal belongings in your cubicles. I have been known to cast into space articles which I persistently find strewn about the wardroom.

"Your schedule will be two hours' study, four hours on watch, six hours off. I will require no specific rate of study progress, but I recommend that you make good use of your time.

"Our destination is Mars. We will presently construct a new sail, then while orbital velocity builds up, you will carefully test and check all equipment aboard. Each of you will compute sail cant and course and work out among yourselves any discrepancies which may appear. I shall take no hand in navigation. I prefer that you involve me in no disaster. If any such occur I shall severely mark down the persons responsible.

"Singing, whistling, humming are forbidden, as are sniffing, nose-picking, smacking the lips, and cracking knuckles. I

disapprove of fear and hysteria, and mark accordingly. No one
dies more than once; we are well aware of the risks of this, our
chosen occupation. There will be no practical jokes. You may
fight, so long as you do not disturb me or break any instruments;
however, I counsel against it, as it leads to resentment, and I have
known cadets to kill each other. I suggest coolness and detach-
ment in your personal relations. Use of the microfilm projector is
of course at your own option. You may not use the radio either
to dispatch or receive messages. In fact I have put the radio out
of commission, as is my practice. I do this to emphasize the fact
that, sink or swim, we must make do with our own resources.
Are there any questions?... Very good. You will find that if you all
behave with scrupulous correctness and accuracy, we shall in due
course return safe and sound, with a minimum of demerits and
no casualties. I am bound to say, however, that in twelve previous
voyages this has failed to occur."

"Perhaps this will be the time, sir," offered Culpepper suavely.

"We shall see. Now you may select your cubicles, stow your
gear, generally make the place shipshape. The carrier will bring
up the new sail tomorrow, and you will go to work."

III

The carrier discharged a great bundle of three-inch tubing: paper-
thin lithium hardened with beryllium, reinforced with filaments
of mono-crystalline iron—a total length of eight miles. The cadets
fitted the tubes end to end, cementing the joints. When the tube
extended a quarter-mile it was bent bow-shaped by a cord stretched
between two ends, and further sections added. As the process
continued the free end curved far out and around, and presently

began to veer back in toward the hull. When the last tube was in place the loose end was hauled down, socketed home, to form a great hoop two miles and a half in diameter.

Henry Belt came out occasionally in his spacesuit to look on, and occasionally spoke a few words of sardonic comment, to which the cadets paid little heed. Their mood had changed; this was exhilaration, to be weightlessly afloat above the bright cloud-marked globe, with continent and ocean wheeling massively below. Anything seemed possible, even the training voyage with Henry Belt! When he came out to inspect their work, they grinned at each other with indulgent amusement. Henry Belt suddenly seemed a rather pitiful creature, a poor vagabond suited only for drunken bluster. Fortunate indeed that they were less naïve than Henry Belt's previous classes! They had taken Belt seriously; he had cowed them, reduced them to nervous pulp. Not this crew, not by a long shot! They saw through Henry Belt! Just keep your nose clean, do your work, keep cheerful. The training voyage won't last but a few months, and then real life begins. Gut it out, ignore Henry Belt as much as possible.

Already the group had made a composite assessment of its members, arriving at a set of convenient labels. Culpepper: smooth, suave, easy-going. Lynch: excitable, argumentative, hot-tempered. Von Gluck: the artistic temperament, delicate with his hands and sensibilities. Ostrander: prissy, finicky, over-tidy. Sutton: moody, suspicious, competitive. Verona: the plugger, rough at the edges, but persistent and reliable.

Around the hull swung the gleaming hoop, and now the carrier brought up the sail, a great roll of darkly shining stuff. When unfolded and unrolled, and unfolded many times more, it became a tough gleaming film, flimsy as gold leaf. Unfolded to its fullest extent it was a shimmering disc, already rippling and bulging to the light of the sun. The cadets fitted the film to the hoop, stretched it taut as a drum-head, cemented it in place. Now the sail must carefully be held edge on to the sun, or it would quickly move away, under a thrust of about a hundred pounds.

From the rim braided-iron threads were led to a ring at the back of the parabolic reflector, dwarfing this as the reflector dwarfed the hull, and now the sail was ready to move.

The carrier brought up a final cargo: water, food, spare parts, a new magazine for the microfilm viewer, mail. Then Henry Belt said, "Make sail."

This was the process of turning the sail to catch the sunlight while the hull moved around Earth away from the sun, canting it parallel to the sun-rays when the ship moved on the sunward leg of its orbit: in short, building up an orbital velocity which in due course would stretch loose the bonds of terrestrial gravity and send Sail 25 kiting out toward Mars.

During this period the cadets checked every item of equipment aboard the vessel. They grimaced with disgust and dismay at some of the instruments: 25 was an old ship, with antiquated gear. Henry Belt seemed to enjoy their grumbling. "This is a training voyage, not a pleasure cruise. If you wanted your noses wiped, you should have taken a post on the ground. I warn you, gentlemen, I have no sympathy for fault-finders. If you wish a model by which to form your own conduct, observe me. I accept every vicissitude placidly. You will never hear me curse or flap my arms in astonishment at the turns of fortune."

The moody introspective Sutton, usually the most diffident and laconic of individuals, ventured an ill-advised witticism. "If we modelled ourselves after you, sir, there'd be no room to move for the whiskey."

Out came the red book. "Extraordinary impudence, Mr. Sutton. How can you yield so easily to malice? You must control the razor edge of your wit; you will make yourself unpopular aboard this ship."

Sutton flushed pink; his eyes glistened, he opened his mouth to speak, then closed it firmly. Henry Belt, waiting politely expectant, turned away. "You gentlemen will perceive that I rigorously obey my own rules of conduct. I am regular as a clock. There is no better, more genial shipmate than Henry Belt. There is not a fairer man alive. Mr. Culpepper, you have a remark to make?"

"Nothing of consequence, sir. I am merely grateful not to be making a voyage with a man less regular, less genial, and less fair than yourself."

Henry Belt considered. "I suppose I can take no exception to the remark. There is indeed a hint of tartness and glancing obloquy—but, well, I will grant you the benefit of the doubt, and accept your statement at its face value."

"Thank you, sir."

"But I must warn you, Mr. Culpepper, that there is a certain ease to your behaviour that gives me cause for distress. I counsel you to a greater show of earnest sincerity, which will minimize the risk of misunderstanding. A man less indulgent than myself might well have read impertinence into your remark and charged you one demerit."

"I understand, sir, and shall cultivate the qualities you mention."

Henry Belt found nothing more to say. He went to the port, glared out at the sail. He swung around instantly. "Who is on watch?"

"Sutton and Ostrander, sir."

"Gentlemen, have you noticed the sail? It has swung about and is canting to show its back to the sun. In another ten minutes we shall be tangled in a hundred miles of guy-wires."

Sutton and Ostrander sprang to repair the situation. Henry Belt shook his head disparagingly. "This is precisely what is meant by the words 'negligence' and 'inattentiveness'. You two have committed a serious error. This is poor spacemanship. The sail must always be in such a position as to hold the wires taut."

"There seems to be something wrong with the sensor, sir," Sutton blurted. "It should notify us when the sail swings behind us."

"I fear I must charge you an additional demerit for making excuses, Mr. Sutton. It is your duty to assure yourself that all the warning devices are functioning properly, at all times. Machinery must never be used as a substitute for vigilance."

Ostrander looked up from the control console. "Someone has turned off the switch, sir. I do not offer this as an excuse, but as an explanation."

"The line of distinction is often hard to define, Mr. Ostrander. Please bear in mind my remarks on the subject of vigilance."

"Yes, sir, but—who turned off the switch?"

"Both you and Mr. Sutton are theoretically hard at work watching for any such accident or occurrence. Did you not observe it?"

"No, sir."

"I might almost accuse you of further inattention and neglect, in this case."

Ostrander gave Henry Belt a long dubious side-glance. "The only person I recall going near the console is yourself, sir. I'm sure you wouldn't do such a thing."

Henry Belt shook his head sadly. "In space you must never rely on anyone for rational conduct. A few moments ago Mr. Sutton unfairly imputed to me an unusual thirst for whiskey. Suppose this were the case? Suppose, as an example of pure irony, that I had indeed been drinking whiskey, that I was in fact drunk?"

"I will agree, sir, that anything is possible."

Henry Belt shook his head again. "That is the type of remark, Mr. Ostrander, that I have come to associate with Mr. Culpepper. A better response would have been, 'In the future, I will try to be ready for any conceivable contingency.' Mr. Sutton, did you make a hissing sound between your teeth?"

"I was breathing, sir."

"Please breathe with less vehemence. A more suspicious man than myself might mark you for sulking and harbouring black thoughts."

"Sorry, sir, I will breathe to myself."

"Very well, Mr. Sutton." Henry Belt turned away and wandered back and forth about the wardroom, scrutinizing cases, frowning at smudges on polished metal. Ostrander muttered something to Sutton, and both watched Henry Belt closely as he moved here and there. Presently Henry Belt lurched toward them. "You show great interest in my movements, gentlemen."

"We were on the watch for another unlikely contingency, sir."

"Very good, Mr. Ostrander. Stick with it. In space nothing is impossible. I'll vouch for this personally."

IV

Henry Belt sent all hands out to remove the paint from the surface of the parabolic reflector. When this had been accomplished, incident sunlight was now focused upon an expanse of photo-electric cells. The power so generated was used to operate plasma jets, expelling ions collected by the vast expanse of sail, further accelerating the ship, thrusting it ever out into an orbit of escape. And finally one day, at an exact instant dictated by the computer, the ship departed from Earth and floated tangentially out into space, off at an angle for the orbit of Mars. At an acceleration of g/100 velocity built up rapidly. Earth dwindled behind; the ship was isolated in space. The cadets' exhilaration vanished, to be replaced by an almost funereal solemnity. The vision of Earth dwindling and retreating is an awesome symbol, equivalent to eternal loss, to the act of dying itself. The more impressionable cadets—Sutton, von Gluck, Ostrander—could not look astern without finding their eyes swimming with tears. Even the suave Culpepper was awed by the magnificence of the spectacle, the sun an aching pit not to be tolerated, Earth a plump pearl rolling on black velvet among a myriad glittering diamonds. And away from Earth, away from the sun, opened an exalted magnificence of another order entirely. For the first time the cadets became dimly aware that Henry Belt had spoken truly of strange visions. Here was death, here was peace, solitude, star-blazing beauty which promised not oblivion in death, but eternity... Streams and spatters of stars... The familiar constellations, the stars with their prideful names presenting themselves like heroes: Achernar, Fomalhaut, Sadal Suud, Canopus...

Sutton could not bear to look into the sky. "It's not that I feel fear," he told von Gluck, "or yes, perhaps it is fear. It sucks at me, draws me out there... I suppose in due course I'll become accustomed to it."

"I'm not so sure," said von Gluck. "I wouldn't be surprised if space could become a psychological addiction, a need—so that whenever you walked on Earth you felt hot and breathless."

Life settled into a routine. Henry Belt no longer seemed a man, but a capricious aspect of nature, like storm or lightning; and like some natural cataclysm, Henry Belt showed no favouritism, nor forgave one jot or tittle of offence. Apart from the private cubicles no place on the ship escaped his attention. Always he reeked of whiskey, and it became a matter of covert speculation as to exactly how much whiskey he had brought aboard. But no matter how he reeked or how he swayed on his feet, his eyes remained clever and steady, and he spoke without slurring in his paradoxically clear sweet voice.

One day he seemed slightly drunker than usual, and ordered all hands into spacesuits and out to inspect the sail for meteoric puncture. The order seemed sufficiently odd that the cadets stared at him in disbelief. "Gentlemen, you hesitate, you fail to exert yourselves, you luxuriate in sloth. Do you fancy yourselves at the Riviera? Into the spacesuits, on the double, and a demerit to the last man dressed!"

The last man proved to be Culpepper. "Well, sir?" demanded Henry Belt. "You have earned yourself a mark. Is it below your dignity to compete?"

Culpepper considered. "Well, sir, that might be the case. Somebody had to get the demerit, and I figured it might as well be me."

"I deplore your attitude, Mr. Culpepper. I interpret it as an act of deliberate defiance."

"Sorry, sir. I don't mean it that way."

"You feel then that I am mistaken?" Henry Belt studied Culpepper carefully.

"Yes, sir," said Culpepper with engaging simplicity. "You are absolutely wrong. My attitude is not one of defiance. I think I would call it fatalism. I look at it this way. If it turns out that I accumulate so many demerits that you hold back my commission, then perhaps I wasn't cut out for the job in the first place."

For a moment Henry Belt had nothing to say. Then he grinned wolfishly. "We shall see, Mr. Culpepper. I assure you that at the present moment I am far from being confident of your abilities. Now, everybody into space. Check hoop, sail, reflector, struts and sensor. You will be adrift for two hours. When you return I want a comprehensive report. Mr. Lynch, I believe you are in charge of this watch. You will present the report."

"Yes, sir."

"One more matter. You will notice that the sail is slightly bellied by the continual radiation pressure. It therefore acts as a focusing device, the focal point presumably occurring behind the cab. But this is not a matter to be taken for granted. I have seen a man burnt to death in such a freak accident. Bear this in mind."

For two hours the cadets drifted through space, propelled by tanks of gas and thrust tubes. All enjoyed the experience except Sutton, who found himself appalled by the immensity of his emotions. Probably least affected was the practical Verona, who inspected the sail with a care exacting enough even to satisfy Henry Belt.

The next day the computer went wrong. Ostrander was in charge of the watch and knocked on Henry Belt's door to make the report.

Henry Belt appeared in the doorway. He apparently had been asleep. "What is the difficulty, Mr. Ostrander?"

"We're in trouble, sir. The computer has gone out."

Henry Belt rubbed his grizzled pate. "This is not an unusual circumstance. We prepare for this contingency by schooling all cadets thoroughly in computer design and repair. Have you identified the difficulty?"

"The bearings which suspend the data separation disks have broken. The shaft has several millimetres play and as a result there is total confusion in the data presented to the analyser."

"An interesting problem. Why do you present it to me?"

"I thought you should be notified, sir. I don't believe we carry spares for this particular bearing."

Henry Belt shook his head sadly. "Mr. Ostrander, do you recall my statement at the beginning of this voyage, that you six gentlemen are totally responsible for the navigation of the ship?"

"Yes, sir. But—"

"This is an applicable situation. You must either repair the computer, or perform the calculations yourself."

"Very well, sir. I will do my best."

V

Lynch, Verona, Ostrander and Sutton disassembled the mechanism, removed the worn bearing. "Confounded antique!" said Lynch. "Why can't they give us decent equipment? Or if they want to kill us, why not shoot us and save us all trouble?"

"We're not dead yet," said Verona. "You've looked for a spare?"

"Naturally. There's nothing remotely like this."

Verona looked at the bearing dubiously. "I suppose we could cast a babbitt sleeve and machine it to fit. That's what we'll have to do—unless you fellows are awfully fast with your math."

Sutton glanced out the port, quickly turned away his eyes. "I wonder if we should cut sail."

"Why?" asked Ostrander.

"We don't want to build up too much velocity. We're already going 30 miles a second."

"Mars is a long way off."

"And if we miss, we go shooting past. Then where are we?"

"Sutton, you're a pessimist. A shame to find morbid tendencies in one so young." This from von Gluck, speaking from the console across the room.

"I'd rather be a live pessimist than a dead comedian."

The new sleeve was duly cast, machined and fitted. Anxiously the alignment of the data disks was checked. "Well," said Verona dubiously, "there's wobble. How much that affects the functioning remains to be seen. We can take some of it out by shimming the mount…"

Shims of tissue paper were inserted and the wobble seemed to be reduced. "Now—feed in the data," said Sutton. "Let's see how we stand."

Coordinates were fed into the system; the indicator swung. "Enlarge sail cant four degrees," said von Gluck, "we're making too much left concentric. Projected course…" he tapped buttons, watched the bright line extend across the screen, swing around a dot representing the centre of gravity of Mars. "I make it an elliptical pass, about twenty thousand miles out. That's at present acceleration, and it should toss us right back at Earth."

"Great. Simply great. Let's go, 25!" This was Lynch. "I've heard of guys dropping flat on their faces and kissing Earth when they put down. Me, I'm going to live in a cave the rest of my life."

Sutton went to look at the data disks. The wobble was slight but perceptible. "Good Lord," he said huskily. "The other end of the shaft is loose too."

Lynch started to spit curses; Verona's shoulders slumped. "Let's get to work and fix it."

Another bearing was cast, machined, polished, mounted. The disks wobbled, scraped. Mars, an ochre disc, shouldered ever closer in from the side. With the computer unreliable the cadets calculated

and plotted the course manually. The results were at slight but
significant variance with those of the computer. The cadets looked
dourly at each other. "Well," growled Ostrander, "there's error. Is it
the instruments? The calculation? The plotting? Or the computer?"

Culpepper said in a subdued voice, "Well, we're not about to
crash head-on, at any rate."

Verona went back to study the computer. "I can't imagine why
the bearings don't work better... The mounting brackets—could
they have shifted?" He removed the side housing, studied the
frame, then went to the case for tools.

"What are you going to do?" demanded Sutton.

"Try to ease the mounting brackets around. I think that's our
trouble."

"Leave them alone! You'll bugger the machine so it'll never
work."

Verona paused, looked questioningly around the group. "Well?
What's the verdict?"

"Maybe we'd better check with the old man," said Ostrander
nervously.

"All well and good—but you know what he'll say."

"Let's deal cards. Ace of spades goes to ask him."

Culpepper received the ace. He knocked on Henry Belt's door.
There was no response. He started to knock again, but restrained
himself.

He returned to the group. "Wait till he shows himself. I'd rather
crash into Mars than bring forth Henry Belt and his red book."

The ship crossed the orbit of Mars well ahead of the looming
red planet. It came toppling at them with a peculiar clumsy gran-
deur, a mass obviously bulky and globular, but so fine and clear
was the detail, so absent the perspective, that the distance and size
might have been anything. Instead of swinging in a sharp elliptical

curve back toward Earth, the ship swerved aside in a blunt hyper-
bola and proceeded outward, now at a velocity of close to fifty
miles a second. Mars receded astern and to the side. A new part
of space lay ahead. The sun was noticeably smaller. Earth could
no longer be differentiated from the stars. Mars departed quickly
and politely, and space seemed lonely and forlorn.

Henry Belt had not appeared for two days. At last Culpepper went
to knock on the door—once, twice, three times: a strange face
looked out. It was Henry Belt, face haggard, skin like pulled taffy.
His eyes were red and glared, his hair seemed matted and more
unkempt than hair a quarter-inch long should be.

But he spoke in his quiet clear voice. "Mr. Culpepper, your
merciless din has disturbed me. I am quite put out with you."

"Sorry, sir. We feared that you were ill."

Henry Belt made no response. He looked past Culpepper,
around the circle of faces. "You gentlemen are unwontedly serious. Has this presumptive illness of mine caused you all distress?"

Sutton spoke in a rush, "The computer is out of order."

"Why then, you must repair it."

"It's a matter of altering the housing. If we do it incorrectly—"

"Mr. Sutton, please do not harass me with the hour-by-hour
minutiae of running the ship."

"But, sir, the matter has become serious; we need your advice.
We missed the Mars turn-around—"

"Well, I suppose there's always Jupiter. Must I explain the basic
elements of astrogation to you?"

"But the computer's out of order—definitely."

"Then, if you wish to return to Earth, you must perform the
calculations with pencil and paper. Why is it necessary to explain
the obvious?"

"Jupiter is a long way out," said Sutton in a shrill voice. "Why can't we just turn around and go home?" This last was almost a whisper.

"I see I've been too easy on you cads," said Henry Belt. "You stand around idly; you chatter nonsense while the machinery goes to pieces and the ship flies at random. Everybody into spacesuits for sail inspection. Come now. Let's have some snap. What are you all? Walking corpses? You, Mr. Culpepper, why the delay?"

"It occurred to me, sir, that we are approaching the asteroid belt. As chief of the watch I consider it my duty to cant sail to swing us around the area."

"You may do this; then join the rest in hull and sail inspection."

"Yes, sir."

The cadets donned spacesuits, Sutton with the utmost reluctance. Out into the dark void they went, and now here was loneliness indeed.

When they returned, Henry Belt had returned to his compartment.

"As Mr. Belt points out, we have no great choice," said Ostrander. "We missed Mars, so let's hit Jupiter. Luckily it's in good position—otherwise we'd have to swing out to Saturn or Uranus—"

"They're off behind the sun," said Lynch. "Jupiter's our last chance."

"Let's do it right then. I say, let's make one last attempt to set those confounded bearings…"

But now it seemed as if the wobble and twist had been eliminated. The disks tracked perfectly, the accuracy monitor glowed green.

"Great!" yelled Lynch. "Feed it the dope. Let's get going! All sail for Jupiter. Good Lord, but we're having a trip!"

"Wait till it's over," said Sutton. Since his return from sail inspection, he had stood to one side, cheeks pinched, eyes staring. "It's not over yet. And maybe it's not meant to be."

The other five pretended not to have heard him. The computer spat out figures and angles. There was a billion miles to travel. Acceleration was less, due to the diminution in the intensity of sunlight. At least a month must pass before Jupiter came close.

VI

The ship, great sail spread to the fading sunlight, fled like a ghost— out, always out. Each of the cadets had quietly performed the same calculation, and arrived at the same result. If the swing around Jupiter were not performed with exactitude, if the ship were not slung back like a stone on a string, there was nothing beyond. Saturn, Uranus, Neptune, Pluto were far around the sun; the ship, speeding at a hundred miles a second, could not be halted by the waning gravity of the sun, nor yet sufficiently accelerated in a con-centric direction by sail and jet into a true orbit. The very nature of the sail made it useless as a brake, always the thrust was outward.

Within the hull seven men lived and thought, and the psychic relationship worked and stirred like yeast in a vat of decaying fruit. The fundamental similarity, the human identity of the seven men, was utterly cancelled; apparent only were the disparities. Each cadet appeared to others only as a walking characteristic, and Henry Belt was an incomprehensible Thing, who appeared from his compartment at unpredictable times, to move quietly here and there with the blind blank grin of an archaic Attic hero.

Jupiter loomed and bulked. The ship, at last within reach of the Jovian gravity, sidled over to meet it. The cadets gave ever more careful attention to the computer, checking and counterchecking the instructions. Verona was the most assiduous at this, Sutton the most harassed and ineffectual. Lynch growled and cursed and sweated; Ostrander complained in a thin peevish voice. Von Gluck worked with the calm of pessimistic fatalism; Culpepper seemed unconcerned, almost debonair, a blandness which bewildered Ostrander, infuriated Lynch, awoke a malignant hate in Sutton. Verona and von Gluck on the other hand seemed to derive strength and refreshment from Culpepper's placid acceptance of the situation. Henry Belt said nothing. Occasionally he emerged from his compartment, to survey the wardroom and the cadets with the detached interest of a visitor to an asylum.

It was Lynch who made the discovery. He signalled it with an odd growl of sheer dismay, which brought a resonant questioning sound from Sutton. "My God, my God," muttered Lynch.

Verona was at his side. "What's the trouble?"

"Look. This gear. When we replaced the disks we de-phased the whole apparatus one notch. This white dot and this other white dot should synchronize. They're one sprocket apart. All the results would check and be consistent because they'd all be off by the same factor."

Verona sprang into action. Off came the housing, off came various components. Gently he lifted the gear, set it back into correct alignment. The other cadets leaned over him as he worked, except Culpepper who was chief of the watch.

Henry Belt appeared. "You gentlemen are certainly diligent in your navigation," he said presently. "Perfectionists, almost."

"We do our best," grated Lynch between set teeth. "It's a damn shame sending us out with a machine like this."

The red book appeared. "Mr. Lynch, I mark you down not for your private sentiments, which are of course yours to entertain, but for voicing them and thereby contributing to an unhealthy atmosphere of despairing and hysterical pessimism."

A tide of red crept up from Lynch's neck. He bent over the computer, made no comment. But Sutton suddenly cried out, "What else do you expect from us? Do you think we're fish or insects? We came out here to learn, not to suffer, or to fly on forever!" He gave a ghastly laugh. Henry Belt listened patiently. "Think of it!" cried Sutton. "The seven of us. In this capsule, forever!"

"All of us must die in due course, Mr. Sutton. I expect to die in space."

"I'm not afraid of death." But Sutton's voice trailed off as he glanced toward the port.

"I am afraid that I must charge you two demerits for your outburst, Mr. Sutton. A good space-man maintains his dignity at all costs, and values it more than his life."

Lynch looked up from the computer. "Well, now we've got a corrected reading. Do you know what it says?"

Henry Belt turned him a look of polite inquiry.

"We're going to miss," said Lynch. "We're going to pass by just as we passed Mars. Jupiter is pulling us around and sending us out toward Gemini."

The silence was thick in the room. Sutton seemed to whisper something, soundlessly. Henry Belt turned to look at Culpepper, who was standing by the porthole, photographing Jupiter with his personal camera.

"Mr. Culpepper?"

"Yes, sir."

"You seem unconcerned by the prospect which Mr. Sutton has set forth."

"I hope it's not imminent, sir."

"How do you propose to avoid it?"

"I imagine that we will radio for help, sir."

"You forget that I have destroyed the radio."

"I remember noting a crate marked 'Radio Parts' stored in the starboard jet-pod."

"I am sorry to disillusion you, Mr. Culpepper. That case is mislabelled."

Ostrander jumped to his feet, left the wardroom. There was the sound of moving crates. A moment of silence. Then he returned. He glared at Henry Belt. "Whiskey. Bottles of whiskey."

Henry Belt nodded. "I told you as much."

"But now we have no radio," said Lynch in an ugly voice.

"We never have had a radio, Mr. Lynch. You were warned that you would have to depend on your own resources to bring us home. You have failed, and in the process doomed me as well as yourself. Incidentally, I must mark you all down ten demerits for a faulty cargo check."

"Demerits," said Ostrander in a bleak voice.

"Now, Mr. Culpepper," said Henry Belt. "What is your next proposal?"

"I don't know, sir."

Verona spoke in a placatory voice. "What would you do, sir, if you were in our position?"

Henry Belt shook his head. "I am an imaginative man, Mr. Verona, but there are certain leaps of the mind which are beyond my powers." He returned to his compartment.

Von Gluck looked curiously at Culpepper. "It is a fact. You're not at all concerned."

"Oh, I'm concerned. But I believe that Mr. Belt wants to get home too. He's too good a space-man not to know exactly what he's doing."

The door from Henry Belt's compartment slid back. Henry Belt stood in the opening. "Mr. Culpepper, I chanced to overhear your remark, and I now note down ten demerits against you. This attitude expresses a complacence as dangerous as Mr. Sutton's utter funk. You rely on my capabilities; Mr. Sutton is afraid to rely on his own. This is not the first time I have cautioned you against this easy vice."

"Very sorry, sir."

Henry Belt looked about the room. "Pay no heed to Mr. Culpepper. He is wrong. Even if I could repair this disaster, I would not raise a hand. For I expect to die in space."

VII

The sail was canted vectorless, edgewise to the sun. Jupiter was a smudge astern. There were five cadets in the wardroom. Culpepper, Verona, and von Gluck sat talking in low voices. Ostrander and Lynch lay crouched, arms to knees, faces to the wall. Sutton had gone two days before. Quietly donning his spacesuit, he had stepped into the exit chamber and thrust himself headlong into space. A propulsion unit gave him added speed, and before any of the cadets could intervene he was gone.

He had left a short note: "I fear the void because of the terrible attraction of its glory. I briefly felt the exaltation when we went out on sail inspection, and I fought it back. Now, since we must die, I will die this way, by embracing this black radiance, by giving myself wholly. Do not be sorry for me. I will die mad, but the madness will be ecstasy."

Henry Belt, when shown the note, merely shrugged. "Mr. Sutton was perhaps too imaginative and emotional to make a sound space-man. He could not have been relied upon in any emergency." And his sardonic glance seemed to include the rest of them.

Shortly thereafter Lynch and Ostrander succumbed to inanition, a kind of despondent helplessness: manic-depression in its most stupefying phase. Culpepper the suave, Verona the pragmatic and von Gluck the sensitive remained.

They spoke quietly to themselves, out of earshot of Henry Belt's room. "I still believe," said Culpepper, "that somehow there is a means to get ourselves out of this mess, and that Henry Belt knows it."

Verona said, "I wish I could think so... We've been over it a hundred times. If we set sail for Saturn or Neptune or Uranus, the outward vector of thrust plus the outward vector of our momentum will take us far beyond Pluto before we're anywhere near. The plasma jets could stop us if we had enough energy, but the shield can't supply it and we don't have another power source..."

Von Gluck hit his fist into his hand. "Gentlemen," he said in a soft delighted voice.

Culpepper and Verona stared at him, absorbing warmth from the light in his face.

"Gentlemen," said von Gluck, "I believe we have sufficient energy at hand. We will use the sail. Remember? It is bellied. It can function as a mirror. It spreads five square miles of surface. Sunlight out here is thin—but so long as we collect enough of it—"

"I understand!" said Culpepper. "We back off the hull till the reactor is at the focus of the sail and turn on the jets!"

Verona said dubiously, "We'll still be receiving radiation pressure. And what's worse, the jets will impinge back on the sail. Effect—cancellation. We'll be nowhere."

"If we cut the centre out of the sail—just enough to allow the plasma through—we'd beat that objection. And as for the radiation pressure—we'll surely do better with the plasma drive."

"What do we use to make plasma? We don't have the stock."

"Anything that can be ionized. The radio, the computer, your shoes, my shirt, Culpepper's camera, Henry Belt's whiskey…"

VIII

The angel-wagon came up to meet Sail 25, in orbit beside Sail 40, which was just making ready to take out a new crew.

Henry Belt said, "Gentlemen, I beg that you leave no trash, rubbish, old clothing aboard. There is nothing more troublesome than coming aboard an untidy ship. While we wait for the lighter to discharge, I suggest that you give the ship a final thorough policing."

The cargo carrier drifted near, eased into position. Three men sprang across space to Sail 40, a few hundred yards behind 25, tossed lines back to the carrier, pulled bales of cargo and equipment across the gap.

The five cadets and Henry Belt, clad in spacesuits, stepped out into the sunlight. Earth spread below, green and blue, white and brown, the contours so precious and dear to bring tears to the eyes. The cadets transferring cargo to Sail 40 gazed at them curiously as they worked. At last they were finished, and the six men of Sail 25 boarded the carrier.

"Back safe and sound, eh, Henry?" said the pilot. "Well, I'm always surprised."

Henry Belt made no answer. The cadets stowed their cargo, and standing by the port, took a final look at Sail 25. The carrier retro-jetted; the two sails seemed to rise above them.

The lighter nosed in and out of the atmosphere, braking, extended its wings, glided to an easy landing on the Mojave Desert.

The cadets, their legs suddenly loose and weak to the unaccustomed gravity, limped after Henry Belt to the carry-all, seated themselves and were conveyed to the administration complex. They alighted from the carry-all, and now Henry Belt motioned the five to the side.

"Here, gentlemen, is where I leave you. I go my way, you go yours. Tonight I will check my red book, and after various adjustments I will prepare my official report. But I believe I can present you an unofficial résumé of my impressions.

"First of all, this is neither my best nor my worst class. Mr. Lynch and Mr. Ostrander, I feel that you are ill-suited either for command or for any situation which might inflict prolonged emotional pressure upon you. I cannot recommend you for space-duty.

"Mr. von Gluck, Mr. Culpepper and Mr. Verona, all of you meet my minimum requirements for a recommendation, although I shall write the words 'Especially Recommended' only beside the names 'Clyde von Gluck' and 'Marcus Verona'. You brought the sail back to Earth by essentially faultless navigation. It means that if I am to fulfil my destiny I must make at least one more voyage into space.

"So now our association ends. I trust you have profited by it." Henry Belt nodded briefly to each of the five and limped off around the building.

The cadets looked after him. Culpepper reached in his pocket and brought forth a pair of small metal objects which he displayed in his palm. "Recognize these?"

"Hmf," said Lynch in a flat voice. "Bearings for the computer disks. The original ones."

"I found them in the little spare-parts tray. They weren't there before."

Von Gluck nodded. "The machinery always seemed to fail immediately after sail check, as I recall."

Lynch drew in his breath with a sharp hiss. He turned, strode away. Ostrander followed him. Culpepper shrugged. To Verona he gave one of the bearings, to von Gluck the other. "For souvenirs—or medals. You fellows deserve them."

"Thanks, Ed," said von Gluck.

"Thanks," muttered Verona. "I'll make a stick-pin of this thing."

The three, not able to look at each other, glanced up into the sky where the first stars of twilight were appearing, then continued on into the building where family and friends and sweethearts awaited them.

THE LONGEST VOYAGE

Richard C. Meredith

Richard Carlton Meredith (1937–79), whose career ended tragically when he died of a brain haemorrhage when he was only 41, was for a brief while acknowledged as an accomplished writer of space opera and time paradoxes. He had trained in the army as a radio engineer, but his passion had always been for the stars and he had wanted to be an astronomer but lacked the ability as a mathematician. His first novel was The Sky is Filled with Ships *(1969), but he established himself with* We All Died at Breakaway Station *(1969); a tense action-packed novel of soldiers trying to survive in an interstellar war. His* Timeliner *series, which began with* At the Narrow Passage *(1973), has aliens seeking to punish humanity by altering history. Throughout his books we meet stoic individuals struggling to cope with adversity, no better demonstrated than in the following story of one man trying to get home on a damaged spaceship.*

This journey has been no brief Moon jump, no six-month trip between Earth and the Mars colony. This has been the longest voyage without landfall that has ever been attempted by a crew of human beings.

Nine Planets, ALAN E. NOURSE

S AYERS CAREFULLY WORKED HIS WAY OUT OF THE AIR LOCK, unsuccessfully trying to avoid bumping his left arm against the rim of the lock. His shoulder brushed against an outside sealing flange; bright streamers of pain tore their way down his arm, searing into the numbness of his fingers. Instinctively he recoiled, throwing himself back into the lock, his helmet clanging loudly against metal.

Cursing bitterly and poetically, he threw his sound arm back across the lock's lip, and pulled himself out slowly. Once clear of the lock, he clipped a line to a small ring set into the ship's hull, and let out a long sigh of relief. He had made it out. Maybe he could even make it back inside, if he decided it was worth the effort.

Looking at the sky, he saw the squashed sphere of grand daddy Jupiter hanging against a backdrop of stars, decorated with gaudy stripes like a beach ball that someone had thrown outward with such force that it had gone into solar orbit. It was something more than eleven, almost twelve degrees in angular diameter, nearly twenty-four times the size of the Moon as seen from Earth. Despite its size, it did not look big and distant, but small and close, as if Sayers could actually reach out and touch it.

You're not as innocent as you look, Sayers said to himself, feeling a sensation that would have been hatred had it been directed at another human being rather than the huge, impersonal planet. You God damned methane and ammonia snowball.

Half the planet was in shadow, its silhouette a darkness against the stars. The bright side was illuminated by a tiny yellow sun, a fourth the size of that same sun on Earth. Sayers remembered someone having told him during his training that Jupiter received less than four one hundredths the amount of light of Earth, and right then he did not doubt it. It looked cold; it was cold. That was the very essence of this end of the universe—cold!

After a while he pulled his eyes away from the shadowed beach ball, and began working back toward the rear of the ship, sometimes floating, sometimes pulling himself along with his hands, slowly paying out the line as he moved.

Priam was in no better shape than he had figured. The rear third of the ship was just no longer there. A flaw, a structural error, a miscalculation—and liquid oxygen had somehow made its way into one of the cesium tanks, and everything had gone off with a hell of a bang. It was that simple, and that deadly.

He was surprised at the number of metallic balloons that remained. He wondered how any of the metalized plastic spheres could have escaped being punctured by fragments during the explosions, yet about half of them were intact.

Sayers looked at the torn hulk of the *Priam* for a long while, thinking how stupid any optimism had been. *Priam* was dead and powerless, a hulk without an engine, a derelict little chunk of metal that had become another satellite of Jupiter, and would probably remain that way for the next few million years, if it were not captured by Europa, whose orbit it crossed.

For a few moments Sayers had an urge to reach up and unsnap the clamps that held his helmet on, to let the air rush out and end this sorry mess once and for all, to bring to as clean a conclusion as he could the ill-fated first expedition to Jupiter.

Mixed with his desire for self destruction were images of a green and blue world over four hundred million miles distant, a world of warmth and sunlight and air, a world where there were people and laughter and no fear of instant death, a dream world so distant in space, so remote in time. And there were memories of fevered dreams of a squashed beach ball with a grinning face hidden in the shadows, and long chains that stretched from it, wrapping their links around Sayers and binding him so that he could never escape.

Hours later, it seemed to him, the inside of his spacesuit filled with the moisture and odour of his own sweat, Sayers turned himself around and began crawling back toward the air lock. During that trip back, pulling himself along with his good hand, the line white and taut in the glow of the distant sun, his mind was as nearly blank as a conscious human mind can be.

He scraped his shattered arm again as he crawled back through the air lock into the ship. Pain, nausea and a dangerous greyness rose up in him, and he bit his swollen lips to keep from losing the small spark of consciousness that remained. That was all he had to which he could cling, and he was not going to allow himself to lose that.

Finally the pain subsided enough for him to slam the inner hatch of the air lock closed, dog it, and then crawl/swim through the vacuum of the ship's forward compartment to the air cycling controls. His right hand, a distant, remote extension of a body his mind happened to possess, reached out toward the controls, hit the toggle switch that started the air pumps, adjusted for air pressure then relaxed.

How much later it was when he pushed himself away from the control panel, he did not know, but it seemed to have been long enough for the air pressure to have risen to a breathable level. The same alien hand came up slowly, and clumsily undid the snaps on his helmet. The helmet lazily floated away across the cabin, and Sayers breathed deeply.

Allowing his body to drift as it would, Sayers relaxed, trying to ignore the pain, trying to ignore everything. His eyelids floated closed with free-fall slowness, and he slept. And while he slept, he dreamed.

His name was Scott W. Sayers, Lieutenant Colonel, USAFS, assigned to NASA, where rank sometimes came fast, and death came as suddenly. A small, dark, thirtyish moon pilot with a perpetually sardonic smile, Scotty had a hankering to see the further ends of space. He volunteered for Project Troy.

Twenty-six men were selected for training for Project Troy; eighteen completed the course and went into the active phase of the project. There were three crews of them, six men for each of the three ships, and Scott Sayers was assigned to the flagship, USNASASS *Priam*. Being an electronic engineer by training, he was given the title Fleet Communications Officer, and since he had grown up on a farm, he was also horticulturist for the *Priam*, in charge of her hydroponic gardens. He was also back-up pilot for ship's captain Commander Ray Coiner.

Little, annoying things had happened even while the ships orbited Earth, but nothing major went wrong until they were 351 days out, almost half way to Jupiter. *Priam, Hector* and *Paris* were in a line, spaced about two miles apart, *Priam* leading. Having just skirted a loose mass of asteroidal debris, space seemed clear enough ahead. At least radar officer Jan Whittinger saw nothing, recorded nothing on his 'scopes.

But something was there, a fragment of rock that reflected only a tiny amount of light, that made only a tiny blip on the radar screens. But it was moving!

"Maybe it was a chunk of a dwarf star like Sirius B," Ray Coiner said later, "zipping through the galaxy for a hundred million years. It had a hell of a lot of mass."

The tiny, massive, speeding meteor shot past *Priam* finally bringing a response from her instruments. Fleet Captain Coiner grabbed for his microphone to radio a warning to the ships behind.

The chance was one out of millions that it would happen, but it did: head on the meteor met the *Paris*, ripping her open, spilling dying men out into space. Six men died as metal and stone met, tore, shattered, vaporized.

Sayers was still in radio contact with Earth then. The weak, fading voice gave the two surviving ships what consolation it could, and told them to go on; two ships could still complete the mission, but for God's sake, be careful.

They were, but perhaps not careful enough.

Seven hundred and seventy-one days out of Earth, the *Priam* and the *Hector* passed the orbit of Hades, Jupiter's outermost moon.

"We've made it," Juan Garza said quietly, jubilantly.

Ganymede, some 665,000 miles from Jupiter, was much as they had expected, a cold, lifeless, useless lump of stone. It was, at best, a place they could orbit while they ran their initial studies of Jupiter. Jan Whittinger broke out his telescopes, spectroscopes, thermocouples, and a hundred other instruments, and with Sayers' inexpert help, began his preliminary studies of grand daddy Jupiter at close hand.

Seventeen days later the first of these observations had been completed, and it was *Hector's* turn to run in as close to the giant planet as practicable, and shoot her three probes down into the methane and ammonia soup that passed for Jupiter's atmosphere.

Hector fired her drives, squirted ionized cesium into space, boosted out of orbit and spiralled in toward Jupiter. Inside the orbit of Amalthea, the closest moon to Jupiter, she began having trouble. A steering jet jammed open, burning fuel at a rate that *Hector* could not afford, and sending the ship into a crazy spiral.

Jack Winters, *Hector's* captain, went outside to see what he could do about it. While he manipulated the jet's external controls, one of its bearing rings gave way. The engine began snapping wildly back and forth, throwing the ship into an even wilder plunge, and washing the instantly roasted body of Captain Winters off into the darkness of space.

The crew of the *Priam* went in to help. Maybe they shouldn't, Sayers thought. They were too far away and there really wasn't anything they could do when they got there—but they *had* to try; God, those were people.

Ray Coiner gave the orders and they boosted toward Jupiter.

They were too late.

Running in as close as they dared, too far into the gravitational field of the giant planet, radar showed *Hector* breaking apart, shattering under the stress of too many forces acting in different directions, spinning down toward Jupiter's atmosphere. The ship's radio was silent and dead—the crew was probably the same.

There were tears in Ray Coiner's eyes when he finally fired the ship's lateral steering jets, turning the ship away from the grand daddy planet. Sayers felt a moistness in the corners of his own eyes, which he quickly wiped away. None of them said very much as the ship made a wide, arcing turn around Jupiter, back toward Jupiter.

The *Priam* lost altitude, too much altitude, as it made its comet-like spin around the giant planet. Coiner fired the cesium ion drive, and the ship began to pick up speed, accelerating outward against the powerful gravitational force of Jupiter. As Coiner moved the controls to maximum, G forces mounted, pressing Sayers back into his acceleration couch.

Suddenly a brilliant, flashing red light came into being on the control panel, a light labelled "Cesium Tank No. 4." The ship and the men inside her were taking more G's than either had been designed to withstand, and some structural weakness of the ship was showing up. Something was leaking; heat was growing in the tank.

A wave of consternation went across Coiner's face. For a moment he remained motionless; then his hand, moving slowly under the tremendous gravitational force, moved toward the controls. He began cutting back the drive.

"We should never have gotten that close," he muttered.

Sayers made some quick calculations in his head as the G forces dropped. "Fuel consumption's too high, Ray," he said aloud.

"Got to cut back," Coiner said, biting off his words savagely. "Something's wrong out there. Got to have a look."

The acceleration dropped to a little less than one gravity. The *Priam* was still moving away from Jupiter, but at a slower rate, a rate that would cost them too much fuel for too little speed.

"Take over, Scotty," Coiner said suddenly, slipping out of the command pilot seat. "Juan and I'd better go out and have a look."

"Outside?" Sayers asked. "While we're accelerating?"

"We don't dare go into orbit," Coiner snapped back, "and we've got to have a look."

He did not speak again as he spun around, motioned Juan Garza to follow him, and then made his way to the air lock.

As the air lock cycled closed behind the two men, Sayers snapped the faceplate of his space helmet closed, and glanced around the now empty control room. The other three crewmen were in the aft compartment, watching their instruments, making their readings, reporting to Sayers the increasing danger.

Once outside Coiner radioed in, asking Sayers for a report. One after another warning lights were coming to life on the control boards. Hydrogen was spilling out into space, mixing with oxygen from a ruptured balloon—something like a fire was burning along the rear third of the ship, starboard side, near the cesium tanks.

"Cut the drive, Scott!" Coiner's voice screamed suddenly. "Now! Hit the retros."

Sayers' hands fell across the controls, panic from Coiner's voice reaching him.

"Don't worry about sequence," Coiner yelled. "Just shut it off!" And that was all Sayers remembered, Coiner's voice crying, "Just shut it off!"

The first thing Sayers remembered after the blow-up was blood, blood everywhere, on everything, a red fog that ran and blurred across the whole universe. After a long, long while he realized that it was blood inside his helmet.

There was little pain, though he knew he was hurt. The blood in his helmet came from a big gash over his right eye, and he knew that if he did not do something about it soon, he would drown in it. His left arm felt strangely numb, and there was an odd joint where no joint should have been.

While he slowly returned to consciousness, he hung a few inches from the rear bulkhead, midway between the deck and the ceiling, in the forward compartment. There was the uncanny silence of vacuum around him, the lonely, dead silence when there is no air to carry the vibrations of sound.

Twisting just enough to reach around and check his suit radio, he spoke into the throat mike. His voice was almost a scream.

"Ray? Jan?" he waited for a moment. "Norman? Harry? Juan?" He waited again, but there was no answer. "Ray, can you hear me?" He ran down the names of the others again, but there was still silence in the headphones, except for the distant crackling of cosmic noise.

Oh, God, he said to himself as the mental numbness moved aside just enough for him to realize what had happened. Not us too?

He shoved away from the bulkhead with his right hand, careful not to let his strangely uncomfortable left arm touch anything. Through the red fog that filled his helmet he could see a frighteningly large gap in one of the side bulkheads, a gap that extended through both the ship's hulls, leaving a clear view of space beyond, and apparently running from the rear of the ship, through the aft crew compartment and ending in the forward one. There was good reason for no air to be in the ship.

The fuel cells still functioned, at least. The forward view screens were operating, showing a vast field of stars and the huge, flattened, striped sphere of Jupiter.

Sayers hung still for a few moments, looking at the screen, peering at the grand daddy planet. It did not seem to be moving against the backdrop of stars, at least not enough to tell, and it did not appear to be swelling or shrinking. Maybe *Priam's* orbit was stable, just maybe.

Tearing his eyes away from the screen, he twisted and pushed himself toward the hatch that connected the two crew compartments, a hatch that was standing open a little way, its whole framework twisted out of shape. It was not open quite wide enough for him to get through, and it took a great deal of effort to get it wide enough with only one hand.

The aft crew compartment was a little larger and more cylindrical in shape than was the conical forward cabin, but it was in no better condition. The rent in the hull was wider, and extended the whole length of the cabin. Like the forward compartment, dozens of loose objects hung in free fall, motionless. There were two spacesuited figures there—and neither of them moved.

"Can anyone hear me?" he said into the throat mike of his spacesuit, not wanting to look closely at the two still forms. "For God's sake, are any of you still alive?"

The radio answered with a faint crackling of stellar noise, but that was all.

Sayers felt a sudden desire to scream. It wasn't fair. Oh, Holy God, it wasn't fair!

Then some coldly rational part of his mind gave him a mental slap. Only a fool expects fairness in this universe, it said. Pull yourself together.

The red fog in his helmet was growing thicker, forming distinct blobs of blood inches from his eyes, entering his nose and mouth with each breath he took, a warm, saline moistness.

Somehow, without consciously doing it, he turned around and pulled himself back into the forward compartment. He pushed the hatch as nearly closed as he could, and wondered how much longer it would take before he really did drown in his own blood.

If I plan to go on living, he said to himself, I'm going to have to get a God damned patch on that hull.

Sensation had begun to return to his arm, a sensation that was mostly pain, a growing, swelling pain that told him that his arm was more than simply broken.

Fighting down the pain, he opened a locker that contained sheets of a thick, durable plastic-like material. Placing several of the sheets across the gap in the bulkhead, he bonded them to the metal with a small, soldering gun-like tool. He repeated the process with the warped hatch, covering the twisted framework with the plastic and bonding it to the bulkhead and deck. After a few checks, he decided that the seals were airtight.

As he propelled himself across the chamber toward the air cycling controls, nausea rose in his stomach, and a greyness came up into his eyes. The whole cabin seemed to expand suddenly, and grow dim as if the fuel cells were failing. He caught his slow flight across the cabin more by instinct than anything else, and fumbled for the air controls.

After his third or fourth attempt, the air pumps came to life; a little green signal light shone through his red-spotted faceplate, through the numb greyness of his mind, signalling proper operation. A gauge began to show the rise in pressure. The gauge became harder to read as his eyes involuntarily went out of focus and the red blobs inside his helmet swelled. Finally he had to guess that the gauge was in the safety zone. He unsnapped the clamps in his helmet.

A cloud of red droplets came away with the helmet, and he gasped for a breath of air that did not taste and smell of blood and sweat and death.

As quickly as he took the first breath of air, he was sick. His stomach made a wild lurch inside him, and its contents, the remains of a forgotten meal, spilled out of him into the air.

After a while his insides settled, leaving him feeling so weak he could hardly move. A sharp, throbbing pain replaced the nausea, and there was enough blood in his vomitings to make him think that he was hurt internally, perhaps not seriously, but badly enough.

"You're in a hell of a spot, fellow," he said aloud, forcing his lips into a smile. "You sure as hell are."

Fumbling around in the cabin, he found a first aid kit. He applied a thick, white cream to the gash in his forehead, and then covered it with a bandage. Then he began working his way out of his spacesuit.

His left arm was broken, badly broken in two places. From a fracture above his elbow a sharp corner of white bone had cut outward through the skin. He felt sick again, awfully sick.

Sayers, like all the crewmen, had been given extensive training in first aid during the preparation for the flight, and even before that he had had experiences where it had been necessary to take quick, and sometimes unorthodox action to save human life. But it had always been someone else who was hurt. Now it was himself on whom he had to work, and that was a different matter altogether.

He lost consciousness several times as he slowly worked the broken bones of his arm back into some semblance of their normal shape, and then splinted the arm stiffly at his side. When that was completed, he allowed himself to fall back into unconsciousness, and stayed that way for a long, long time.

For a day, maybe two—he was not sure—he did not move except to drink from the water canister of his spacesuit and to relieve himself. Otherwise he slept in a haze of pain and periodic coughing, soothed by ampules of drugs he found in the first aid kit. He had dreams, terrible dreams, but when he awoke he found that reality was just a little worse than the worst of the dreams.

Sayers did not die, though there were times when he thought he would, and even wished he would. Finally the pain began to fade, or perhaps he had just grown used to it, and he began to wonder just exactly what his situation was.

The ship's instruments told him a few things when he had the strength and the will to interpret them: the cesium tanks had exploded. How? Why? Hydrogen and oxygen balloons had split under the acceleration of escaping from Jupiter; liquid oxygen, as well as combining with the hydrogen, had spilled back, found its way through a stress crack into the cesium; then a violent oxidization had begun, a reaction that grew, blasting open other cesium tanks, tearing open more balloons of liquid oxygen and hydrogen, creating a tremendous, flaming explosion in the airlessness of space. Now *Priam* was a wreck, without ionic jet engines, without its cesium fuel. It was that simple.

About two-thirds of the way to the rear of the ship had been the ring of metallic plastic balloons which had contained liquid oxygen, to replenish the crew's air and other ship's functions, liquid hydrogen, a coolant for the engines, and water. About half of those balloons had been ruptured and their contents strewn half way to Jupiter.

The hull was torn by a gap that extended half the length of the ship. Two of the four sections of the hydroponic gardens had been depressurized, though the other two sections were still airtight, and their contents apparently in good condition.

Radar reported that the wreck of the *Priam* was in a stable elliptical orbit around Jupiter. The kick of the explosion and her own inertia had carried the ship far beyond the spot where Ray Coiner had commanded that the engines be shut off. The average distance was in the neighbourhood of 420,000 miles from the planet, or just a little over the distance of Europa, and one revolution around would last something like 3 days and 14 or 15 hours. Sayers would probably never see Europa, except as a bright star, since his orbit was at quite an angle to hers. It would probably take thousands or millions of years before the derelict happened to cross Europa's path when the moon was anywhere near.

Food supplies were more than ample for one person for a long time, and as long as the remaining hydroponic gardens were tended, they would continue to supply fresh food and help replenish the air. Even with half the stores of air and water gone, there was enough to last Sayers at least ten years; the water might last even longer than that since a lot of the original supply had been intended for use in operating the drive units, and they no longer existed. Highly efficient reclamation and recycling equipment could make a gallon of water do the work of several dozen before it was finally lost from the system.

Sayers could survive for a long time in orbit around Jupiter. But so what? he asked himself. No one was coming after him. It was merely a matter of delaying the inevitable. He was like a patient with a terminal disease; the ultimate end could be put off, but not avoided, and he wondered whether putting it off was worth the trouble.

He sat looking at the banks of instruments for what seemed to be hours, and would probably have continued to stare had not the very basic sensation of hunger gotten the better of him.

His stomach had returned to enough like normal for the desire for food to have come back, and sooner or later, unless he decided to starve himself to death, he would have to get into his spacesuit, pull the seals off the connecting hatch, and go through the aft compartment into the galley.

He delayed it as long as he could, not wanting to have to put the spacesuit back on, knowing it would be painful to his broken arm, not wanting to see the two bodies that hung silently in the rear compartment. At last he gave in, and cleaned the blood out of his helmet. Then he began to pull his spacesuit on. It was difficult, but not painful, until he began stretching the tough fabric up over his broken arm. The arm was taped to his side, and bent at the elbow so that his forearm came across his stomach. His numb left hand bending around his right side. The added girth to his torso made a tight fit for the spacesuit, and Sayers thought he could feel the broken bone ends move as he zippered the suit shut.

Clamping his helmet tight, he went to the air cycling controls, reduced the air pressure to zero and saw the green operating light fade out, replaced by a red one. He pulled the sealing patch off the hatch, worked it as wide open as he could, and pulled himself through.

He paused for a moment, his breath coming in hot gasps, and surveyed the compartment. It had not changed. The two space-suited figures had not moved.

Before he looked for food, he told himself, he would have to do something about them. Burial in space? He could not just slip them out of the air lock and let them float in orbit around the ship. Then he thought of the airless sections of the hydroponic gardens. Those tanks of chemicals were a poor facsimile of soil, but at least things had grown there once. Perhaps it was fitting that his friends lie there.

Despite himself he looked at the faces inside the helmets as he slowly, painfully moved them through the corridor to the hydroponic gardens. Norman Hudson was the first one—big, ugly, red faced, but with a mind... Dammit! he yelled to himself. Cut it out!

He placed Hudson's body inside one of the ruptured sections of the gardens, and then went back.

Harry Isaacs had died suddenly, painlessly, and for Harry's sake, he was glad of it.

Ray and Juan had been outside, he told himself as he moved Isaacs' body in beside Hudson's. They had gotten it when the tanks exploded. Norm and Harry had been killed by the concussion that had not quite killed Sayers. But what had happened to Jan Whittinger?

Whittinger had been in the aft compartment with the other two, bent over his instruments, plotting their orbit back to Ganymede. Maybe he had been sucked out through the gap in the hull when the cabin depressurized. Maybe he was floating out there somewhere, still alive, his radio inoperative. Maybe... That's enough! Sayers told himself. The gap was not large enough to pass a human being without touching the edges of the ragged metal—and it took very little imagination to visualize what would have happened to a spacesuit passing through that opening. Jan was not alive, no more than Harry and Norm. Jan was dead. They were all dead, God dammit, dead!

Sayers felt very little hunger after that.

He forced himself to go into the galley, gather up several packages of food and a canister of water, and then half-floated, half-swam back into the forward compartment. After re-sealing the hatch, he cut the air cycler back on and removed his helmet. Somehow he opened his mouth, forced in food, and gagged it down his throat.

While he ate, some small and distant part of his mind said: No situation is ever really hopeless, not unless you're dead.

Platitudes, the surface of his mind replied angrily, that's just exactly what the hell I need, platitudes.

But he remembered an incident, fifteen or sixteen years before, when he was just a kid. They had lived on the northwest coast of Florida then, right on the Gulf of Mexico, and during the summer he spent every day on the beach.

His father had a small boat with an outboard motor that he used for fishing, and young Scott used for water skiing. He took it out in the narrow bay near his home two or three times a week, seldom going far from shore.

One day, when all his friends were otherwise occupied, Scott was out alone in the boat, feeling a little braver than usual. He drifted farther from shore than ever before, out of the bay into the unusually calm waters of the Gulf. About the time he lost sight of the land, a sudden summer storm came up, lashing him with cold rain, obscuring the afternoon sun. By the time the storm was over, he had completely lost his orientation, and could not see the sun through the heavy clouds that remained in the sky.

He began running aimlessly, first one way, and then another, trying to catch some glimpse of the distant shore, and after a while the inevitable happened—he ran out of fuel, and still without sighting land. When darkness came, he sat in the middle of an endless ocean.

That was the longest night Scotty Sayers ever spent in his life. Death seemed to hover over him like a dark angel, beating its taloned wings in his face. He did not ever think he would see solid land again. Saying his childhood prayers, he resigned himself to whatever fate awaited lost sailors.

A few hours before dawn the overcast began to break apart, and finally, one after another, stars began to appear. At last the Big Dipper was complete and he followed its pointer star to Polaris. He knew where north was. He began rowing with the boat's single oar, rowing until his arms were so sore and stiff he did not think he could continue to move, but he did; he kept rowing.

When dawn came, the sky was clear, and on the horizon he could see white sandy beaches, and a house or two. He came ashore five miles from home. He was at home when his father's search party returned. His punishment was swift, stern and just, but he had learned his lesson; he had learned several lessons.

That little incident, stupid and minor as it was, had taught him to never give up hope. Maybe that sounds inane and trite, he told himself, but it's true. Maybe there *are* situations you can't get out of, but you can never be sure that *this* is one of them. Keep trying—really, what have you got to lose?

He had not taken off his spacesuit while he ate, and when he had completed forcing the food down into his unwilling stomach, he slipped his helmet back on, went to the air lock, found that the outer hatch was jammed open, went back and cut off the air pumps, then wormed his way through the air lock and out into space.

The instruments had told him the condition of the ship, but he wanted to see it for himself. Maybe things were not quite as bad as they seemed.

They were.

After coming back into the ship and resting fitfully, Sayers pulled himself back out of his spacesuit, located a clipboard, pencil and paper, and began writing down his assets.

The better part of the ship was still intact, though the hull needed patching. He still had power and most of the instruments functioned. Food was not a problem; the frozen and dehydrated supplies were meant to last for years, and the two remaining sections of the hydroponic garden supplemented that. Air, from both the oxygen given off from the gardens and that in the remaining metallic balloons, would last a decade. Water was equally well supplied. He even had several hundred gallons of liquid hydrogen, though he could not see the value of that. One good spacesuit and replacement units were in the lockers. He was amply outfitted with tools, though he did not know what he could build. He had a tremendously powerful radio, but not powerful enough to contact Earth or the Mars station.

The debit side of the list was shorter, but even at that, far too long: Ray, Juan, Norman, Harry, Jan—dead; engines—destroyed; fuel—gone. That seemed quite a sufficient list.

He took a second piece of paper and stared down at the blank, white surface for a long while. Then he wrote:

"Problem: in orbit around J.

"Solution: build up sufficient velocity to break away and fall into solar orbit like a comet.

"How achieve: ???"

It's pretty simple when you write it down, he thought. But what in God's name do I do for an engine and fuel?

"$2H_2 + O_2 = 2H_2O$," he wrote. "And a release of energy," he said aloud. "But how much?" He did not remember his basic chemistry well enough to come up with any meaningful figures, but he was sure that it was not enough to do him any real good. Anyway, what would he do for a combustion chamber?

"Where does that leave you?" he asked.

He quickly began sketching an egg-shaped chamber on the bottom of the paper. Punch a hole in one end, fit a cone-shaped nozzle, and I've got an engine, he thought. I could build that from the materials I've got.

But that thought brought him back to the original problem—fuel. What did he have to burn besides oxygen and hydrogen? "Nothing, not a God damned thing!"

His drawing made him think of something he had seen in a history book, a crude steam engine built by an ancient Greek named Hero, or something like that. It had been a hollow sphere, mounted on pivots, with an "L"-shaped nozzle on either side, facing in opposite directions. When the chamber had water placed in it, heated and began to build up steam pressure, it rotated as the vapour jetted out of the nozzles. Do away with one nozzle, he thought, straighten out the other and flare it a little, and I've got a jet engine, a steam jet.

Sayers smiled to himself. I've got water, more than I'll ever need, and enough hydrogen and oxygen to make God-only-knows how much more. So I've got fuel, after a fashion.

"Where does that get you, fellow?" he asked himself. "How do you go about heating the water. Got that much fuel in your lighter?"

He thought of running wires from the ship's electrical system out to the rear of the ship where he would construct his "steam jet." But how much electrical power have I got available? And how much would it take to give me the kind of heat I'd need? Not enough, he answered himself, not nearly enough.

"Heat?" he said aloud, suddenly grabbing the paper from the clipboard and wadding it in his hand. "Where the hell do I get heat out here?"

He looked up at one of the view screens over the forward control panel. In the lower right hand corner was a tiny yellow disc, a fourth the size of Earth's sun, 484,000,000 miles away.

Sitting right in the middle of Hell's ninth ring, he thought, out here where methane and ammonia are normally liquid, and I need heat.

"You've got talent, Scotty," he said aloud, "real talent, boy."

Somehow that seemed funny to him, too funny. A strange, savage laughter came up in his throat, a laughter he suddenly found he could not control.

"God damn you," he yelled between bursts of laughter, shaking his fist at the cold, remote disc of the sun. "God damn you. God damn you!"

Suddenly the laughter died in his throat, and for a few moments Sayers hung in free fall before the view screen, peering at the tiny yellow disc of Sol.

"Maybe you've got some use after all," he said aloud, very, very slowly.

Weeks, months, perhaps even years later—Sayers did not really know—he sat before the control board, watching the huge bulk of Jupiter as he swung around it, out of its shadow back into the pale light of the distant sun.

His left hand lay strapped to the arm of his control seat, his fingers in a strange, motionless position. There was a pale waxiness to that hand and arm, a flabbiness to the flesh that the rest of his body did not share.

His face was dark and lined and thick, covered with a growth of dark beard. His NASA uniform was tattered rags, soiled and ugly. But there was a bright gleam to his eyes, and a hard smile on his lips.

"Okay," he said aloud, for he had grown quite accustomed to talking to himself, "let's see what happens."

A large, crude wheel had been built into the control panel, a wheel that was connected to a geared-down pointer and to a chain drive that went back through the cabin, through a rubber-sealed opening in the bulkhead, vanishing into the rear of the ship.

Sayers estimated the position of the sun and then began to turn the wheel slowly with his right hand, turning it until the pointer lined up with the sun. Then he waited, his eyes peering intently at a gauge that was crudely lettered "Steam Pressure."

For hours he did not move, did nothing but watch the red needle of the gauge as it slowly, terribly slowly began to climb from its zero position. But it did move, by God, it moved.

Three quarters of the way across the face of the gauge there was a red mark, and Sayers did not move until the needle crept up to that mark. Then he caught his breath. There was silence.

The sound that passed through the ship was a mere vibration, a sudden cough and a shudder that pressed Sayers back into his seat only slightly, but that was enough.

"God damn!" he yelled jubilantly. "It works. I'm going home. By God, I'm going home."

The NASA spaceship *Priam* had never been a pretty sight. It had been designed for efficiency, not beauty—an ungainly collection of tubes and spheres, braces and supports. But now it was stranger and uglier looking than ever before, like a huge bat-winged thing spewing behind it a cloud of white vapour that vanished into space.

Two huge, parabolically curved crescents of metallic plastic, the remnants of burst balloons, sprouted from either side of the naked framework. An "L"-shaped arm came out of the ship's stripped structure for each wing. The short leg of the "L" was connected to a crude chain drive which ran from the interior of the ship; the long leg was connected to the wing; and the whole affair could be rotated so that the concave portions of the crescent wings always aimed toward a large, roughly egg-shaped chamber that had been welded into the spot where the *Priam's* ion drive had once been.

The parabolic wings were not the most efficient mirrors men had ever devised, but at least they did work: gathering the faint light of the distant sun, focusing its weak rays on the metal egg, heating it and its contents until the pressure of the vaporizing water grew great enough to blow off its valves and spew a jet of steam out into space.

Sayers knew it was crude and inefficient, the whole mess, and delivered an infinitesimal fraction of the power the ship's ionic jets would have given him. But at least it was power, and that is what he needed.

Of water he had plenty, maybe even enough to give him the boost he needed. It would take a long time, God, a hell of a long time, as the weak jet slowly increased his speed, slowly pushed him out into a widening spiral, slowly pushed him out to the point where Sol's distant gravitational field would rival, then surpass that of Jupiter, and he would begin to fall sunward, Earthward.

Maybe he would run out of water before he escaped from Jupiter's gravitational field. He did not know. But so be it. He was trying, and to die trying was a hell of a lot better than to die without giving it a chance.

Maybe I'll never get close to Earth, Sayers thought as he slowly turned the crank and kept the mirrors directed into the sun, but if I can just get within radio range, that'll be enough. Just let me get close enough.

Sayers sat back in the control chair and looked up at the huge disc of Jupiter on one of the auxiliary view screens.

"I'll beat you, God damn you," he said, "or die trying. But I think I'll beat you."

The longest voyage had begun, the long voyage back toward the raging solar furnace, and a green and blue planet called Earth.

THE SHIP WHO SANG

Anne McCaffrey

Anne McCaffrey (1926–2011) has become inextricably associated with dragons, because of her long-running and highly popular series set on the planet Pern. This began with the award-winning novella "Weyr Search" (1967) which was incorporated into the first novel of the series, Dragonflight (1968). Because of dragons, the series is often thought of as fantasy, but it is far from that. The dragons are the predominant fauna on a world colonized long ago by humans with whom they form a close telepathic, almost symbiotic bond. The Pern series would eventually run to over twenty books, some written with, or by, her son Todd McCaffrey, and they have rather overshadowed her other work. Early in her career, years before Pern, she created the idea of the mind-ship or brain-ship, where an adapted human becomes the operational heart of a spaceship and works in harmony with the ship's captain. This pairing is known colloquially as Brain and Brawn which is the overall name for the series that emerged from this first story, 'The Ship Who Sang' (1961). McCaffrey later regarded it as her best story.

S HE WAS BORN A THING AND AS SUCH WOULD BE CONDEMNED if she failed to pass the encephalograph test required of all newborn babies. There was always the possibility that though the limbs were twisted, the mind was not, that though the ears would hear only dimly, the eyes see vaguely, the mind behind them was receptive and alert.

The electro-encephalogram was entirely favourable, unexpectedly so, and the news was brought to the waiting, grieving parents. There was the final, harsh decision: to give their child euthanasia or permit it to become an encapsulated "brain," a guiding mechanism in any one of a number of curious professions. As such, their offspring would suffer no pain, live a comfortable existence in a metal shell for several centuries, performing unusual service to Central Worlds.

She lived and was given a name, Helva. For her first three vegetable months she waved her crabbed claws, kicked weakly with her clubbed feet and enjoyed the usual routine of the infant. She was not alone for there were three other such children in the big city's special nursery. Soon they all were removed to Central Laboratory School where their delicate transformation began.

One of the babies died in the initial transferral but of Helva's "class," seventeen thrived in the metal shells. Instead of kicking feet, Helva's neural responses started her wheels; instead of grabbing with hands, she manipulated mechanical extensions. As she matured, more and more neural synapses would be adjusted to operate other mechanisms that went into the maintenance and running of a space ship. For Helva was destined to be the "brain" half of a scout ship, partnered with a man or a woman, whichever she chose, as the mobile half. She would be among the elite of her kind. Her initial intelligence tests registered above normal and her adaptation index was unusually high. As long as her development within her shell lived up to expectations, and there were no side-effects from the pituitary tinkering, Helva would live a rewarding, rich and unusual life, a far cry from what she would have faced as an ordinary, "normal" being.

However, no diagram of her brain patterns, no early I.Q. tests recorded certain essential facts about Helva that Central must eventually learn. They would have to bide their official time and see, trusting that the massive doses of shell-psychology would suffice her, too, as the necessary bulwark against her unusual confinement and the pressures of her profession. A ship run by a human brain could not run rogue or insane with the power and resources Central had to build into their scout ships. Brain ships were, of course, long past the experimental stages. Most babes survived the perfected techniques of pituitary manipulation that kept their bodies small, eliminating the necessity of transfers from smaller to larger shells. And very, very few were lost when the final connection was made to the control panels of ship or industrial combine. Shell people resembled mature dwarfs in size whatever their natal deformities were, but the well-oriented brain would not have changed places with the most perfect body in the Universe.

So, for happy years, Helva scooted around in her shell with her classmates, playing such games as Stall, Power-Seek, studying her lessons in trajectory, propulsion techniques, computation, logistics, mental hygiene, basic alien psychology, philology, space history, law, traffic, codes: all the et ceteras that eventually became compounded into a reasoning, logical, informed citizen. Not so

obvious to her, but of more importance to her teachers, Helva
ingested the precepts of her conditioning as easily as she absorbed
her nutrient fluid. She would one day be grateful to the patient
drone of the subconscious-level instruction.

Helva's civilization was not without busy, do-good associations,
exploring possible inhumanities to terrestrial as well as extraterrestrial
citizens. One such group got all incensed over shelled "children"
when Helva was just turning fourteen. When they were forced
to, Central Worlds shrugged its shoulders, arranged a tour of the
Laboratory Schools and set the tour off to a big start by showing
the members case histories, complete with photographs. Very few
committees ever looked past the first few photos. Most of their
original objections about "shells" were overridden by the relief
that these hideous (to them) bodies *were* mercifully concealed.

Helva's class was doing Fine Arts, a selective subject in her
crowded programme. She had activated one of her microscopic
tools which she would later use for minute repairs to various parts
of her control panel. Her subject was large—a copy of the Last
Supper—and her canvas, small—the head of a tiny screw. She had
tuned her sight to the proper degree. As she worked she absent-
mindedly crooned, producing a curious sound. Shell people used
their own vocal chords and diaphragms but sound issued through
microphones rather than mouths. Helva's hum then had a curious vibrancy, a warm, dulcet quality even in its aimless chromatic
wanderings.

"Why, what a lovely voice you have," said one of the female
visitors.

Helva "looked" up and caught a fascinating panorama of regular, dirty craters on a flaky pink surface. Her hum became a gurgle
of surprise. She instinctively regulated her "sight" until the skin
lost its cratered look and the pores assumed normal proportions.

"Yes, we have quite a few years of voice training, madam," remarked Helva calmly. "Vocal peculiarities often become excessively irritating during prolonged intra-stellar distances and must be eliminated. I enjoyed my lessons."

Although this was the first time that Helva had seen unshelled people, she took this experience calmly. Any other reaction would have been reported instantly.

"I meant that you have a nice singing voice… dear," the lady amended.

"Thank you. Would you like to see my work?" Helva asked, politely. She instinctively sheered away from personal discussions but she filed the comment away for further meditation.

"Work?" asked the lady.

"I am currently reproducing the Last Supper on the head of a screw."

"O, I say," the lady twittered.

Helva turned her vision back to magnification and surveyed her copy critically.

"Of course, some of my colour values do not match the old Master's and the perspective is faulty but I believe it to be a fair copy."

The lady's eyes, unmagnified, bugged out.

"Oh, I forget," and Helva's voice was really contrite. If she could have blushed, she would have. "You people don't have adjustable vision."

The monitor of this discourse grinned with pride and amusement as Helva's tone indicated pity for the unfortunate.

"Here, this will help," suggested Helva, substituting a magnifying device in one extension and holding it over the picture.

In a kind of shock, the ladies and gentlemen of the committee bent to observe the incredibly copied and brilliantly executed Last Supper on the head of a screw.

"Well," remarked one gentleman who had been forced to accompany his wife, "the good Lord can eat where angels fear to tread."

"Are you referring, sir," asked Helva politely, "to the Dark Age discussions of the number of angels who could stand on the head of a pin?"

"I had that in mind."

"If you substitute 'atom' for 'angel,' the problem is not insoluble, given the metallic content of the pin in question."

"Which you are programmed to compute?"

"Of course."

"Did they remember to program a sense of humour, as well, young lady?"

"We are directed to develop a sense of proportion, sir, which contributes the same effect."

The good man chortled appreciatively and decided the trip was worth his time.

If the investigation committee spent months digesting the thoughtful food served them at the Laboratory School, they left Helva with a morsel as well.

"Singing" as applicable to herself required research. She had, of course, been exposed to and enjoyed a music appreciation course which had included the better known classical works such as "Tristan und Isolde," "Candide," "Oklahoma," "Nozze di Figaro," the atomic age singers, Eileen Farrell, Elvis Presley and Geraldine Todd, as well as the curious rhythmic progressions of the Venusians, Capellan visual chromatics and the sonic concerti of the Altairians. But "singing" for any shell person posed considerable technical difficulties to be overcome. Shell people were schooled to examine every aspect of a problem or situation before making a prognosis. Balanced properly between optimism and practicality, the non-defeatist attitude of the shell people led them to extricate themselves, their ships and personnel, from bizarre situations. Therefore to Helva, the problem that she couldn't open her mouth to sing, among other restrictions, did not bother her. She would work out a method, by-passing her limitations, whereby she could sing.

She approached the problem by investigating the methods of sound reproduction through the centuries, human and instrumental. Her own sound production equipment was essentially more instrumental than vocal. Breath control and the proper enunciation of vowel sounds within the oral cavity appeared to require the most development and practice. Shell people did not, strictly speaking, breathe. For their purposes, oxygen and other gases were not drawn from the surrounding atmosphere through the medium of lungs but sustained artificially by solution in their shells. After experimentation, Helva discovered that she could manipulate her diaphragmic unit to sustain tone. By relaxing the throat muscles and expanding the oral cavity well into the frontal sinuses, she could direct the vowel sounds into the most felicitous position for proper reproduction through her throat microphone. She compared the results with tape recordings of modern singers and was not unpleased although her own tapes had a peculiar quality about them, not at all unharmonious, merely unique. Acquiring a repertoire from the Laboratory library was no problem to one trained to perfect recall. She found herself able to sing any role and any song which struck her fancy. It would not have occurred to her that it was curious for a female to sing bass, baritone, tenor, alto, mezzo, soprano and coloratura as she pleased. It was, to Helva, only a matter of the correct reproduction and diaphragmic control required by the music attempted.

If the authorities remarked on her curious avocation, they did so among themselves. Shell people were encouraged to develop a hobby so long as they maintained proficiency in their technical work.

On the anniversary of her sixteenth year in her shell, Helva was unconditionally graduated and installed in her ship, the XH-834. Her permanent titanium shell was recessed behind an even more indestructible barrier in the central shaft of the scout ship. The neural, audio, visual and sensory connections were made and sealed. Her extendibles were diverted, connected or augmented and the final, delicate-beyond-description brain taps were completed while Helva remained anaesthetically unaware of the proceedings. When she awoke, she *was* the ship. Her brain and intelligence controlled every function from navigation to such loading as a scout ship of her class needed. She could take care of herself and her ambulatory half, in any situation already recorded in the annals of Central Worlds and any situation its most fertile minds could imagine.

Her first actual flight, for she and her kind had made mock flights on dummy panels since she was eight, showed her complete mastery of the techniques of her profession. She was ready for her great adventures and the arrival of her mobile partner.

There were nine qualified scouts sitting around collecting base pay the day Helva was commissioned. There were several missions which demanded instant attention but Helva had been of interest to several department heads in Central for some time and each man was determined to have her assigned to *his* section. Consequently no one had remembered to introduce Helva to the prospective partners. The ship always chose its own partner. Had there been another "brain" ship at the Base at the moment, Helva would have been guided to make the first move. As it was, while Central wrangled among itself, Robert Tanner sneaked out of the pilots' barracks, out to the field and over to Helva's slim metal hull.

"Hello, anyone at home?" Tanner wisecracked.

"Of course," replied Helva logically, activating her outside scanners. "Are you my partner?" she asked hopefully, as she recognized the Scout Service uniform.

"All you have to do is ask," he retorted hopefully.

"No one has come. I thought perhaps there were no partners available and I've had no directives from Central."

Even to herself Helva sounded a little self-pitying but the truth was she was lonely, sitting on the darkened field. Always she had had the company of other shells and more recently, technicians by the score. The sudden solitude had lost its momentary charm and become oppressive.

"No directives from Central is scarcely a cause for regret, but there happen to be eight other guys biting their fingernails to the quick just waiting for an invitation to board you, you beautiful thing."

Tanner was inside the central cabin as he said this, running appreciative fingers over her panel, the scout's gravity-couch, poking his head into the cabins, the galley, the head, the pressured-storage compartments.

"Now, if you want to give Central a shove and do *us* a favour all in one, call up the Barracks and let's have a ship-warming partner-picking party. Hmmmm?"

Helva chuckled to herself. He was so completely different from the occasional visitors or the various Laboratory technicians she had encountered. He was so gay, so assured, and she was delighted by his suggestion of a partner-picking party. Certainly it was not against anything in her understanding of regulations.

"Cencom, this is XH-834. Connect me with Pilot Barracks."

"Visual?"

"Please."

A picture of lounging men in various attitudes of boredom came on her screen.

"This is XH-834. Would the unassigned scouts do me the favour of coming aboard?"

Eight figures galvanized into action, grabbing pieces of wearing apparel, disengaging tape mechanisms, disentangling themselves from bedsheets and towels.

Helva dissolved the connection while Tanner chuckled gleefully and settled down to await their arrival.

Helva was engulfed in an unshell-like flurry of anticipation. No actress on her opening night could have been more apprehensive, fearful or breathless. Unlike the actress, she could throw no hysterics, china objets d'art or greasepaint to relieve her tension. She could, of course, check her stores for edibles and drinks, which she did, serving Tanner from the virgin selection of her commissary.

Scouts were colloquially known as "brawns" as opposed to their ship "brains." They had to pass as rigorous a training programme as the brains and only the top one percent of each contributory world's highest scholars were admitted to Central Worlds Scout Training Program. Consequently the eight young men who came pounding up the gantry into Helva's hospitable lock were unusually fine-looking, intelligent, well-coordinated and adjusted young men, looking forward to a slightly drunken evening, Helva permitting, and all quite willing to do each other dirt to get possession of her.

Such a human invasion left Helva mentally breathless, a luxury she thoroughly enjoyed for the brief time she felt she should permit it.

She sorted out the young men. Tanner's opportunism amused but did not specifically attract her; the blond Nordsen seemed too simple; dark-haired Al-atpay had a kind of obstinacy with which she felt no compassion: Mir-Ahnin's bitterness hinted an inner

darkness she did not wish to lighten although he made the biggest
outward play for her attention. Hers was a curious courtship—this
would be only the first of several marriages for her, for brawns
retired after 75 years of service, or earlier if they were unlucky.
Brains, their bodies safe from any deterioration, served 200 years,
and were then permitted to decide for themselves if they wished
to continue. Helva had actually spoken to one shell person three
hundred and twenty-two years old. She had been so awed by the
contact she hadn't presumed to ask the personal questions she
had wanted to.

Her choice did not stand out from the others until Tanner
started to sing a scout ditty, recounting the misadventures of the
bold, dense, painfully inept Billy Brawn. An attempt at harmony
resulted in cacophony and Tanner wagged his arms wildly for
silence.

"What we need is a roaring good lead tenor. Jennan, besides
palming aces, what do you sing?"

"Sharp," Jennan replied with easy good humour.

"If a tenor is absolutely necessary, I'll attempt it," Helva
volunteered.

"My good *woman*," Tanner protested.

"Sound your 'A'," laughed Jennan.

Into the stunned silence that followed the rich, clear, high "A,"
Jennan remarked quietly, "Such an A Caruso would have given the
rest of his notes to sing."

It did not take them long to discover her full range.

"All Tanner asked for was one roaring good lead tenor," Jennan
complained jokingly, "and our sweet mistress supplies us an entire
repertory company. The boy who gets this ship will go far, far, far."

"To the Horsehead Nebulae?" asked Nordsen, quoting an old
Central saw.

"To the Horsehead Nebulae and back, we shall make beautiful music," countered Helva chuckling.

"Together," Jennan amended. "Only you'd better make the music and with my voice, I'd better listen."

"I rather imagined it would be I who listened," suggested Helva.

Jennan executed a stately bow with an intricate flourish of his crush-brimmed hat. He directed his bow towards the central control pillar where Helva *was*. Her own personal preference crystallized at that precise moment and for that particular reason: Jennan, alone of the men, had addressed his remarks directly at her physical presence, regardless of the fact that he knew she could pick up his image wherever he was in the ship and regardless of the fact that her body was behind massive metal walls. Throughout their partnership, Jennan never failed to turn his head in her direction no matter where he was in relation to her. In response to this personalization, Helva at that moment and from then on always spoke to Jennan only through her central mike, even though that was not always the most efficient method.

Helva didn't know that she fell in love with Jennan that evening. As she had never been exposed to love or affection, only the drier cousins, respect and admiration, she could scarcely have recognized her reaction to the warmth of his personality and consideration. As a shell-person, she considered herself remote from emotions largely connected with physical desires.

"Well, Helva, it's been swell meeting you," said Tanner suddenly as she and Jennan were arguing about the Baroque quality of "Come All Ye Sons of Art." "See you in space some time, you lucky dog, Jennan. Thanks for the party, Helva."

"You don't have to go so soon?" pleaded Helva, realizing belatedly that she and Jennan had been excluding the others from this discussion.

"Best man won," Tanner said, wryly. "Guess I'd better go get a tape on love ditties. May need 'em for the next ship, if there're any more at home like you."

Helva and Jennan watched them leave, both a little confused.

"Perhaps Tanner's jumping to conclusions?" Jennan asked.

Helva regarded him as he slouched against the console, facing her shell directly. His arms were crossed on his chest and the glass he held had been empty for some time. He was handsome, they all were; but his watchful eyes were unwary, his mouth assumed a smile easily, his voice (to which Helva was particularly drawn) was resonant, deep and without unpleasant overtones or accent.

"Sleep on it, at any rate, Helva. Call me in the morning if it's your op."

She called him at breakfast, after she had checked her choice through Central. Jennan moved his things aboard, received their joint commission, had his personality and experience file locked into her reviewer, gave her the coordinates of their first mission and the XH-834 officially became the JH-834.

Their first mission was a dull but necessary crash priority (Medical got Helva), rushing a vaccine to a distant system plagued with a virulent spore disease. They had only to get to Spica as fast as possible.

After the initial, thrilling forward surge at her maximum speed, Helva realized her muscles were to be given less of a workout than her brawn on this tedious mission. But they did have plenty of time for exploring each other's personalities. Jennan, of course, knew what Helva was capable of as a ship and partner, just as she knew what she could expect from him. But these were only facts and Helva looked forward eagerly to learning that human side of her partner which could not be reduced to a series of symbols. Nor could the give and take of two personalities be learned from a book. It has to be experienced.

"My father was a scout, too, or is that programmed?" began Jennan their third day out.

"Naturally."

"Unfair, you know. You've got all my family history and I don't know one blamed thing about yours."

"I've never known either," Helva confided. "Until I read yours, it hadn't occurred to me I must have one, too, someplace in Central's files."

Jennan snorted. "Shell psychology!"

Helva laughed. "Yes, and I'm even programmed against curiosity about it. You'd better be, too."

Jennan ordered a drink, slouched into the gravity couch opposite her, put his feet on the bumpers, turning himself idly from side to side on the gimbals.

"Helva—a made-up name…"

"With a Scandinavian sound."

"You aren't blonde," Jennan said positively.

"Well, then, there're dark Swedes."

"And blonde Turks and this one's harem is limited to one."

"Your woman in purdah, yes, but you can comb the pleasure houses—" Helva found herself aghast at the edge to her carefully trained voice.

"You know," Jennan interrupted her, deep in some thought of his own, "my father gave me the impression he was a lot more married to his ship, the Silvia, than to my mother. I know I used to think Silvia was my grandmother. She was a low number so she must have been a great-great-grandmother at least. I used to talk to her for hours."

"Her registry?" asked Helva, unwitting of the jealousy for everyone and anyone who had shared his hours.

"422. I think she's TS now. I ran into Tom Burgess once."

Jennan's father had died of a planetary disease, the vaccine for which his ship had used up in curing the local citizens.

"Tom said he'd got mighty tough and salty. You lose your sweetness and I'll come back and haunt you, girl," Jennan threatened.

Helva laughed. He startled her by stamping up to the control panel, touching it with light, tender fingers.

"I *wonder* what you look like," he said softly, wistfully.

Helva had been briefed about this natural curiosity of scouts. She didn't know anything about herself and neither of them ever would or could.

"Pick any form, shape and shade and I'll be yours obliging," she countered as training suggested.

"Iron Maiden, I fancy blondes with long tresses," and Jennan pantomined Lady Godiva-like tresses. "Since you're immolated in titanium, I'll call you Brunhilda, my dear," and he made his bow.

With a chortle, Helva launched into the appropriate aria just as Spica made contact.

"What'n'ell's that yelling about? Who are you? And unless you're Central Worlds Medical go away. We've got a plague with no visiting privileges."

"My ship is singing, we're the JH-834 of Worlds and we've got your vaccine. What are our landing coordinates?"

"Your *ship* is singing?"

"The greatest S.A.T.B. in organized space. Any request?"

The JH-834 delivered the vaccine but no more arias and received immediate orders to proceed to Leviticus IV. By the time they got there, Jennan found a reputation awaiting him and was forced to defend the 834's virgin honour.

"I'll stop singing," murmured Helva contritely as she ordered up poultices for his third black eye in a week.

"You will not," Jennan said through gritted teeth. "If I have to black eyes from here to the Horsehead to keep the snicker out of the title, we'll be the ship who sings."

After the "ship who sings" tangled with a minor but vicious narcotic ring in the Lesser Magellanics, the title became definitely respectful. Central was aware of each episode and punched out a "special interest" key on JH-834's file. A first-rate team was shaking down well.

Jennan and Helva considered themselves a first-rate team, too, after their tidy arrest.

"Of all the vices in the universe, I *hate* drug addiction," Jennan remarked as they headed back to Central Base. "People can go to hell quick enough without that kind of help."

"Is that why you volunteered for Scout Service? To redirect traffic?"

"I'll bet my official answer's on your review."

"In far too flowery wording. 'Carrying on the traditions of my family which has been proud of four generations in Service' if I may quote you your own words."

Jennan groaned. "I was *very* young when I wrote that and I certainly hadn't been through Final Training and once I was in Final Training, my pride wouldn't let me fail...

"As I mentioned, I used to visit Dad on board the Silvia and I've a very good idea she might have had her eye on me as a replacement for my father because I had had massive doses of scout-oriented propaganda. It took. From the time I was seven, I was going to be a scout or else." He shrugged as if deprecating a youthful determination that had taken a great deal of mature application to bring to fruition.

"Ah, so? Scout Sahir Silan on the JS-422 penetrating into the Horsehead Nebulae?"

Jennan chose to ignore her sarcasm.

"With *you*, I may even get that far but even with Silvia's nudging *I* never day-dreamed myself *that* kind of glory in my wildest flights of fancy. I'll leave the whoppers to your agile brain henceforth. I have in mind a smaller contribution to Space History."

"So modest?"

"No. Practical. We also serve, et cetera." He placed a dramatic hand on his heart.

"Glory hound!" scoffed Helva.

"Look who's talking, my Nebulae-bound friend. At least I'm not greedy. There'll only be one hero like my dad at Parsaea, but I *would* like to be remembered for some kudo. Everyone does. Why else do or die?"

"Your father died on his way back from Parsaea, if I may point out a few cogent facts. So he could never have known he was a hero for damning the flood with his ship. Which kept Parsaean colony from being abandoned. Which gave them a chance to discover the anti-paralytic qualities of Parsaea. Which *he* never knew."

"*I* know," said Jennan softly.

Helva was immediately sorry for the tone of her rebuttal. She knew very well how deep Jennan's attachment to his father had been. On his review a note was made that he had rationalized his father's loss with the unexpected and welcome outcome of the Affair at Parsaea.

"Facts are not human, Helva, My father was and so am I. And *basically*, so are you. Check over your dial, 834. Amid all the wires attached to you is a heart, an underdeveloped human heart. Obviously!"

"I apologize, Jennan," she said contritely.

Jennan hesitated a moment, threw out his hands in acceptance and then tapped her shell affectionately.

"If they ever take us off the milkruns, we'll make a stab at the Nebulae, huh?"

As so frequently happened in the Scout Service, within the next hour they had orders to change course, not to the Nebulae, but to a recently colonized system with two habitable planets, one tropical, one glacial. The sun, named Ravel, had become unstable; the spectrum was that of a rapidly expanding shell, with absorption lines rapidly displacing toward violet. The augmented heat of the primary had already forced evacuation of the nearer world, Daphnis. The pattern of spectral emissions gave indication that the sun would sear Chloe as well. All ships in the immediate spatial vicinity were to report to Disaster Headquarters on Chloe to effect removal of the remaining colonists.

The JH-834 obediently presented itself and was sent to outlying areas on Chloe to pick up scattered settlers who did not appear to appreciate the urgency of the situation. Chloe, indeed, was enjoying the first temperatures above freezing since it had been flung out of its parent. Since many of the colonists were religious fanatics who had settled on rigorous Chloe to fit themselves for a life of pious reflection, Chloe's abrupt thaw was attributed to sources other than a rampaging sun.

Jennan had to spend so much time countering specious arguments that he and Helva were behind schedule on their way to the fourth and last settlement.

Helva jumped over the high range of jagged peaks that surrounded and sheltered the valley from the former raging snows as well as the present heat. The violent sun with its flaring corona was just beginning to brighten the deep valley as Helva dropped down to a landing.

"They'd better grab their toothbrushes and hop aboard," Helva commented. "HQ says speed it up."

"All women," remarked Jennan in surprise as he walked down to meet them. "Unless the men on Chloe wear furred skirts."

"Charm 'em but pare the routine to the bare essentials. And turn on your two-way private."

Jennan advanced smiling, but his explanation of his mission was met with absolute incredulity and considerable doubt as to his authenticity. He groaned inwardly as the matriarch paraphrased previous explanations of the warming sun.

"Revered mother, there's been an overload on that prayer circuit and the sun is blowing itself up in one obliging burst. I'm here to take you to the spaceport at Rosary—"

"That Sodom?" the worthy woman glowered and shuddered disdainfully at his suggestion. "We thank you for your warning but we have no wish to leave our cloister for the rude world. We must go about our morning meditation which has been interrupted—"

"It'll be permanently interrupted when that sun starts broiling. You must come now," Jennan said firmly.

"Madame," said Helva, realizing that perhaps a female voice might carry more weight in this instance than Jennan's very masculine charm.

"Who spoke?" cried the nun, startled by the bodiless voice.

"I, Helva, the ship. Under my protection you and your sisters-in-faith may enter safely and be unprofaned by association with a male. I will guard you and take you safely to a place prepared for you."

The matriarch peered cautiously into the ship's open port.

THE SHIP WHO SANG

"Since only Central Worlds is permitted the use of such ships, I acknowledge that you are not trifling with us, young man. However, we are in no danger here."

"The temperature at Rosary is now 99°," said Helva. "As soon as the sun's rays penetrate directly into this valley, it will also be 99°, and it is due to climb to approximately 180° today. I notice your buildings are made of wood with moss chinking. Dry moss. It should fire around noontime."

The sunlight was beginning to slant into the valley through the peaks and the fierce rays warmed the restless group behind the matriarch. Several opened the throats of their furry parkas.

"Jennan," said Helva privately to him, "our time is very short."

"I can't leave them, Helva. Some of those girls are barely out of their teens."

"Pretty, too. No wonder the matriarch doesn't want to get in."

"Helva."

"It will be the Lord's will," said the matriarch stoutly and turned her back squarely on rescue.

"To burn to death?" shouted Jennan as she threaded her way through her murmuring disciples.

"They want to be martyrs? Their opt, Jennan," said Helva dispassionately. "*We* must leave and that is no longer a matter of option."

"How can I leave, Helva?"

"Parsaea?" Helva flung tauntingly at him as he stepped forward to grab one of the women. "You can't drag them *all* aboard and we don't have time to fight it out. Get on board, Jennan, or I'll have you on report."

"They'll die," muttered Jennan dejectedly as he reluctantly turned to climb on board.

"You can risk only so much," Helva said sympathetically. "As it is we'll just have time to make a rendezvous. Lab reports a critical speed-up in spectral evolution."

Jennan was already in the airlock when one of the younger women, screaming, rushed to squeeze in the closing port. Her action set off the others and the others stampeded through the narrow opening. Even crammed back to breast, there was not enough room inside for all the women. Jennan broke out spacesuits to the three who would have to remain with him in the airlock. He wasted valuable time explaining to the matriarch that she must put on the suit because the airlock had no independent oxygen or cooling units.

"We'll be caught," said Helva grimly to Jennan on their private connection. "We've lost 18 minutes in this last-minute rush. I am now overloaded for maximum speed and I must attain maximum speed to outrun the heat-wave."

"Can you lift? We're suited."

"Lift? Yes," she said, doing so. "Run? I stagger."

Jennan, bracing himself and the women, could feel her sluggishness as she blasted upward. Heartlessly, Helva applied thrust as long as she could, despite the fact that the gravitational force mashed her cabin passengers brutally and crushed two fatally. It was a question of saving as many as possible. The only one for whom she had any concern was Jennan and she was in desperate terror about his safety. Airless and uncooled, protected by only one layer of metal, not three, the airlock was not going to be safe for the four trapped there, despite their spacesuits. These were only the standard models, not built to withstand the excessive heat to which the ship would be subjected.

Helva ran as fast as she could but the incredible wave of heat from the explosive sun caught them halfway to cold safety.

She paid no heed to the cries, moans, pleas and prayers in her cabin. She listened only to Jennan's tortured breathing, to the missing throb in his suit's purifying system and the sucking of the overloaded cooling unit. Helpless, she heard the hysterical screams of his three companions as they writhed in the awful heat. Vainly, Jennan tried to calm them, tried to explain they would soon be safe and cool if they could be still and endure the heat. Undisciplined by their terror and torment, they tried to strike out at him despite the close quarters. One flailing arm became entangled in the leads to his power pack and the damage was quickly done. A connection, weakened by heat and the dead weight of the arm, broke.

For all the power at her disposal, Helva was helpless. She watched as Jennan fought for his breath, as he turned his head beseechingly towards *her*, and died.

Only the iron conditioning of her training prevented Helva from swinging around and plunging back into the cleansing heart of the exploding sun. Numbly she made rendezvous with the refugee convoy. She obediently transferred her burned, heat-prostrated passengers to the assigned transport.

"I will retain the body of my scout and proceed to the nearest base for burial," she informed Central dully.

"You will be provided escort," was the reply.

"I have no need of escort," she demurred.

"Escort is provided, XH-834," she was told curtly.

The shock of hearing Jennan's initial severed from her call number cut off her half-formed protest. Stunned, she waited by the transport until her screens showed the arrival of two other slim brain ships. The cortege proceeded homeward at unfuneral speeds.

"834? The ship who sings?"

"I have no more songs."

"Your scout was Jennan."

"I do not wish to communicate."

"I'm 422."

"Silvia?"

"Silvia died a long time ago. I'm 422. Currently MS," the ship rejoined curtly. "AH-640 is our other friend, but Henry's not listening in. Just as well—he wouldn't understand it if you wanted to turn rogue. But I'd stop *him* if he tried to delay you."

"Rogue?" the term snapped Helva out of her apathy.

"Sure. You're young. You've got power for years. Skip. Others have done it. 732 went rogue two years ago after she lost her scout on a mission to that white dwarf. Hasn't been seen since."

"I never heard about rogues," gasped Helva.

"As it's exactly the thing we're conditioned against, you sure wouldn't hear about it in school, my dear," 422 said.

"Break conditioning?" cried Helva, anguished, thinking longingly of the white, white furious hot heart of the sun she had just left.

"For you I don't think it would be hard at the moment," 422 said quietly, her voice devoid of her earlier cynicism. "The stars are out there, winking."

"Alone?" cried Helva from her heart.

"Alone!" 422 confirmed bleakly.

Alone with all of space and time. Even the Horsehead Nebulae would not be far enough away to daunt her. Alone with a hundred years to live with her memories and nothing... nothing more.

"Was Parsaea worth it?" she asked 422 softly.

"Parsaea?" 422 came back, surprised. "With his father? Yes. We were there, at Parsaea when we were needed. Just as you... and his son… were at Chloe. When you were needed. The crime is always not knowing where need is and not being there."

"But *I* need *him*. Who will supply my need?" said Helva bitterly…

"834," said 422 after a day's silent speeding, "Central wishes your report. A replacement awaits your opt at Regulus Base. Change course accordingly."

"A replacement?" That was certainly not what she needed… a reminder inadequately filling the void Jennan left. Why, her hull was barely cool of Chloe's heat. Atavistically, Helva wanted time to mourn Jennan.

"Oh, none of them are impossible if *you're* a good ship," 422 remarked philosophically. "And it is just what you need. The sooner the better."

"You told them I wouldn't go rogue, didn't you?" Helva said heavily.

"The moment passed you even as it passed me after Parsaea, and before that, after Glen Arhur, and Betelgeuse."

"We're conditioned to go on, aren't we? We *can't* go rogue. You were testing."

"Had to. Orders. Not even Psycho knows why a rogue occurs. Central's very worried, and so, daughter, are your sister ships. I asked to be your escort. I… don't want to lose you both."

In her emotional nadir, Helva could feel a flood of gratitude for Silvia's rough sympathy.

"We've all known this grief, Helva. It's no consolation but if we couldn't feel with our scouts, we'd only be machines wired for sound."

Helva looked at Jennan's still form stretched before her in its shroud and heard the echo of his rich voice in the quiet cabin.

"Silvia! I *couldn't* help him," she cried from her soul.

"Yes, dear. I know," 422 murmured gently and then was quiet.

The three ships sped on, wordless, to the great Central Worlds base at Regulus. Helva broke silence to acknowledge landing instructions and the officially tendered regrets.

The three ships set down simultaneously at the wooded edge where Regulus' gigantic blue trees stood sentinel over the sleeping dead in the small Service cemetery. The entire Base complement approached with measured step and formed an aisle from Helva to the burial ground. The honour detail, out of step, walked slowly into her cabin. Reverently they placed the body of her dead love on the wheeled bier, covered it honourably with the deep blue, star-splashed flag of the Service. She watched as it was driven slowly down the living aisle which closed in behind the bier in last escort.

Then, as the simple words of interment were spoken, as the atmosphere planes dipped wings in tribute over the open grave, Helva found voice for her lonely farewell.

Softly, barely audible at first, the strains of the ancient song of evening and requiem swelled to the final poignant measure until black space itself echoed back the sound of the song the ship sang.

O'MARA'S ORPHAN

James White

James White (1928–1999) was born and lived in Belfast and worked initially in a tailoring firm before moving on to the aircraft industry. His first story was published in 1953 and he was a mainstay of the British science-fiction magazines for the next decade. He was a gifted and ingenious writer who, having lived through the Troubles in Northern Ireland, never lost his belief in humanity. In a career lasting over forty years he produced a wide variety of novels and stories but is best remembered for his series featuring the Sector Twelve General Hospital, a huge space habitat run by and intended to look after every known alien species. The series began with the eponymous "Sector General" (1957) and eventually ran to twelve books, starting with Hospital Station *(1962), exploring a remarkable diversity of creatures and problems, as the following story shows.*

I

THE ALIEN OCCUPYING O'MARA'S SLEEPING COMPARTMENT weighed roughly half a ton, possessed six short, thick appendages which served both as arms or legs and had a hide like flexible armour plate. Coming as it did from Hudlar, a four-G world with an atmospheric pressure nearly seven times Earth normal, such ruggedness of physique was to be expected. But despite its enormous strength the being was helpless, O'Mara knew, because it was barely six months old, it had just seen its parents die in a construction accident, and its brain was sufficiently well developed for the sight to have frightened it badly.

"I've b-b-brought the kid," said Waring, one of the section's tractor-beam operators. He hated O'Mara, and with good reason, but he was trying not to gloat. "C-C-Caxton sent me. He says your leg makes you unfit for normal duty, so you can look after the young one until somebody arrives from its home planet. He's on his way over n-now..."

Waring trailed off. He began checking the seals of his spacesuit, obviously in a hurry to get out before O'Mara could mention the accident. "I brought some of its food with me," he ended quickly. "It's in the airlock."

O'Mara nodded without speaking. He was a young man cursed with the kind of physique which insured him winning every fight he had ever been in, and there had been a great many of them recently, and a face which was as square, heavy and roughly formed as was his over-muscled body. He knew that if he allowed himself to show how much that accident had affected him, Waring would think that he was simply putting on an act. Men who were put together as he was, O'Mara had long ago discovered, were not supposed to have any of the softer emotions.

Immediately Waring departed he went to the airlock for the glorified paint-sprayer with which Hudlarians away from their home planet were fed. While checking the gadget and its spare food tanks he tried to go over the story he would have to tell Caxton when the section chief arrived. Staring moodily through the airlock port at the bits and pieces of the gigantic jigsaw puzzle spread across fifty cubic miles of space outside, he tried to think. But his mind kept ducking away from the accident and slipping instead into generalities and events which were in the far past or future.

The vast structure which was slowly taking shape in Galactic Sector Twelve, midway between the rim of the parent galaxy and the densely populated systems of the Greater Magellanic Cloud, was to be a hospital—a hospital to end all hospitals. Hundreds of different environments would be accurately reproduced here, any extreme of heat, cold, pressure, gravity, radiation or atmosphere necessary for the patients and staff it would contain. Such a tremendous and complex structure was far beyond the resources of any one planet, so that hundreds of worlds had each fabricated sections of it and transported them to the assembly point.

But fitting the jigsaw together was no easy job.

Each of the worlds concerned had their copies of the master plan. But errors occurred despite this—probably through the plan having to be translated into so many different languages and systems of measurement. Sections which should have fitted snugly together very often had to be modified to make them join properly, and this necessitated moving the sections together and apart several times with massed tractor and pressor beams. This was very tricky work for the beam operators, because while the weight of the sections out in space was nil, their mass and inertia was tremendous.

And anyone unlucky enough to be caught between the joining faces of two sections in the process of being fitted became, no matter how tough a life-form they happened to be, an almost perfect representation of a two-dimensional body.

The beings who had died belonged to a tough species, physiological classification FROB to be exact. Adult Hudlarians weighed in the region of two Earth tons, possessed an incredibly hard but flexible tegument which, as well as protecting them from their own native and external pressures, allowed them to live and work comfortably in any atmosphere of lesser pressure down to and including the vacuum of space. In addition they had the highest radiation tolerance level known, which made them particularly invaluable during power pile assembly.

The loss of two such valuable beings from his section would, in any case, have made Caxton mad, quite apart from other considerations. O'Mara sighed heavily, decided that his nervous system demanded a more positive release than that, and swore. Then he picked up the feeder and returned to the bedroom.

Normally the Hudlarians absorbed food directly through their skin from the thick, soupy atmosphere of their planet, but on any other world or in space a concentrated food compound had to be sprayed onto the absorbent hides at certain intervals. The young e-t was showing large bare patches and in other places the previous food coating had worn very thin. Definitely, thought O'Mara, the infant was due for another feed. He moved as close as seemed safe and began to spray carefully.

The process of being painted with food seemed to be a pleasant one for the young FROB. It ceased to cower in the corner and began blundering excitedly about the small bedroom. For O'Mara it became a matter of trying to hit a rapidly moving object while practising violent evasive manoeuvres himself, which set his injured leg throbbing more painfully than ever. His furniture suffered, too.

Practically the whole interior surface of his sleeping compartment was covered with the sticky, sharp-smelling food compound, and also the exterior of the now-quiescent young alien, when Caxton arrived.

"What's going on?" said the section chief.

Space construction men as a class were simple, uncomplicated personalities whose reactions were easily predictable. Caxton was the type who always asked what was going on even when, as now, he knew—and especially when such unnecessary questions were meant simply to needle somebody. In the proper circumstances the section chief was probably a quite likable individual, O'Mara thought, but between Caxton and himself those circumstances had yet to come about.

O'Mara answered the question without showing the anger he felt, and ended, "... After this I think I'll keep the kid in space, and feed it there..."

"You will not!" Caxton snapped. "You'll keep it here with you, all the time. But more about that later. At the moment I want to know about the accident. Your side of it, that is."

His expression said that he was prepared to listen, but that he already doubted every word that O'Mara would say in advance.

"Before you go any further," Caxton broke in after O'Mara had completed two sentences, "you know that this project is under Monitor Corps jurisdiction. Usually the Monitors let us settle any trouble that crops up in our own way, but this case involves extra-terrestrials and they'll have to be brought in on it. There'll be an investigation." He tapped the small, flat box hanging from his chest. "It's only fair to warn you that I'm taping everything you say."

O'Mara nodded and began giving his account of the accident in a low monotone. It was a very weak story, he knew, and stressing any particular incident so as to point it up in his favour would make it sound even more artificial. Several times Caxton opened his mouth to speak, but thought better of it. Finally he said:

"But did anyone *see* you doing these things? Or even see the two e-ts moving about in the danger area while the warning lights were burning? You have a neat little story to explain this madness on their part—which, incidentally, makes you quite a hero—but it could be that you switched on the lights *after* the accident, that it was your negligence regarding the lights which caused it, and that all this about the straying youngster is a pack of lies designed to get you out of a very serious charge—"

"Waring saw me," O'Mara cut in.

Caxton stared at him intently, his expression changing from suppressed anger to one of utter disgust and scorn. Despite himself O'Mara felt his face heating up.

"Waring, eh?" said the section chief tonelessly. "A nice touch, that. You know, and we all know, that you have been riding Waring constantly, needling him and playing on his disability to such an extent that he must hate you like poison. Even if he did see you, the court would expect him to keep quiet about it. And if he did not see you, they would think that he had and was keeping quiet about it anyway.

"O'Mara, you make me sick."

Caxton wheeled and stamped towards the airlock. With one foot through the inner seal he turned again.

"You're nothing but a trouble-maker, O'Mara," he said angrily, "a surly, quarrelsome lump of bone and muscle with just enough skill to make you worth keeping. You may think that it was technical ability which got you these quarters on your own. It wasn't, you're good but not that good! The truth is that nobody else in my section would share accommodation with you…"

The section chief's hand moved to the cut-off switch on his recorder. His voice, as he ended, became a quiet, deadly thing.

"… And O'Mara, if you let any harm come to that youngster, if anything happens to it at all, the Monitors won't even get the chance to try you."

The implications behind those final words were clear, O'Mara thought angrily as the section chief left; he was sentenced to live with this organic half-ton tank for a period that would feel like eternity no matter how short it was. Everybody knew that exposing Hudlarians to space was like putting a dog out for the night—there were no harmful effects at all. But what some people knew and what they felt were two vastly different things and O'Mara was dealing here with the personalities of simple, uncomplicated, over-sentimental and very angry construction men.

When he had joined the project six months before, O'Mara found that he was doomed again to the performance of a job which, while important in itself, gave him no satisfaction and was far below his capabilities. Since school his life had been a series of such frustrations. Personnel officers could not believe that a young man with such square, ugly features and shoulders so huge that his head looked moronically small by comparison could be interested in *subtle* subjects like psychology or electronics. He had gone into space in the hope of finding things different, but no. Despite constant efforts during interviews to impress people with his quite considerable knowledge, they were too dazzled by his muscle-power to listen, and his applications were invariably stamped "Approved Suitable for Heavy, Sustained Labour."

On joining this project he had decided to make the best of what promised to be another boring, frustrating job—he decided to become an unpopular character. As a result his life had been anything but boring. But now he was wishing that he had not been so successful at making himself disliked.

What he needed most at this moment was friends, and he hadn't a single one.

O'Mara's mind was dragged back from the dismal past to the even less pleasant present by the sharp all-pervading odour of the Hudlarian's food compound. Something would have to be done about that, and quickly. He hurriedly got into his lightweight suit and went through the lock.

II

His living quarters were in a tiny sub-assembly which would one day form the theatre, surgical ward and adjoining storage compartments of the hospital's low-gravity MSVK section. Two small rooms with a connecting section of corridor had been pressurized and fitted with artificial gravity grids for O'Mara's benefit, the rest of the structure remaining both airless and weightless. He drifted along short, unfinished corridors whose ends were open to space, staring into the bare, angular compartments which slid past. They were all full of trailing plumbing and half-built machinery the purpose of which it was impossible to guess without actually taking an MSVK educator tape. But all the compartments he examined were either too small to hold the alien or they were open in one direction to space. O'Mara swore with restraint but great feeling, pushed himself out to one of the ragged edges of his tiny domain and glared around him.

Above, below and all around him out to a distance of ten miles floated pieces of hospital, invisible except for the bright blue lights scattered over them as a warning to ship traffic in the area. It was a little like being at the centre of a dense globular star cluster, O'Mara thought, and rather beautiful if you were in a mood to appreciate it. He wasn't, because on most of those floating sub-assemblies there were pressor-beam men on watch, placed there to fend off sections which threatened to collide. These men would see and report it to Caxton if O'Mara took his baby alien outside even for feeding.

The only answer apparently, he told himself disgustedly as he retraced his way, was nose-plugs.

Inside the lock he was greeted by a noise like a tinny foghorn. It blared out in long, discordant blasts with just enough interval in between to make him dread the arrival of the next one. Investigation revealed bare patches of hide showing through the last coat of food, so presumably his little darling was hungry again. O'Mara went for the sprayer.

When he had about three square yards covered there was an interruption. Dr. Pelling arrived.

The project doctor took off his helmet and gauntlets only, flexed the stiffness out of his fingers and growled, "I believe you hurt your leg. Let's have a look."

Pelling could not have been more gentle as he explored O'Mara's injured leg, but what he was doing was plainly a duty rather than an act of friendship. His voice was reserved as he said, "Severe bruising and a couple of pulled tendons is all—you were lucky. Rest. I'll give you some stuff to rub on it. Have you been redecorating?"

"What...?" began O'Mara, then saw where the doctor was looking. "That's food compound. The little so-and-so kept moving while I was spraying it. But speaking of the youngster, can you tell me—"

"No, I can't," said Pelling. "My brain is overloaded enough with the ills and remedies of my own species without my trying to stuff it with FROB physiology tapes. Besides, they're tough—nothing *can* happen to them!" He sniffed loudly and made a face. "Why don't you keep it outside?"

"Certain people are too soft-hearted," O'Mara replied bitterly. "They are horrified by such apparent cruelties as lifting kittens by the scruff of the neck..."

"Humph," said the doctor, looking almost sympathetic. "Well, that's your problem. See you in a couple of weeks."

"Wait!" O'Mara called urgently, hobbling after the doctor with one empty trouser leg flapping. "What if something does happen? And there has to be rules about the care and feeding of these things, simple rules. You can't just leave me to... to..."

"I see what you mean," said Pelling. He looked thoughtful for a moment, then went on, "There's a book kicking around my place somewhere, a sort of Hudlarian first aid handbook. But it's printed in Universal..."

"I read Universal," said O'Mara.

Pelling looked surprised. "Bright boy. All right, I'll send it over." He nodded curtly and left.

O'Mara closed the bedroom door in the hope that this might cut down the intensity of the food smell, then lowered himself carefully into the living room couch for what he told himself was a well-deserved rest. He settled his leg so that it ached almost comfortably and began trying to talk himself into an acceptance

of the situation. The best he could achieve was a seething, philo-
sophical calm.

But he was so weary that even the effort of feeling angry
became too much for him. His eyelids dropped and a warm dead-
ness began creeping up from his hands and feet. O'Mara sighed,
wriggled, and prepared to sleep...

The sound which blasted him out of his couch had the stri-
dent, authoritative urgency of all the alarm sirens that ever were
and a volume which threatened to blow the bedroom door off its
runners. O'Mara grabbed instinctively for his spacesuit, dropped
it with a curse as he realized what was happening, then went for
the sprayer.

Junior was hungry again...!

During the eighteen hours which followed it was brought home
to O'Mara how much he did not know about infant Hudlarians. He
had spoken many times to its parents via Translator, and the baby
had been mentioned often, but somehow they had not spoken of
the important things. Sleep, for instance.

Judging from recent observation and experience, infant FROBs
did not sleep. In the all too short intervals between feeds they
blundered around the bedroom smashing all items of furniture
which were not metal and bolted down—and these they bent
beyond recognition or usefulness—or they huddled in a corner
knotting and unknotting their tentacles. Probably this sight of a
baby doing the equivalent of playing with its fingers would have
brought coos of delight from an adult Hudlarian, but it merely
made O'Mara sick and cross-eyed.

And every two hours, plus or minus a few minutes, he had
to feed the brute. If he was lucky it lay quiet, but more often he
had to chase it around with the sprayer. Normally FROBs of this
age were too weak to move about—but that was under Hudlar's

crushing gravity-pull and pressure. Here in conditions which were to it less than one quarter-G, the infant Hudlarian could move. And it was having fun.

O'Mara wasn't: his body felt like a thick, clumsy sponge saturated with fatigue. After each feed he dropped onto the couch and let his bone-weary body dive blindly into unconsciousness. He was so utterly and completely spent, he told himself after every spraying, that he could not possibly hear the brute the next time it complained—he would be too deeply out. But always that blaring, discordant foghorn jerked him at least half awake and sent him staggering like a drunken puppet through the motions which would end that horrible, mind-wrecking din.

After nearly thirty hours of it O'Mara knew he couldn't take much more. Whether the infant was collected in two days or two months the result as far as he was concerned would be the same; he would be a raving lunatic. Unless in a weak moment he took a walk outside without his suit. Pelling would never have allowed him to be subjected to this sort of punishment, he knew, but the doctor was an ignoramus where the FROB life-form was concerned. And Caxton, only a little less ignorant, was the simple, direct type who delighted in this sort of violent practical joke, especially when he considered that the victim deserved everything he got.

But just suppose the section chief was a more devious character than O'Mara had suspected? Suppose he knew exactly what he was sentencing him to by leaving the infant Hudlarian in his charge? O'Mara cursed tiredly, but he had been at it so constantly for the last ten or twelve hours that bad language had ceased to be an emotional safety valve. He shook his head angrily in a vain attempt to dispel the weariness which clogged his brain.

Caxton wasn't going to get away with it.

He was the strongest man on the whole project, O'Mara knew, and his reserves of strength must be considerable. All this fatigue and nervous twitching was simply in his mind, he told himself insistently, and a couple of days with practically no sleep meant nothing to his tremendous physique—even after the shaking up he'd received in the accident. And anyway, the present situation with the infant couldn't get any worse, so it must soon begin to improve. He would beat them yet, he swore. Caxton would not drive him mad, or even to the point of calling for help.

This was a challenge, he insisted with weary determination. Up to now he had bemoaned the fact that no job had fully exploited his capabilities. Well, this was a problem which would tax both his physical stamina and deductive processes to the limit. An infant had been placed in his charge and he intended taking care of it whether it was here for two weeks or two months. What was more, he was going to see that the kid was a credit to him when its foster parents arrived...

After the forty-eighth hour of the infant FROB's company and the fifty-seventh since he had had a good sleep, such illogical and somewhat maudlin thinking did not seem strange to O'Mara at all.

Then abruptly there came a change in what O'Mara had accepted as the order of things. The FROB after complaining, was fed, and refused to shut up!

O'Mara's first reaction was a feeling of hurt surprise; this was against the *rules*. They cried, you fed them, they stopped crying—at least for a while. This was so unfair that it left him too shocked and helpless to react.

The noise was bedlam, with variations. Long, discordant blasts of sound beat over him. Sometimes the pitch and volume varied in an insanely arbitrary manner and at others it had a grinding,

staccato quality as if broken glass had got into its vocal gears. There
were intervals of quiet, varying between two seconds and half a
minute, during which O'Mara cringed waiting for the next blast.
He stuck it for as long as he could—a matter of ten minutes or
so—then he dragged his leaden body off the couch again.

"What the blazes is *wrong* with you?" O'Mara roared against
the din. The FROB was thoroughly covered by food compound
so it couldn't be hungry.

Now that the infant had seen him the volume and urgency of
its cries increased. The external, bellows-like flap of muscle on the
infant's back—used for sound production only, the FROBs being
non-breathers—continued swelling and deflating rapidly. O'Mara
jammed the palms of his hands against his ears, an action which
did no good at all, and yelled, *"Shut up!"*

He knew that the recently orphaned Hudlarian must still be
feeling confused and frightened, that the mere process of feeding
it could not possibly fulfil all of its emotional needs—he knew all
this and felt a deep pity for the being. But these feelings were in
some quiet, sane and civilized portion of his mind and divorced
from all the pain and weariness and frightful onslaughts of sound
currently torturing his body. He was really two people, and while
one of him knew the reason for the noise and accepted it the
other—the purely physical O'Mara—reacted instinctively and
viciously to stop it.

"Shut up! SHUT UP!" screamed O'Mara, and started swinging
with his fists and feet.

Miraculously, after about ten minutes of it, the Hudlarian
stopped crying.

O'Mara returned to the couch shaking. For those ten minutes
he had been in the grip of a murderous, uncontrollable rage. He
had punched and kicked savagely until the pain from his hands

and injured leg forced him to stop using those members, but he had gone on kicking and screeching invective with the only other weapons left to him, his good leg and tongue. The sheer viciousness of what he had done shocked and sickened him.

It was no good telling himself that the Hudlarian was tough and might not have felt the beating; the infant had stopped crying so he must have got through to it somehow. Admittedly Hudlarians were hard and tough, but this was a baby and babies had weak spots. Human babies, for instance, had a very soft spot on the top of their heads...

When O'Mara's utterly exhausted body plunged into sleep his last coherent thought was that he was the dirtiest, lowest louse that had ever been born.

Sixteen hours later he awoke. It was a slow, natural process which brought him barely above the level of unconsciousness. He had a brief feeling of wonder at the fact that the infant was not responsible for waking him before he drifted back to sleep again. The next time he wakened was five hours later and to the sound of Waring coming through the airlock.

"Dr. P-Pelling asked me to bring this," he said, tossing O'Mara a small book. "And I'm not doing you a favour, understand—it's just that he said it was for the good of the youngster. How is it doing?"

"Sleeping," said O'Mara.

Waring moistened his lips. "I'm-I'm supposed to check. C-C-Caxton says so."

"Ca-Ca-Caxton would," mimicked O'Mara.

He watched the other silently as Waring's face grew a deeper red. Waring was a thin young man, sensitive, not very strong, and the stuff of which heroes were made. On his arrival O'Mara had been overwhelmed with stories about this tractor-beam operator.

There had been an accident during the fitting of a power pile and Waring had been trapped in a section which was inadequately shielded. But he had kept his head and, following instructions radioed to him from an engineer outside, had managed to avert a slow atomic explosion which nevertheless would have taken the lives of everyone in his section. He had done this while all the time fully convinced that the level of radiation in which he worked would, in a few hours time, certainly cause his death.

But the shielding had been more effective than had been thought and Waring did not die. The accident had left its mark on him, however, they told O'Mara. He had blackouts, he stuttered, his nervous system had been subtly affected, they said, and there were other things which O'Mara himself would see and was urged to ignore. Because Waring had saved all their lives and for that he deserved special treatment. That was why they made way for him wherever he went, let him win all fights, arguments and games of skill or chance, and generally kept him wrapped in a swathe of sentimental cottonwool.

And that was why Waring was a spoiled, insufferable, simpering brat.

Watching his white-lipped face and clenched fists, O'Mara smiled. He had never let Waring win at anything if he could possibly help it, and the first time the tractor-beam man had started a fight with him had also been the last. Not that he had hurt him, he had been just tough enough to demonstrate that fighting O'Mara was not a good idea.

"Go in and have a look," O'Mara said eventually. "Do what Ca-Ca-Caxton says."

They went in, observed the gently twitching infant briefly and came out. Stammering, Waring said that he had to go and headed for the airlock. He didn't often stutter these days, O'Mara

knew; probably he was scared the subject of the accident would
be brought up.

"Just a minute," said O'Mara. "I'm running out of food compound, will you bring—"

"G-get it yourself!"

O'Mara stared at him until Waring looked away, then he said
quietly, "Caxton can't have it both ways. If this infant has to be
cared for so thoroughly that I'm not allowed to either feed or
keep it in airless conditions, it would be negligence on my part to
go away and leave it for a couple of hours to get food. Surely you
see that. The Lord alone knows what harm the kid might come
to if it was left alone. I've been made responsible for this infant's
welfare so I insist..."

"B-b-but it won't—"

"It only means an hour or so of your rest period every second
or third day," said O'Mara sharply. "Cut the bellyaching. And stop
sputtering at me, you're old enough to talk properly."

Waring's teeth came together with a click. He took a deep, shuddering breath then with his jaws still clenched furiously together he
exhaled. The sound was like an airlock valve being cracked. He said:

"It... will... take... all of... my next two rest periods. The FROB
quarters... where the food is kept... are being fitted to the main
assembly the day after tomorrow. The food compound will have
to be transferred before then."

"See how easy it is when you try," said O'Mara, grinning. "You
were a bit jerky at first there, but I understood every word. You're
doing fine. And by the way, when you're stacking the food tanks
outside the airlock will you try not to make too much noise in
case you wake the baby?"

For the next two minutes Waring called O'Mara dirty names
without repeating himself or stuttering once.

"I said you were doing fine," said O'Mara reprovingly. "You don't have to show off."

III

After Waring left, O'Mara thought about the dismantling of the Hudlarian's quarters. With gravity grids set to four-Gs and what few other amenities they required the FROBs had been living in one of the key sections. If it was about to be fitted to the main assembly then the completion of the hospital structure itself could only be five or six weeks off. The final stages, he knew, would be exciting. Tractor men at their safe positions—depressions actually on the joining faces—tossing thousand-ton loads about the sky, bringing them together gently while fitters checked alignment or adjusted or prepared the slowly closing faces for joining. Many of them would disregard the warning lights until the last possible moment, and take the most hair-raising risks imaginable, just to save the time and trouble of having their sections pulled apart and rejoined again for a possible re-fitting.

O'Mara would have liked to be in on the finish, instead of baby-sitting!

Thought of the infant brought back the worry he had been concealing from Waring. It had never slept this long before—it must be twenty hours since it had gone to sleep, or he had kicked it to sleep. FROBs were tough, of course, but wasn't it possible that the infant was not simply asleep but unconscious through concussion...?

O'Mara reached for the book which Pelling had sent and began to read.

It was slow, heavy going but at the end of two hours O'Mara knew a little about the handling of Hudlarian babies, and the knowledge brought both relief and despair. Apparently his fit of temper and subsequent kicking had been a good thing—FROB babies needed constant petting and a quick calculation of the amount of force used by an adult of the species administering a gentle pat to its offspring showed that O'Mara's furious attack had been a very weak pat indeed. But the book warned against the dangers of over-feeding, and O'Mara was definitely guilty on this count. Seemingly the proper thing to do was to feed it every five or six hours during its waking period and use physical methods of soothing—patting, that was—if it appeared restless or still hungry. Also it appeared that FROB infants required, at fairly frequent intervals, a bath.

On the home planet this involved something like a major sand-blasting operation, but O'Mara thought that this was probably due to the pressure and stickiness of the atmosphere. Another problem which he would have to solve was how to administer a hard enough consoling pat. He doubted very much if he could fly into a temper to order every time the baby needed its equivalent of a nursing.

But at least he would have plenty of time to work out something, because one of the things he had found out about them was that they were wakeful for two full days at a stretch, and slept for five.

During the first five-day period of sleep O'Mara was able to devise methods of petting and bathing his charge, and even had a couple of days free to relax and gather his strength for the two days of hard labour ahead when the infant woke up. It would have been a killing routine for a man of ordinary strength, but O'Mara discovered that after the first two weeks of it he seemed to make the necessary physical and mental adjustment to it. And at the end of four weeks the pain and stiffness had gone out of his leg and he had no worries regarding the baby at all.

Outside, the project neared completion. The vast, three-dimensional jigsaw puzzle was finished except for a few unimportant pieces around the edges. A Monitor Corps investigator had arrived and was asking questions—of everybody, apparently, except O'Mara.

He couldn't help wondering if Waring had been questioned yet, and if he had what the tractor man had said. The investigator was a psychologist, unlike the mere Engineer officers already on the project, and very likely no fool. O'Mara thought that he, himself, was no fool either; he had worked things out and by rights he should feel no anxiety over the outcome of the Monitor's investigations. O'Mara had sized up the situation here and the people in it, and the reactions of everyone were predictable. But it all depended on what Waring told that Monitor.

You're turning yellow! O'Mara thought in angry self-disgust. *Now that your pet theories are being put to the test you're scared silly they won't work. You want to crawl to Waring and lick his boots!*

And that course, O'Mara knew, would be introducing a wild variable into what should be a predictable situation, and it would almost certainly wreck everything. Yet the temptation was strong nevertheless.

It was at the beginning of the sixth week of his enforced guardianship of the infant, while he was reading up on some of the weird and wonderful diseases to which baby FROBs were prone, his airlock telltale indicated a visitor. He got off the couch quickly and faced the opening seal, trying hard to look as if he hadn't a worry in the world.

But it was only Caxton.

"I was expecting the Monitor," said O'Mara.

Caxton grunted. "Hasn't seen you yet, eh? Maybe he figures it would be a waste of time. After what we've told him he probably thinks the case is open and shut. He'll have cuffs with him when he comes."

O'Mara just looked at him. He was tempted to ask Caxton if the Corpsman had questioned Waring yet, but it was only a small temptation.

"My reason for coming," said Caxton harshly, "is to find out about the water. Stores department tells me you've been requisitioning treble the amount of water that you could conceivably use. You starting an aquarium or something?"

Deliberately O'Mara avoided giving a direct answer. He said, "It's time for the baby's bath, would you like to watch?"

He bent down, deftly removed a section of floor plating and reached inside.

"What are you doing?" Caxton burst out. "Those are the gravity grids, you're not allowed to touch—"

Suddenly the floor took on a thirty degree list. Caxton staggered against a wall, swearing. O'Mara straightened up, opened the inner seal of the airlock, then started up what was now a stiff gradient towards the bedroom. Still insisting loudly that O'Mara was neither allowed nor qualified to alter the artificial gravity settings, Caxton followed.

Inside, O'Mara said, "This is the spare food sprayer with the nozzle modified to project a high pressure jet of water." He pointed the instrument and began to demonstrate, playing the jet against a small area of the infant's hide. The subject of the demonstration was engaged in pushing what was left of one of O'Mara's chairs into even more unrecognizable shapes, and ignored them.

"You can see," O'Mara went on, "the area of skin where the food compound has hardened. This has to be washed at intervals because it clogs the being's absorption mechanism in those areas, causing the food intake to drop. This makes a young Hudlarian very unhappy and, ah, noisy..."

O'Mara trailed off into silence. He saw that Caxton wasn't looking at the infant but was watching the water which rebounded from its hide streaming along the now steeply slanted bedroom floor, across the living room and into the open airlock. Which was just as well, because O'Mara's sprayer had uncovered a patch of the youngster's hide which had a texture and colour he had never seen before. Probably there was nothing to worry about, but it was better not to have Caxton see it and ask questions.

"What's that up there?" said Caxton, pointing towards the bedroom ceiling.

In order to give the infant the petting it deserved O'Mara had had to knock together a system of levers, pulleys and counterweights and suspend the whole ungainly mass from the ceiling. He was rather proud of the gadget; it enabled him to administer a good, solid pat—a blow which would have instantly killed a human being—anywhere on that half-ton carcass. But he doubted if Caxton would appreciate the gadget. Probably the section chief would swear that he was torturing the baby and forbid its use.

O'Mara started out of the bedroom. Over his shoulder he said, "Just lifting tackle."

He dried up the wet patches of floor with a cloth which he threw into the now partly waterfilled airlock. His sandals and coveralls were wet so he threw them in, also, then he closed the inner seal and opened the outer. While the water was boiling off into the vacuum outside he readjusted the gravity grids so that the floor was flat and the walls vertical again, then he retrieved his sandals, coveralls and cloth which were now bone dry.

"You seem to have everything well organized," said Caxton grudgingly as he fastened his helmet. "At least you're looking after the youngster better than you did its parents. See it stays that way.

"The Monitor will be along to see you at hour nine tomorrow," he added, and left.

O'Mara returned quickly to the bedroom for a closer look at the coloured patch. It was a pale bluish grey and in that area the smooth, almost steel-hard surface of the skin had taken on a sort of crackle finish. O'Mara rubbed the patch gently and the FROB wriggled and gave a blast of sound that was vaguely interrogatory.

"You and me both," said O'Mara absently. He couldn't remember reading about anything like this, but then he had not read all the book yet. The sooner he did so the better.

The chief method of communicating between beings of different species was by means of a Translator, which electronically sorted and classified all sense-bearing sounds and reproduced them in the native language of its user. Another method, used when large amounts of accurate data of a more subjective nature had to be passed on, was the Educator tape system. This transferred bodily all the sensory impressions, knowledge and personality of one being into the mind of another. Coming a long way third both in popularity and accuracy was the written language which was somewhat extravagantly called Universal.

Universal was of use only to beings who possessed brains linked to optical receptors capable of abstracting knowledge from patterns of markings on a flat surface—in short, the printed page. While there were many species with this ability, the response to colour in each species was very rarely matched. What appeared to be a bluish-grey patch to O'Mara might look like anything from yellow-grey to dirty purple to another being, and the trouble was that the other being might have been the author of the book.

One of the appendices gave a rough colour-equivalent chart, but it was a tedious, time-consuming job checking back on it, and his knowledge of Universal was not perfect anyway.

Five hours later he was still no nearer diagnosing the FROB's ailment, and the single blue-grey patch on its hide had grown to twice its original size and been joined by three more. He fed the infant, wondering anxiously whether that was the right thing to do in a case like this, then returned quickly to his studies.

According to the handbook there were literally hundreds of mild, short-lived diseases to which young Hudlarians were subject. This youngster had escaped them solely because it had been fed on tanked food compound and had avoided the air-borne bacteria so prevalent on its home planet. Probably this disease was nothing worse than the Hudlarian equivalent of a dose of measles, O'Mara told himself reassuringly, but it *looked* serious. At the next feeding the number of patches had grown to seven and they were a deeper, angrier blue, also the baby was continually slapping at itself with its appendages. Obviously the coloured patches itched badly. Armed with this new datum O'Mara returned to the book.

And suddenly he found it. The symptoms were given as rough, discoloured patches on the tegument with severe itching due to unabsorbed food particles. Treatment was to cleanse the irritated patches after each feed so as to kill the itching and let nature take care of the rest. The disease was a very rare one on Hudlar these days, the symptoms appeared with dramatic suddenness and it ran its course and disappeared equally quickly. Provided ordinary care was taken of the patient, the book stated, the disease was not dangerous.

O'Mara began converting the figures into his own time and size scale. As accurately as he could come to it the coloured patches should grow to about eighteen inches across and he could expect anything up to twelve of them before they began to fade. This would occur, calculating from the time he had noticed the first spot, in approximately six hours.

He hadn't a thing to worry about.

IV

At the conclusion of the next feeding O'Mara carefully sprayed the blue patches clean, but still the young FROB kept slapping furiously at itself and quivering ponderously. Like a kneeling elephant with six angrily waving trunks, he thought. O'Mara had another look at the book, but it still maintained that under ordinary conditions the disease was mild and short-lived, and that the only palliative treatment possible was rest and seeing that the affected areas were kept clean.

Kids, thought O'Mara distractedly, *were a blasted worrisome thing...!*

All that quivering and slapping looked wrong, common sense told him, and should be stopped. Maybe the infant was scratching through sheer force of habit, though the violence of the process made this seem doubtful, and a distraction of some kind would make it stop. Quickly O'Mara chose a fifty-pound weight and used his lifting tackle to swing it to the ceiling. He began raising and dropping it rhythmically over the spot which he had discovered gave the infant the most pleasure—an area two feet back of the hard, transparent membrane which protected its eyes. Fifty pounds dropping from a height of eight feet was a nice gentle pat to a Hudlarian.

Under the patting the FROB grew less violent in its movements. But as soon as O'Mara stopped it began lashing at itself worse than ever, and even running full tilt into walls and what was left of the furniture. During one frenzied charge it nearly escaped into the living room, and the only thing which stopped it was the fact that it was too big to go through the door. Up to that moment O'Mara did not realize how much weight the FROB had put on in five weeks.

Finally sheer fatigue made him give up. He left the FROB threshing and blundering about in the bedroom and threw himself on to the couch outside to try to think.

According to the book it was now time for the blue patches to begin to fade. But they weren't fading—they had reached the maximum number of twelve and instead of being eighteen or less inches across they were nearly double that size. They were so large that at the next feeding the absorption area of the infant would have shrunk by a half, which meant that it would be further weakened by not getting enough food. And everyone knew that itchy spots should not be scratched if the condition was not to spread and become more serious…

A raucous foghorn note interrupted his thoughts. O'Mara had experience enough to know by the sound that the infant was badly frightened, and by the relative decrease in volume that it was growing weak as well.

He needed help badly, but O'Mara doubted very much if there was anyone available who could furnish it. Telling Caxton about it would be useless—the section chief would only call in Pelling and Pelling was much less informed on the subject of Hudlarian children than was O'Mara, who had been specializing in the subject for the past five weeks. That course would only waste time and not help the kid at all, and there was a strong possibility that—despite the presence of a Monitor investigator—Caxton would see to it that something pretty violent happened to O'Mara for allowing the infant to take sick, for that was the way the section chief would look at it.

Caxton didn't like O'Mara. Nobody liked O'Mara.

If he had been well-liked on the project nobody would have thought of blaming him for the infant's sickness, or immediately and unanimously assumed that he was the one responsible for the death of its parents. But he had made the decision to appear a pretty lousy character, and he had been too damned successful.

Maybe he really was a despicable person and that was why the role had come so easy to him. Perhaps the constant frustration of never having the chance to really use the brain which was buried in his ugly, muscle-bound body had gradually soured him, and the part he thought he was playing was the real O'Mara.

If only he had stayed clear of the Waring business. That was what had them really mad at him.

But this sort of thinking was getting him nowhere. The solution of his own problems lay—in part, at least—in showing that he was responsible, patient, kind and possessed the various other attributes which his fellow men looked on with respect. To do that he must first show that he could be trusted with the care of a baby.

He wondered suddenly if the Monitor could help. Not personally; a Corps psychologist officer could hardly be expected to know about obscure diseases of Hudlar children, but through his organization. As the Galaxy's police, maid-of-all-work and supreme authority generally, the Monitor Corps would be able to find at short notice a being who would know the necessary answers. But again, that being would almost certainly be found on Hudlar itself, and the authorities there already knew of the orphaned infant's position and help had probably been on the way for weeks. It would certainly arrive sooner than the Monitor could bring it. Help might arrive in time to save the infant, but again maybe it might not.

The problem was still O'Mara's.

About as serious as a dose of measles.

But measles, in a human baby, could be very serious if the patient was kept in a cold room or in some other environment which, although not deadly in itself, could become lethal to an organism whose resistance was lowered by disease or lack of food. The handbook had prescribed rest, cleansing and nothing else. Or had it? There might be a large and well-hidden assumption there. The kicker was that the patient under discussion was residing on its home world at the time of the illness. Under ordinary conditions like that the disease probably was mild and short-lived.

But O'Mara's bedroom was not, for a Hudlarian baby with the disease, anything like normal conditions.

With that thought came the answer, if only he wasn't too late to apply it. Abruptly O'Mara pushed himself out of the couch and hurried to the spacesuit locker. He was climbing into the heavy duty model when the communicator beeped at him.

"O'Mara," Caxton's voice brayed at him when he had acknowledged, "the Monitor wants to talk to you. It wasn't supposed to be until tomorrow but—"

"Thank you, Mr. Caxton," broke in a quiet, firmer voice. There was a pause, then: "My name is Craythorne, Mr. O'Mara. I had planned to see you tomorrow as you know, but I managed to clear up some other work which left me time for a preliminary chat..."

What, thought O'Mara fulminatingly, *a damned awkward time you had to pick!* He finished putting on the suit but left the gauntlets and helmet off. He began tearing into the panel which covered the air-supply controls.

"... To tell you the truth," the quiet voice of the Monitor went on, "your case is incidental to my main work here. My job is to arrange accommodation and so on for the various life-forms who will shortly be arriving to staff this hospital, and to do everything possible to avoid friction developing between them when they do come. There are a lot of finicky details to attend to, but at the moment I'm free.

"And I'm curious about you, O'Mara. I'd like to ask some questions."

This is one smooth operator! thought one half of O'Mara's mind. The other half noted that the air-supply controls were set to suit the conditions he had in mind. He left the panel hanging loose and began pulling up a floor section to get at the artificial gravity grid underneath. A little absently he said, "You'll have to excuse me if I work while we talk. Caxton will explain—"

"I've told him about the kid," Caxton broke in, "and if you think you're fooling him by pretending to be the harassed mother type…!"

"I understand," said the Monitor. "I'd also like to say that forcing you to live with an FROB infant when such a course was unnecessary comes under the heading of cruel and unusual punishment, and that about ten years should be knocked off your sentence for what you've taken this past five weeks—that is, of course, if you're found guilty.

"And now, I always think it's better to see who one is talking to. Can we have vision, please?"

The suddenness with which the artificial gravity grids switched from one to two-Gs caught O'Mara by surprise. His arms folded under him and his chest thumped the floor. A frightened bawl from his patient in the next room must have disguised the noise he made from his listeners because they didn't mention it. He did the great granddaddy of all press-ups and heaved himself to his knees.

He fought to keep from gasping. "Sorry, my vision transmitter is on the blink."

The Monitor was silent just long enough to let O'Mara know that he knew he was lying, and that he would disregard the lie for the moment. He said finally, "Well, at least you can see me," and O'Mara's vision plate lit up.

It showed a youngish man with close-cropped hair whose eyes seemed twenty years older than the rest of his features. The shoulder tabs of a Major were visible on the trim, dark-green tunic and the collar bore a caduceus. O'Mara thought that in different circumstances he would have liked this man.

"I've something to do in the next room," O'Mara lied again. "Be with you in a minute."

He began the job of setting the antigravity belt on his suit to two-Gs repulsion, which would exactly counteract the floor's present attraction and allow him to increase the pull to four-Gs without too much discomfort to himself. He would then reset the belt for three-Gs, and that would give him back a normal gravity apparent of one-G.

At least that was what should have happened.

Instead the G-belt or the floor grids or both started producing half-G fluctuations, and the room went mad. It was like being in an express elevator which was constantly being started and stopped. The frequency of the surges built up rapidly until O'Mara was being shaken up and down so hard his teeth rattled. Before he could react to this a new and more devastating complication occurred. As well as variations in strength the floor grids were no longer acting at right angles to their surface, but yawed erratically from ten to thirty degrees from the vertical. No storm-tossed ship had ever pitched and rolled as viciously as this. O'Mara staggered, grabbed frantically for the couch, missed and was flung heavily against the wall. The next surge sent him skidding against the opposite wall before he was able to switch off the G-belt.

The room settled down to a steady gravity-pull of two-Gs again.

"Will this take long?" asked the Monitor suddenly.

O'Mara had almost forgotten the Major during the past hectic seconds. He did his best to make his voice sound both natural and as if it was coming from the next room as he replied, "It might. Could you call back later?"

"I'll wait," said the Monitor.

For the next few minutes O'Mara tried to forget the bruising he had received despite the protection given him by the heavy spacesuit, and concentrate on thinking his way out of this latest mess. He was beginning to see what must have happened.

When two antigravity generators of the same power and frequency were used close together, a pattern of interference was set up which affected the stability of both. The grids in O'Mara's quarters were merely a temporary job and powered by a generator similar to the one used in his suit, though normally a difference in frequency was built in against the chance of such instability occurring. But O'Mara had been fiddling with the grid settings constantly for the past five weeks—every time the infant had a bath, to be exact—so that he must have unknowingly altered the frequency...

He didn't know what he had done wrong and there wasn't enough time to try fixing it if he had known. Gingerly, O'Mara switched on his G-belt again and slowly began increasing power. It registered over three-quarters of a G before the first signs of instability appeared.

Four-Gs less three-quarters made a little over three-Gs. It looked, O'Mara thought grimly, like he was going to have to do this the hard way...

V

O'Mara closed his helmet quickly, then strung a cable from his suit mike to the communicator so that he would be able to talk without Caxton or the Monitor realizing that he was sealed inside his suit. If he was to have time to complete the treatment they must not suspect that there was anything out of the ordinary going on here. Next came the final adjustments to the air-pressure regulator and gravity grids.

Inside two minutes the atmospheric pressure in the two rooms had multiplied six times and the gravity apparent was four-Gs—the nearest, in fact, that O'Mara could get to "ordinary conditions" for a Hudlarian. With shoulder muscles straining and cracking with the effort—for his underpowered G-belt took only three-quarters of a gravity off the four-G pull in the room—he withdrew the incredibly awkward and ponderous thing which his arm had become from the grid servicing space and rolled heavily onto his back.

He felt as if his baby was sitting on his chest, and large, black blotches hung throbbing before his eyes. Through them he could see a section of ceiling and, at a crazy angle, the vision panel. The face in it was becoming impatient.

"I'm back, Major," gasped O'Mara. He fought to control his breathing so that the words would not be squeezed out too fast. "I suppose you want to hear my side of the accident?"

"No," said the Monitor. "I've heard the tape Caxton made. What I'm curious about is your background prior to coming here. I've checked up and there is something which doesn't quite fit…"

A thunderous eruption of noise blasted into the conversation. Despite the deeper note caused by the increased air pressure O'Mara recognized the signal for what it was; the FROB was angry and hungry.

With a mighty effort O'Mara rolled onto his side, then propped himself up on his elbows. He stayed that way for a while gathering strength to roll over onto his hands and knees. But when he finally accomplished this he found that his arms and legs were swelling and felt as if they would burst from the pressure of blood piling up in them. Gasping, he eased himself down flat onto his chest. Immediately the blood rushed to the front of his body and his vision began to red out.

He couldn't crawl on hands and knees nor wriggle on his stomach. Most certainly, under three-Gs, he could not stand up and walk. What else was there?

O'Mara struggled onto his side again and rolled back, but this time with his elbows propping him up. The neck-rest of his suit supported his head, but the insides of the sleeves were very lightly padded and his elbows hurt. And the strain of holding up even part of his three times heavier than normal body made his heart pound. Worst of all, he was beginning to black out again.

Surely there must be some way to equalize, or at least distribute, the pressures in his body so that he could stay conscious and move. O'Mara tried to visualize the layout of the acceleration chairs which had been used in ships before artificial gravity came along. It had been a not-quite-prone position, he remembered suddenly, with the knees drawn up...

Inching along on his elbows, bottom and feet, O'Mara progressed snail-like towards the bedroom. His embarrassment of riches where muscles were concerned was certainly of use now—in these conditions any ordinary man would have been plastered helplessly against the floor. Even so it took him fifteen minutes to reach the food sprayer in the bedroom, and during practically every second of the way the baby kept up its ear-splitting racket. With the increased pressure the noise was so tremendously loud and deep that every bone in O'Mara's body seemed to vibrate to it.

"I'm trying to talk to you!" the Monitor yelled during a lull. "Can't you keep that blasted kid shut up!"

"It's hungry," said O'Mara. "It'll quieten down when it's fed…"

The food sprayer was mounted on a trolley and O'Mara had fitted a pedal control so as to leave both hands free for aiming. Now that his patient was immobilized by four gravities he didn't have to use his hands. Instead he was able to nudge the trolley into position with his shoulders and depress the pedal with his elbow. The high-pressure jet tended to bend floorwards owing to the extra gravity but he did finally manage to cover the infant with food. But cleaning the affected areas of food compound was another matter. The water jet, which handled very awkwardly from floor level, had no accuracy at all. The best he could manage was to wash down the wide, vivid blue patch—formed from three separate patches which had grown together—which covered nearly one quarter of its total skin area.

After that O'Mara straightened out his legs and lowered his back gently to the floor. Despite the three-Gs acting on him, the strain of maintaining that half-sitting position for the last half hour made him feel almost comfortable.

The baby had stopped crying.

"What I was about to say," said the Monitor heavily, when the silence looked like lasting for a few minutes, "was that your record on previous jobs does not fit what I find here. Previously you were, as you are now, a restless, discontented type, but you were invariably popular with your colleagues and only a little less so with your superiors—this last being because your superiors were sometimes wrong and you never were…"

"I was every bit as smart as they were," said O'Mara tiredly, "and proved it often. But I didn't *look* intelligent, I had mucker written all over me!"

It was strange, O'Mara thought, but he felt almost disinterested in his own personal trouble now. He couldn't take his eyes off the angry blue patch on the infant's side. The colour had deepened and also the centre of the patch seemed to have swelled. It was as if the super-hard tegument had softened and the FROB's enormous internal pressure had produced a swelling. Increasing the gravity and pressure to the Hudlarian normal should, he hoped, halt that particular development—if it wasn't a symptom of something else entirely.

O'Mara had thought of carrying his idea a step further and spraying the air around the patient with food compound. On Hudlar the natives' food was comprised of tiny organisms floating in their super-thick atmosphere, but then again the handbook expressly stated that food particles must be kept away from the affected areas of tegument, so that the extra gravity and pressure should be enough…

"… Nevertheless," the Monitor was saying, "if a similar accident had happened on one of your previous jobs, your story would have been believed. Even if it had been your fault they would have rallied round to defend you from outsiders like myself.

"What caused you to change from a friendly, likable type of personality to *this*…?"

"I was bored," said O'Mara shortly.

There had been no sound from the infant yet, but he had seen the characteristic movements of the FROB's appendages which foretold of an outburst shortly to come. And it came. For the next ten minutes speech was, of course, impossible.

O'Mara heaved himself onto his side and rolled back onto his now raw and bleeding elbows. He knew what was wrong; the infant had missed its usual after-feed nursing. O'Mara humped his way slowly across to the two counterweight ropes of the gadget he had devised for petting the infant and prepared to remedy this omission. But the ends of the ropes hung four feet above the floor.

Lying propped by one elbow and straining to raise the dead weight of his other arm, O'Mara thought that the rope could just as easily have been four miles away. Sweat poured off his face and body with the intensity of the effort and slowly, trembling and wobbling so much that his gauntleted hand went past it first time, he reached up and grabbed hold. Still gripping it tightly he lowered himself gently back bringing the rope with him.

The gadget operated on a system of counterweights, so that there was no extra pull needed on the controlling ropes. A heavy weight dropped neatly onto the infant's back, administering a reassuring pat. O'Mara rested for a few minutes, then struggled up to repeat the process with the other rope, the pull on which would also wind up the first weight ready for use again.

After about the eighth pat he found that he couldn't see the end of the rope he was reaching for, though he managed to find it all the same. His head was being kept too high above the level of the rest of his body for too long a time and he was constantly on the point of blacking out. The diminished flow of blood to his brain was having other effects, too...

"... There, there," O'Mara heard himself saying in a definitely maudlin voice. "You're all right now, pappy will take care of you. There now, shush..."

The funny thing about it was that he really did feel a responsibility and a sort of angry concern for the infant. He had saved it once only to let *this* happen! Maybe the three-Gs which jammed him against the floor, making every breath a day's work and the smallest movement an operation which called for all the reserves of strength he possessed, was bringing back the memory of another kind of pressure—the slow, inexorable movement together of two large, inanimate and uncaring masses of metal.

The accident.

As fitter-in-charge of that particular shift O'Mara had just switched on the warning lights when he had seen the two adult Hudlarians chasing after their offspring on one of the faces being joined. He had called them through his Translator, urging them to get to safety and leave him to chase the youngster clear—being much smaller than its parents the slowly closing faces would take longer to reach it, and during those extra few minutes O'Mara would have been able to herd it out of danger. But either their Translators were switched off or they were reluctant to trust the safety of their child to a diminutive human being. Whatever the reason they remained between the faces until it was too late. O'Mara had to watch helplessly as they were trapped and crushed by the joining structures.

The sight of the young one, still unharmed because of its smaller girth, floundering about between the bodies of its late parents sent O'Mara into belated action. He was able to chase it out of danger before the sections came close enough to trap it, and had just barely made it himself. For a few heart-stopping seconds back there O'Mara had thought he would have to leave a leg behind.

★

This was no place for kids anyway, he told himself angrily as he looked at the quivering, twitching body with the patches of vivid, scabrous blue. People shouldn't be allowed to bring kids out here, even tough people like the Hudlarians.

But Major Craythorne was speaking again.

"… Judging by what I hear going on over there," said the Monitor acidly, "you're taking very good care of your charge. Keeping the youngster happy and healthy will definitely be a point in your favour…"

Happy and healthy, thought O'Mara as he reached towards the rope yet again. *Healthy…!*

"… But there are other considerations," the quiet voice went on. "Were you guilty of negligence in not switching on the warning lights until after the accident occurred, which is what you are alleged to have done? And your previous record notwithstanding, here you have been a surly, quarrelsome bully and your behaviour towards Waring especially…!"

The Monitor broke off, looked faintly disapproving, then went on, "A few minutes ago you said that you did all these things because you were bored. Explain that."

"Wait a minute, Major," Caxton broke in, his face appearing suddenly behind Craythorne's on the screen. "He's stalling for some reason, I'm sure of it. All those interruptions, this gasping voice he's using and this shush-a-bye-baby stuff is just an act to show what a great little nurse-maid he is. I think I'll go over and bring him back here to answer you face to face—"

"That won't be necessary," said O'Mara quickly. "I'll answer any questions you want, right now."

He had a horrible picture of Caxton's reaction if the other saw the infant in its present state; the sight of it made O'Mara feel queasy and he was used to it now. Caxton wouldn't stop to think, or wait for explanations, or ask himself if it was fair to place an e-t in charge of a human who was completely ignorant of its physiology or weaknesses. He would just react. Violently.

And as for the Monitor...

O'Mara thought that he might get out of the accident part, but if the kid died as well he hadn't a hope. The infant had had a mild though uncommon disease which should have responded to treatment days ago, and instead had become progressively worse, so it would die anyway if O'Mara's last desperate try at reproducing its home planet's conditions did not come off. What he needed now was time. According to the book, about four to six hours of it.

Suddenly the futility of it all hit him. The infant's condition had not improved—it heaved and twitched and generally looked to be the most desperately ill and pitiable creature that had ever been born. O'Mara swore helplessly. What he was trying to do now should have been tried days ago, his baby was as good as dead, and continuing this treatment for another five or six hours would probably kill or cripple him for life. And it would serve him right!

VI

The infant's appendages curled in the way O'Mara knew meant that it was going to cry again, and grimly he began pushing himself onto his elbows for another patting session. That was the very least he could do. And even though he was convinced that going on was useless, the kid had to be given the chance. O'Mara had to have time to finish the treatment without interruptions, and to insure that he would have to answer this Monitor's questions in a full and satisfactory manner. If the kid started crying again he wouldn't be able to do that.

"... For your kind co-operation," the Major was saying drily. "First off, I want an explanation for your sudden change of personality."

"I was bored," said O'Mara. "Hadn't enough to do. Maybe I'd become a bit of a sorehead, too. But the main reason for setting out to be a lousy character was that there was a job I could do here which could not be done by a nice guy. I've studied a lot and think of myself as a pretty good rule-of-thumb psychologist..."

Suddenly came disaster. O'Mara's supporting elbow slipped as he was reaching for the counterweight rope and he crashed back to the floor from a distance of two-and-a-half feet. At three-Gs this was equivalent to a fall of seven feet. Luckily he was in a heavy duty suit with a padded helmet so he did not lose consciousness. But he did cry out, and instinctively held onto the rope as he fell.

That was his mistake.

One weight dropped, the other swung up too far. It hit the ceiling with a crash and loosened the bracket which supported the light metal girder which carried it. The whole structure began to sag, and slip then was suddenly yanked floorwards by four-Gs onto the infant below. In his dazed state O'Mara could not guess at the amount of force expended on the infant—whether it was a harder than usual pat, the equivalent of a sharp smack on the bottom, or something very much more serious. The baby was very quiet afterwards, which worried him.

"... For the third time," shouted the Monitor, "what the blazes is going on in there?"

O'Mara muttered something which was unintelligible even to himself, then Caxton joined in.

"There's something fishy going on, and I bet it involves the kid! I'm going over to see—"

"No, wait!" said O'Mara desperately. "Give me six hours..."

"I'll see you," said Caxton, "in ten minutes."

"Caxton!" O'Mara shouted. "If you come through my airlock you'll kill me! I'll have the inner seal jammed open and if you open the outer one you'll evacuate the place. Then the Major will lose his prisoner."

There was a sudden silence, then:

"What," asked the Monitor quietly, "do you want the six hours for?"

O'Mara tried to shake his head to clear it, but now that it weighed three times heavier than normal he only hurt his neck. What *did* he want six hours for? Looking around him he began to wonder, because both the food sprayer and its connecting water tank had been wrecked by the fall of tackle from the ceiling. He could neither feed, wash, nor scarcely see his patient for fallen wreckage, so all he could do for six hours was watch and wait for a miracle.

"I'm going over," said Caxton doggedly.

"You're not," said the Major, still polite but with a no-nonsense tone. "I want to get to the bottom of this. You'll wait outside until I've spoken with O'Mara alone.

"Now O'Mara, *what... is... happening?*"

Flat on his back again O'Mara fought to gain enough breath to carry on an extended conversation. He had decided that the best thing to do would be to tell the Monitor the exact truth, and then appeal to him to back O'Mara up in the only way possible which might save the infant—by leaving him alone for six hours. But O'Mara was feeling very low as he talked, and his vision was so poor that he couldn't tell sometimes whether his eyelids were open or shut. He did see someone hand the Major a note, but Craythorne didn't read it until O'Mara had finished speaking.

"You are in a mess," Craythorne said finally. He briefly looked sympathetic then his tone hardened again. "And ordinarily I should be forced to do as you suggest and give you that six hours. After all, you have the book and so you know more than we do. But the situation has changed in the last few minutes. I've just had word that two Hudlarians have arrived, one of them a doctor.

"You had better step down, O'Mara. You tried, but now let some skilled help salvage what they can from the situation.

"For the kid's sake," he added.

It was three hours later. Caxton, Waring and O'Mara were facing the Major across the Monitor's desk. Craythorne had just come in.

He said briskly, "I'm going to be busy for the next few days so we'll get this business settled quickly. First, the accident.

"O'Mara, your case depends entirely on Waring's corroboration for your story. Now there seems to be some pretty devious thinking here on your part. I've already heard Waring's evidence, but to satisfy my own curiosity I'd like to know what *you* think he said?"

"He backed up my story," said O'Mara wearily. "He had no choice."

He looked down at his hands, still thinking about the desperately sick infant he had left in his quarters. He told himself again that he wasn't responsible for what had happened, but deep inside he felt that if he had shown more flexibility of mind and had started the pressure treatment sooner the kid would have been all right now. But the result of the accident enquiry didn't seem to matter now, one way or the other, and neither did the Waring business.

"*Why* do you think he had no choice?" prodded the Monitor sharply.

Caxton had his mouth open, looking confused. Waring would not meet O'Mara's eyes and he was beginning to blush.

"When I came here," O'Mara said dully, "I was looking out for a secondary job to fill my spare time, and hounding Waring was it. He is the reason for my being an obnoxious type, that was the only way I could go to work on him. But to understand that you have to go a bit farther back.

"Because of that power pile accident," O'Mara went on, "all the men of his section were very much in Waring's debt—you've probably heard the details by now. Waring himself was a mess. Physically he was below par—had to get shots to keep his blood-count up, was just about strong enough to work his control console, and was fairly wallowing in self-pity. Psychologically he was a wreck. Despite all Pelling's assurances that the shots would only be necessary for a few more months he was convinced that he had pernicious anaemia. He also believed that he had been made sterile, again despite everything the doctor told him, and this conviction made him act and talk in a way which would give any normal man the creeps—because that sort of thing is pathological and there wasn't anything like that wrong with him.

"When I saw how things were I started to ridicule him every chance I got. I hounded him unmercifully. So the way I see it he had no other choice but to support my story. Simple gratitude demanded it."

"I begin to see the light," said the Major. "Go on."

"The men around him were very much in his debt," O'Mara continued. "But instead of putting the brakes on, of giving him a good talking to, they smothered him with sympathy. They let him win all fights, card-games or whatever, and generally treated him like a little tin god.

"I did none of these things.

"Whenever he lisped or stuttered or was awkward about anything," O'Mara went on, "whether it was due to one of his mental and self-inflicted disabilities or a physical one which he honestly couldn't help, I jumped on him hard with both feet. Maybe I was too hard sometimes, but remember that I was one man trying to undo the harm that was being done by fifty. Naturally he hated my guts, but he always knew exactly where he was with me. And I never pulled punches. On the very few occasions when he was able to get the better of me, he knew that he had won despite everything I could do to stop him—unlike his friends who let him beat them at everything and in so doing made his winning meaningless. That was exactly what he needed for what ailed him, somebody to treat him as an equal and make no allowances at all.

"So when this trouble came," O'Mara ended, "I was pretty sure he would begin to see what I'd been doing for him—consciously as well as subconsciously—and that simple gratitude plus the fact that basically he is a decent type would keep him from withholding the evidence which would clear me. Was I right?"

"You were," said the Major. He paused to quell Caxton who had jumped to his feet, protesting, then continued, "Which brings us to the FROB infant.

"Apparently your baby caught one of the mild but rare diseases which can only be treated successfully on the home planet," Craythorne went on. He smiled suddenly. "At least, that was what they thought until a few hours ago. Now our Hudlarian friends state that the proper treatment has already been initiated by you and that all they have to do is wait for a couple of days and the infant will be as good as new.

"But they're very annoyed with you, O'Mara," the Monitor continued. "They say that you've rigged special equipment for petting and soothing the kid and that you've done this much more often than is desirable. The baby has been overfed and spoiled shamelessly, they say, so much so that at the moment it prefers human beings to members of its own species—"

Suddenly Caxton banged the desk. "You're not going to let him get away with this," he shouted, red-faced. "Waring doesn't know what he's saying sometimes…"

"Mr. Caxton," said the Monitor sharply, "all the evidence available proves that Mr. O'Mara is blameless, both at the time of the accident and while he was looking after the infant later. However, I am not quite finished with him here, so perhaps you two would be good enough to leave…"

Caxton stormed out followed more slowly by Waring. At the door the tractor-beam man paused, addressed one printable and three unprintable words to O'Mara, grinned suddenly and left. The Major sighed.

"O'Mara," he said sternly, "you're out of a job again, and while I don't as a rule give unasked for advice I would like to remind you of a few facts. In a few weeks time the staff and maintenance engineers for this hospital will be arriving and they will be comprised of practically every known species in the galaxy. My job is to settle them in and keep friction from developing between them so that eventually they will work together as a team. No textbook rules have been written to cover this sort of thing yet, but before they sent me here my superiors said that it would require a good rule-of-thumb psychologist with plenty of common sense who was not afraid to take calculated risks. I think it goes without saying that two such psychologists would be even better…"

O'Mara was listening to him all right, but he was thinking of that grin he'd got from Waring. Both the infant and Waring were going to be all right now, he knew, and in his present happy state of mind he could refuse nothing of anybody. But apparently the Major had mistaken his abstraction for something else.

"… Dammit I'm offering you a job! You *fit* here, can't you see that? This is a hospital, man, and you've cured our first patient…!"

Eric Frank Russell

Eric Frank Russell (1905–1978) was once regarded as one of the Big Three of British science fiction, alongside Arthur C. Clarke and John Wyndham, but his reputation has faded since he more-or-less stopped writing in 1965. His career began in 1937, his earliest stories being in imitation of Stanley G. Weinbaum, but he also had a fascination for Charles Fort's proposal that we were all the property of an alien race that controls our lives. He channelled these ideas into the novel Sinister Barrier *which led the first issue of* Unknown, *the new companion magazine to* Astounding SF, *in 1939. The novel, which finally appeared in book form in 1943, was extremely popular and Russell utilized Fortean theories again in* Dreadful Sanctuary *(serial, 1948).*

He was the first British writer to win the prestigious Hugo Award for his short story "Allamagoosa" (1955), a typically British satire about bureaucracy in space. It has often been claimed that he was the favourite writer of John W. Campbell, Jr., the editor of Astounding SF, *and many of his stories in the 1950s appeared in that magazine. His short fiction was collected in* Deep Space *(1954),* Far Stars *(1961),* Dark Tides *(1962) and the linked series,* Men, Martians and Machines *(1955). The following story poses the problem: what do you do when you jump through hyperspace and come out in the middle of nowhere?*

THE ROCKET CAME SHIVERING OUT OF HYPERSPACE AND solidified. Metallic coldness slid over its surface, starting from the prow, spreading to the tail. The pale ghosts of forty main propulsors were the last to gain concrete form. They hardened, were a quadruple ring of tubes ready to blast eight miles of fire.

Lawder, peering through the bow observation port, wiped his eyes. He had been there much longer than usual, much longer. A nervous hand put out for binoculars. The high-powered glasses could not have been of much use, the way they shook. He put them down, wiped his eyes again.

"What's eating you?" Santel was watching him. "Something wrong?"

"Plenty."

It brought Santel upright, running long fingers through red hair. He stalked to the port, stared through.

"Well?" invited Lawder.

"Impossible!"

"Ha!" Lawder said.

Santel tried the binoculars, resting wrists on the port's thick rim to steady the field of vision.

"Well?" Lawder persisted.

"Impossible," maintained Santel.

"You deny the evidence of your own eyes?"

"First impressions can be misleading."

"We're lost." Lawder sat down, viewed his boots without seeing them. His thin face twitched. "Lost souls."

"Shut up!"

"When I was a kid I once put three flies in a bottle. Then I rammed home the cork. That's us, flies in a bottle."

"Shut up!" repeated Santel more loudly. His red hair was stiff, bristly. He had another look through the port. "I'm telling Vanderveen."

"I threw the bottle in a lake. That was thirty years ago, several fly-lifetimes ago. In a lake, cold and dark, without a shore. They're still there maybe. Still there, corked in."

Switching the intercom, Santel spoke into its mike. His voice was hoarse.

"Captain, there's something funny. Better come up and see."

"I can see from here," boomed the loud-speaker.

"Huh?"

"There are four windows in this navigation room. They are there to be looked through. I have looked."

"What do you make of it?"

"Nothing."

"Lost," murmured Lawder. "Become as if we had never been. Another lonely line on the list of missing ships. Memories that thin with the years and eventually drift away."

"One can only make nothing of nothing," said Captain Vanderveen. "Who's that mumbling in there?"

"Lawder."

"Who else could it be?" shouted Lawder at the loud-speaker. "There are only we three. All together and all alone. Just three of us. You and me and Santel."

"How can three be alone?" inquired Vanderveen gently. "Only one man can be alone, or one woman, one child."

"Woman—we'll never see one." Lawder's knuckles were white. "Child—we'll never know one."

"Take it easy," advised Santel, looking at him.

"There's a quart of Tralian alodine in the second drawer," came Vanderveen's voice. "Give him a double shot. I'll be along in a minute."

Lawder gulped it down, breathed heavily. After a while, he said, "Sorry, Santel."

"It's all right."

"Sort of shook me up a bit."

"I know."

"You don't know." He showed the signet ring on his left hand. "She gave me this two months back. I gave her pinfire opals from Procyon Seven. We were to be married soon. This was to be my last trip."

"So!" Santel's eyebrows lifted slightly.

"It will be my last all right!"

"Now, now," soothed Santel.

"My last, forever. She can wait, watching the calendar, haunting the spaceports, scanning the arrival-lists, hoping, praying. She can grow old and grey. Or find someone else. Someone who'll come back to her, laughing, with gifts." His hand went out. "Give me that bottle again." He gurgled lengthily, held it up, eyed its dark glass. "Flies. That's us."

"Your childhood conscience is biting back at you," Santel diagnosed. "You shouldn't have done it."

"Didn't you ever cork them in?"

"No."

"Or pull off their wings and watch them crawl?"

"No."

"You're lucky."

"So it seems." Dryly, Santel nodded toward the port.

★

Vanderveen lumbered in—a huge man, portly, with a great spade-beard.

"So you have gazed through the windows and do not like it." He was probably the only experienced deep-spacer who persisted in referring to observation ports as windows. "You look only through these and not through the others. How silly."

They reacted eagerly. "You have something, captain?"

"Nothing. Through every window it is the same. There is nothing."

They relaxed, disappointed.

"There is now only one unobserved direction," he went on. "That is tailward. One of you had better put on a spacesuit. No need to go through the bow lock. The main drivers are cold and will give direct rearward view."

Santel dressed himself. They tightened the neck-bolts of his helmet. He went out.

Every sound of his motion could be heard throughout the ship, faithfully conducted, a little amplified. The clump of his boots. The clang of the engine room's airtight doors. A thin, shrill whistle of air being pumped away before he opened the inspection-trap of a vacuum-filled combustion chamber. Slithering noises, outward then inward. All the former sounds reversed.

He returned. They knew the answer before they unwound the neck-bolts. It was depicted on his face behind the armour-glass visor. The helmet came off. A dampness lay over his forehead.

"It's a heck of a lot worse when you look straight out at it." Santel split his suit down the front, wriggled like a crab escaping its shrunken shell. "And it's wrong, terribly wrong."

"Blackness," chattered Lawder, flourishing his bottle. "Sheer, solid, unrelieved blackness. Not a spark. Not one gold or silver gleam. Not a pale pink rocket trail. Not a phantom comet."

Vanderveen stood by a port, pawing his beard.

"No suns, no planets, no green fields, no singing birds," Lawder went on. He poured generously down his gullet. "The Lord hath given and the Lord hath taken away."

"He's getting drunk," warned Santel.

"Let him." Vanderveen did not look around. "He to his inward comforts—we to ours."

Santel said steadily. "Maybe I'm slower on the uptake. I don't yet feel ready for despair."

"Of course not. You're an engineer and therefore have an engineer's mind. You know we can try the hyperdrive and chance where it takes us. Or the rockets. We have vanished from the ken of men but we're not yet beaten."

"Yeah, the hyperdrive." It hit home in Lawder's brain. "Twenty light-years in one hour. That will save us. What gets in can always come out." He grinned around, momentarily happy.

"Like an airplane plunging into the sea," suggested Santel. "Gets in. Doesn't like it. Up she goes."

Lawder swayed close to him, a glass bludgeon in his grip, swinging it hot-handed.

"You don't care if we not here forever. What've *you* got to go back to? One lousy room in a stinking hostel for lousy space-men. A month ashore picking your teeth and snoring through a library of slumber-educators for the big-ship rating you'll never get. Living and longing for the spaceways that will land you no place when your day is done, and—"

"That will do, Lawder," snapped Vanderveen.

"As for you—" Lawder turned on him.

"THAT WILL DO!" Vanderveen's beard stuck out. His big hands were bunched.

Savagely, Lawder swung the bottle, sobbing, "Talk to me like that!"

The captain grunted deep down in his chest, thrust out a huge paw. No more. He did no more than that, but it sent the other headlong across the room.

Silence. They stared at the body slumped in a corner, eyes shut, breathing slowly and without sound. Turning, they looked through the port. Silence. Blackness. No faraway lanterns. No faint, aureate glow of a Milky Way. Only the utter deadliness of the day before Creation. They were bodies on a forgotten barge becalmed in an ageless, endless sea. A sable sea. Dark and peaceful, as death.

"Space-men don't get that way." Santel jerked a thumb toward the corner. "He can't be normal."

"He has someone waiting. That means much."

Santel cocked an eye at him. "What of you?"

"I'm not soon to be married." The captain viewed the dark, seeing only the past. "Besides, I am different. You are different. That is our beauty as men, that all are different. Each does his best with what the good Lord has given him. He can do no more."

"No, sir," agreed Santel, very respectfully.

Lawder came round after a bit, blinked blearily, made no remark. Crawling into his bunk, he snored for four hours. He awoke, had a look at the chronometer.

"You guys been standing there all that time?"

"Most of it."

"Gaping at jet-black nothingness? What good will it do you?"

Santel did not bother to answer.

"We've been thinking," said Vanderveen. "Hard."

"Yeah?" Lawder crawled out, stood up, tenderly felt around his chops. "Who socked me?"

"Maybe I did. Or maybe Santel did. Or maybe you conked yourself with that bottle you were waving around."

"I get it. Nobody's telling."

"So long as I'm captain there are going to be no recriminations, no animosities. Not while we're stuck in this fix. We're too small a bunch, too alone."

Lawder eyed him, licked dry lips. "I guess so. Well, I'll go get me a drink. I feel dehydrated."

"Easy on the water," advised Vanderveen.

"Huh?"

"There is only so much."

Easy on the water—there is only so much. That was today, the first day. Tomorrow, next week, next month—what? Rationing by count of drops, every one more precious than its predecessor. Each man's measure watched by other eyes, lingering on every glistening globule, seeing it stretch, drop, and hearing its sweet, delicious *plop*.

And three minds growing increasingly bemused by the simple mathematics of the situation: a two-way split goes farther than a three-way deal. Higher calculus: all for one is more than for two. How much consumable blood in somebody else's body? Would the biggest one hold the most? How many warm pints in Vanderveen?

The captain's gaze was on him as he went for his drink. It would have been easier to bear had it been accusing, suspicious or threatening. But it was not. It was cool, calm, courageous. That made it hard, so hard. Lawder contented himself with a mere suck rolled around his mouth. He came slowly back.

"Are we going to squat here until we're mummified? Why don't we take to hyperdrive again."

Vanderveen's thick finger pointed outside. "Because we don't know which way to shoot. Direction is a path relative to visible things. There is nothing visible, therefore no means of relating ourselves to anything, no sense of direction."

"We know how we're sitting. All we need do is back out along the line we came in."

"I wish it were that easy." If the captain was worried he did not show it. "We don't know how we're sitting or even whether we are sitting. We may be motionless or not. We may have rotated a hundred times, longitudinally or axially, and remained unaware of it. We may be skidding some place in a straight line, at high velocity, or we may be spiralling around an enormous radius. There's just no way of telling."

"But the instruments—"

"Were designed for the space-time continuum in which they were made. Right now we need *new* instruments for a totally different set of circumstances."

"All right, I'll give you that. But we've still got the hyperdrive." Lawder gestured urgently. "It can jerk us through four successive layers of hyperspace, four coexisting universes. They won't all be blotted out like this hell-hole. They'll have lights, beacons, calling us home."

"Beacons," echoed Santel moodily. "One red dwarf, old, sterile and planetless, would look like heaven to me."

"We can try, can't we?" insisted Lawder. "Can't we?"

"We can." Vanderveen was thoughtful, reluctant. "But if we choose wrongly—"

"We'll be another mighty jump still deeper into the dark," Santel finished for him. "Then we'll go nuts and make another, and another. Getting farther and farther away trying to get nearer. Struggling harder and sinking deeper like flies trapped in sticky beer."

"Flies!" Lawder shouted it at the top of his voice. "You throw those up to me? Why, you—!"

Vanderveen moved forward, almost touching him chest to chest. "Be quiet! Listen!" His fingers combed a moment at his great beard. "We have a multitude of choices. Right, left, forward, backward, up, down and thousands of intermediates. Plus the other coordinates which make the number of chances a string of figures ten yards long. Only one of those may be correct. Only one may be salvation, life, home, the green fields, the friendly sun, the warmth and fellowship of other men. Any of the others may make confusion worse confounded, our damnation more damned. Do you get that?"

"Yes." It came out in a whisper.

"Very well. Give me a direction and we'll try it."

"Me?" Lawder was shaken. "Why me?"

"You're the bellyacher," said Santel.

The captain turned on him. "That was unnecessary." Again to Lawder, "Go on, choose!"

"How?" Lawder stalled for time, fearful of error.

"Point." Vanderveen's lips uttered it again, commandingly. *"Point!"*

Perspiring freely, Lawder stuck out an arm at random. It was like signalling the death trap to be sprung.

"Give me a three-figure number," Vanderveen ordered.

"237."

"A letter."

"B."

"And an angle."

"Forty-seven degrees."

To Santel, "You heard what he said. Set them up along the line he picked. Switch immediately you're ready."

Ceremoniously, Santel dragged a tiny woollen monkey from his breast pocket, patted it three times, kissed it once and stuffed it back. He sat at the control board, adjusted it, switched.

The others stood waiting as if it were normal for the hyperdrive to be subject to delay. It was merely that its unexpected lack of response took some time to sink into their minds. Not a shudder, not a shake. No queer, flesh-tingling twist such as always accompanied ultra-rapid transition from one scheme of things to another. Not even the faintest tremor in the fabric of the ship.

Scowling to himself, Santel set the controls anew, tried again, reset, had a third go. He disappeared into the engine room, came back after twenty minutes, tried the controls.

"It won't work." His face came round over one shoulder, showing features strained and mystified. "There is nothing wrong with the apparatus. Everything is as it ought to be. Yet it doesn't function."

Lawder burst out, "It has *got* to."

"In that case," suggested Santel, leaving the board, "you make it function."

"I'm not the engineer. That's your job."

"Well, I've flopped on it. I can't put right something that isn't wrong. I can't cure mechanical or electronic faults that don't exist. See if you can do better."

"Let me try." Vanderveen pushed past, sat at the board, patiently set up a dozen series of coordinates. He switched each one. The vessel did not stir. Its ports remained black and blank as if immersed in soot. "No luck." He arose heavily, without emotion, but looking somehow aged and tired. "The drive is out for keeps."

Santel raked his red hair. "I don't like this, captain. Hyperdrive operates from space to space. In theory, there is only one place where it could not work."

"Well?"

"And that place is purely imaginary."

"Well?"

"Unspace, or not-space, or whatever you care to call it. Somewhere devoid of spatial properties."

"Bunk!" Lawder chipped in emphatically. "Everywhere has got to be within one continuum or another. Where could not-space be?"

Vanderveen said, "Outside the whole of Creation."

Momentarily it hypnotized both of them. They stood there, side by side, viewing him with dazed eyes, their thoughts stirred to turmoil, their tongues locked and growing dry.

Finally, Lawder found voice. "The big boats can go faster and farther than us. They can cross gulfs between island universes, hyperspatially. They've skipped from one galaxy to another and found more beyond. Always there are more beyond, sparkling in the dark. Creation has no limits."

"Hasn't it?"

"No," declared Lawder flatly.

"Can you *think* of it without limits?"

"The human mind can't really conceive infinity. So what?"

"So you're dogmatically asserting that which you cannot conceive." Vanderveen studied him beneath thick brows. "Not that that proves or disproves anything."

"Do some proving of your own," Lawder invited. He was getting excited as his mind absorbed the dreadful implications of the captain's viewpoint.

Vanderveen said quietly, "The hyperdrive is extremely efficient when it works, but it's not one hundred per cent reliable. It operates in and through any space. Here it does not work. Neither is light transmitted anywhere immediately outside this ship. Neither does the radio respond."

"The radio!" Lawder smacked his forehead in self-reproof. "I forgot it."

"We tried it while you were snoring. It remains as silent as the grave." Clasping hands behind him, the captain paced the room. "We are some place that is not space as we understand it. Somewhere cold and sterile. Somewhere devoid of all gravitational and electromagnetic phenomena. That which stands outside of all creative forces. Negativity. Ultima Thule. The place that God forgot." He stared at them, his beard sticking forward. "The hyperdrive hit a rut and we got tossed right out of mundane existence."

"That's how it's beginning to look to me," Santel admitted.

"All the things with which we are familiar—light, gravitation, air, food, warmth, company and so on—are confined within this vessel. Outside is nothing—except, possibly, faraway and buried deep in the dark, the forty-odd ships which have vanished without word or trace in the three thousand years since hyperdrive came into general use."

"Gone forever," droned Santel, finding morbid pleasure in it. "Forever, forever, amen!"

Lawder declaimed furiously, "We'll show up. We'll come driving back in a blaze of glory. We won't stay stuck until kingdom come. Do you know why?" He glowered at one, then at the other, inviting contradiction. "Because I'm going to start the rockets."

"Useless," Santel told him. "One hour of hyperdrive covers more distance than the rockets could make up in twenty years, even if the fuel—"

"Damn the fuel! May you both burn with it!"

They were silent. Their eyes followed him as he took the pilot's seat, operated the injectors, pressed the firing stud. The ship roared and shuddered.

"See?" He came out of the seat, yelled above the noise, did a little dance of triumph. "See?"

"See?" shouted Santel even louder. He pointed to the meters. Their fingers quivered in sympathy with the vessel's trembling, but that was all. No forward thrust. No velocity. No acceleration rate. Only the thermometer responded. It began to climb rapidly. Warmth poured forward from the tail end, there being almost no radiation outward.

"Cut it off, Lawder," commanded Vanderveen, anxiously noting the rise of the red line. "Cut it off. If it goes on too long we'll be roasted alive."

"Roast," howled Lawder, doing a crazy jig and ignoring the meters. "Who cares? We're going back. Home. Among the flowers. Winifred there, smiling, happy." The rockets bellowed. The warmth built up. Sweat began to run down his cheeks and was not noticed in his exultation. Winifred, for me. Home. We're on the way."

"Space-happy," commented Santel, grim.

"Lawder, I said cut it off!"

"Back to the suns, the moons, the seas, the clouds. Back to people, millions of them. Thanks to me. The bottle is uncorked, thanks to me."

"CUT IT OFF!" Vanderveen lumbered forward, hair lank, beard dripping. The red line was three-quarters up.

"Never! Never! We're going back, I tell you. Whether you like it or not." His eyes went cunning as they saw the captain's approach. "Keep away. The rockets will run, without your orders. Keep away!" Pulling open the pilot's drawer, he made a grab inside, got something heavy and metallic blue.

A thin stab of fire came from Vanderveen's hip.

Lawder posed by the drawer, one hand propped on it. He gazed at Vanderveen, his face wet, his eyes softening. The rockets thumped and thundered. He went slowly to his knees, pulling the drawer out and spilling its contents. Leaping behind him, Santel stopped the flow to the main propulsors.

In the deep silence that followed, Lawder said apologetically, "I only want home... Winifred. You understand?" His voice was like a child's. He shook his head blindly, keeled over, ceased to breathe.

"Last trip." Santel stood over him, looking down. "It was his last trip."

Vanderveen mopped his forehead. "I intended to make a near miss and frighten him. It was a bad shot."

"It was fate."

"A bad shot," persisted Vanderveen. "I had little time to think." He turned away sadly. "The pain was his, but the punishment was mine. I have slaughtered part of myself."

Santel watched him go out, slow-footed.

No man is an island.

Five weeks. Eight-forty Earth-hours. Twenty intergalactic time-units. Eons in a berillisteel bottle. And still the impenetrable dark outside, thick, cloying, the dark that has never known light or life.

Santel mooched into the navigation room, flopped into a seat. He was thin, pale, had the gauntness of one cooped up with trouble too long.

"The food is all right. Enough for a year. What's the use of it without a year's oxygen?"

Busily writing at his desk, Vanderveen did not reply.

"If we had been fitted up with half an acre of oxygen-producing Sirian cacti, like the big boats carry, we'd have been O.K. in that respect. Tending them would give us something to do. We could concentrate our worrying upon the water."

Scribble, scribble continued Vanderveen.

"Reckon the water will last us about three weeks unless we reduce our takings still further."

No response.

"After that—curtains!" He mooned irritably at the captain's broad back. "Well, aren't you interested?"

Vanderveen sighed, put down his pen, swivelled round in his seat. "We share and share alike—to the end."

"That's understood," agreed Santel.

"It is not understood." The other's eyes were keen, penetrating as they looked into his. "You have tried to deceive me. For the last ten days you have taken less than your share. I know, for I have checked up on it." He paused, added, "So I have taken similarly less. That makes us quits."

Flushing, Santel said, "There was no need for you to do that."

"Why not?"

"You are twice my size. You need more."

"More life?" He waited for the reply that did not come. "I am older than you. I have had more life."

Santel changed the subject with the alacrity of the out-argued. "Writing, writing, always writing. Is it necessary?"

"I am entering the log, in full detail."

"It won't be read for a million years—if ever. We have departed the mortal coil. We're dead but not quite ready to lie down—though it won't be long now! That makes log-filling a waste of effort, doesn't it?"

"It is my duty."

"Duty!" sniffed Santel. "Did Lawder think of duty?"

"In a way." The captain mused a moment. "He had an all-absorbing ambition, natural, harmless, involving a woman and an Earthbound home. He had worked hard for it over many years, been denied it over many years, at last found it almost within reach. In the crisis he did his duty to his dreams, but because his dream was not ours we thought him a little crazy." He gestured to the log. "So I have written that he died in the line of duty. It is all that I can do for him."

"And it's a waste of effort," maintained Santel.

"For five weeks you have been trying various combinations on the hyperdrive. Isn't that equally a waste of effort?"

"One must do something or go nuts. Besides, it is better to live in hope than die in despair."

"Precisely!" Vanderveen twisted back to his desk, resumed writing, his pen going *scratch-scratch*. "So I accept to the very last my responsibilities as ship commander. And remote though the chance may be, a full and complete account of what occurred may be useful to somebody some day. If it served to save the skin of only one ignorant Savage it would not be in vain."

Log-filling. It may be useful some day, somewhere, somehow. The dull grind of routine when life has dribbled away to a mere three weeks, perhaps less. The multi-million to one hope of providing salvation for some barbarian a thousand generations unborn. An impossible long-shot aimed to help one ship, one sailor at a far-distant time when hyperdrives might be hopelessly antiquated and all the multitudinous existences accurately measured, weighed, estimated.

"The least one can do," added Vanderveen, by way of afterthought, "is one's duty to the last—as one deems it."

Santel stood up, staring over his shoulder, seeing the rim of beard that jutted from the stubborn chin. *Scratch-scratch* went the pen. It was like the scratchings of man-hordes at the foundations of Creation. Striving and scratching to bare the treasures and secrets hidden therein; dying and scratching and never giving up.

And it was like the scratching of his dry tongue upon his dry palate. Water. Three weeks. Twice three are six. Three threes are nine. Mistress Mary, quite contrary, how does your garden grow? Water, it needs water. Three weeks. Twice three are six.

"So I have taken similarly less. That makes us quits."

Quietly, Santel went out, closing the door. His gait was stiff, robot-like, his features set. His eyes were on something faraway and insignificant. His dream, his own dream. A scrap of paper. An unimportant roll of vellum bearing the great trans-cosmic seal above his own name. Engineer First Class. Perhaps the name would have been written with a scratchy pen. All this for that. His dream. How futile.

A little later a thin whistle of air sounded from the front. It rose and fell, sobbing without loudness, in imitation of one who weeps muffled and alone.

Vanderveen heard the last wail of it, dropped his pen. Puzzled, apprehensive, he went to the door, pulled it open.

"Santel!"

Silence.

"Are you there?"

An awful hush.

"SANTEL!"

He raced to the bow, steel-shod boots clattering, his beard jutting forward, his eyes anxious.

There it was, the forward air lock. Fastened on the inside, open on the outside, open to the eternal dark. He looked around, big hands clasping and unclasping. Three spacesuits hanging nearby, bulgy but slack, like iron men drained of their insides. A note stuck to the middle one.

"I have nobody. You have many, Good-bye."

Taking it down, he carried it back to the navigation room, sat a long, long time fingering the note and gazing blankly at the wall. Finally, he picked up his pen.

Another six and a half weeks. Twenty-six intergalactic time-units.

Vanderveen wrote slowly, laboriously, with screwed-up eyes and many pauses for breath. He was not engaged upon the log. That official tome lay to one side, discarded, finished with the day's entry. In that respect, duty was done, to the last. But he was still writing.

The calendar hung upon the wall, its various sector indicators all an Earth-month out of date. The chronometer had stopped. A dozen oxygen inlets were wide open and empty, not a whiff of life coming through their tubes from the depleted tanks at back. The utter blackness of nonexistence still lay over the ports, ready for invasion and further conquest when the ship's dimming lights at last flickered and went out.

Laboriously he put down, "I am not alone while I can see your face within my mind. I am not alone while I have memories of you. I thank you, dearest, for these things you have given me, because of which I am not alone." He paused to assert his will over his failing hand. "But now I must finish with fondest love to you and the children, from their affectionate father Conraad V—"

He struggled hard to complete the name, and failed.

The dark came in.

The multitudinous years, the long-rolling eons cannot be measured in death. There is no time beyond the pale of living things.

So there was no sense of bygone centuries or millennia when Vanderveen awoke. There was only intensely brilliant light and much pain and many glistening things in which coloured fluids trembled and bubbled. Also, there were voices within his mind.

"We can do no more. It's now or never. Cut out that switch and let's see if he keeps going."

Pain was all over, along every nerve and artery, in every muscle, but gradually subsiding. The soundless voices were becoming strong.

Something nearby gave a loud click. A torturing throb within him ceased. Only the slight pulsation of his heart could be felt. He was weak, befuddled and curiously tired.

"VANDERVEEN!"

It struck commandingly into the depths of his brain, forcing him to open his eyes, thrust away his lassitude.

He was lying flat on a surface soft, warm and resilient. Three men stood by his side. He knew instinctively that they were men though not like any he had ever known. None had possessed such great optics or exuded such mental power.

"You can hear?"

A whisper. "Yes."

"Beyond the Rim nothing changes, nothing deteriorates. That has saved you."

"Saved?" He strove to comprehend.

"You have been resuscitated."

Questions formed haltingly in his mind. Where am I? Who are these? How did I get here?

They must have been able to read his thoughts, for they responded, "There can be no deliberate escape from non-space. But Creation expands into it at tremendous rate. Eventually its limits reached your vessel—and life reclaimed its own."

That was far too much for him to absorb at such a moment. He made no attempt to grapple with the concept, but listened as they went on.

"So ships come back now and again, centuries apart, like relics from the dawn of history. Yours proved to be a treasure of value beyond compute, for it contained essential data which will enable us to prevent further disappearances. There will be no more lost vessels, no more, no more."

It did not gratify him. There were other fears that prevented him from linking up yesterday's duty with today's reward.

"My wife," he got out in an agony of apprehension.

They shook sad heads, went silent.

He tried to sit up. "My children."

One patted his hand, smiled at him. "We are your children."

Of course, they must be. He sank back, closed his eyes. My children. He who serves mankind is part of mankind—and mankind's children are his very own.

A watcher turned a huge scanner, swung it nearer, showed the waiting and hopeful world that the man from seventeen thousand years ago lived once again.

And as it focused upon him, Captain Vanderveen slept knowing that he was not alone.

THE VOYAGE THAT LASTED 600 YEARS

Don Wilcox

If we are to explore other star systems in the hope of finding inhabitable planets and other intelligent life, in all probability we will have to rely on a generation starship to get there. Although our nearest neighbouring star, Proxima Centauri, is "only" 4.2 light-years away, even if we could travel at one-tenth the speed of light, it would clearly take us 42 years, and there's no point in sending well-trained astronauts at the peak of their careers and aged in their thirties, if they're going to be in their mid-seventies when they get there, always assuming they remain mentally stable. If we could master suspended animation, astronauts might be able to sleep for most of the journey and, hopefully, not age, but the alternative is to have a starship which is the home to successive generations. Life on a generation starship has been the subject of many stories, as discussed in the introduction, and the one regarded as the first to explore this idea and its consequences in detail is the following.

Cleo Eldon Wilcox (1905–2000), who went on to teach a creative writing course, was one of the great sf pulpsters, writing primarily for Amazing Stories *and* Fantastic Adventures, *the two giant pulps edited by that renegade sf showman, Raymond A. Palmer. Palmer didn't want sophisticated, introspective science fiction. He wanted action and adventure. "Gimme bang-bang," was his instruction to Wilcox. In fact, Wilcox was capable of sophistication and introspection but used it sparingly. Instead, he churned out story after story throughout the 1940s often under a variety of pen names. None of his work was collected during his lifetime but more recently a friend of the family, Von Rothenberger, assembled two volumes as* The Best of Don Wilcox *(2016–17) which at last showcases his remarkable imagination.*

T HEY GAVE US A GALA SEND-OFF, THE KIND THAT KEEPS YOUR heart bobbing up at your tonsils.

"It's a long, long way to the Milky Way!" the voices sang out. The band thundered the chorus over and over. The golden trumpaphones blasted our eardrums wide open. Thousands of people clapped their hands in time.

There were thirty-three of us—that is, there was supposed to be. As it turned out, there were thirty-five.

We were a dazzling parade of red, white and blue uniforms. We marched up the gangplank by couples, every couple a man and wife, every couple young and strong, for the selection had been rigid.

Captain Sperry and his wife and I—I being the odd man—brought up the rear. Reporters and cameramen swarmed at our heels. The microphones stopped us. The band and the crowd hushed.

"This is Captain Sperry telling you good-bye," the amplified voice boomed. "In behalf of the thirty-three, I thank you for your grand farewell. We'll remember this hour as our last contact with our beloved Earth."

The crowd held its breath. The mighty import of our mission struck through every heart.

"We go forth into space to live—and to die," the captain said gravely. "But *our children's children*, born in space and reared in the light of our vision, will carry on our great purpose. And in centuries to come, *your children's children* may set forth for the Robinello planets, knowing that you will find an American colony already planted there."

The captain gestured good-bye and the multitude responded with a thunderous cheer. Nothing so daring as a six-century non-stop flight had ever been undertaken before.

An announcer nabbed me by the sleeve and barked into the microphone,

"And now one final word from Professor Gregory Grimstone, the one man who is supposed to live down through the six centuries of this historic flight and see the journey through to the end."

"Ladies and gentlemen," I choked, and the echo of my swallow blobbed back at me from distant walls, "as Keeper of the Traditions, I give you my word that the S.S. *Flashaway* shall carry your civilization through to the end, unsoiled and unblemished!"

A cheer stimulated me and I drew a deep breath for a burst of oratory. But Captain Sperry pulled at my other sleeve.

"That's all. We're set to slide out in two minutes."

The reporters scurried down the gangplank and made a centre rush through the crowd. The band struck up. Motors roared sullenly.

One lone reporter who had missed out on the interviews blitzkrieged up and caught me by the coattail.

"Hold it, Butch. Just a coupla words so I can whip up a column of froth for the *Star*— Well, I'll be damned! If it ain't 'Crackdown' Grimstone!"

I scowled. The reporter before me was none other than Bill Broscoe, one of my former pupils at college and a star athlete. At heart I knew that Bill was a right guy, but I'd be the last to tell him so.

"Broscoe!" I snarled. "Tardy as usual. You finally flunked my history course, didn't you?"

"Now, Crackdown," he whined, "don't go hopping on me. I won that Thanksgiving game for you, remember?"

★

He gazed at my red, white and blue uniform.

"So you're off for Robinello," he grinned.

"Son, this is my last minute on Earth, and *you* have to haunt me, of all people—"

"So you're the one that's taking the refrigerated sleeper, to wake up every hundred years—"

"And stir the fires of civilization among the crew—yes. Six hundred years from now when your bones have rotted, I'll still be carrying on."

"Still teaching 'em history? God forbid!" Broscoe grinned.

"I hope I have better luck than I did with you."

"Let 'em off easy on dates, Crackdown. Give them 1066 for William the Conqueror and 2066 for the *Flashaway* takeoff. That's enough. Taking your wife, I suppose?"

At this impertinent question I gave Broscoe the cold eye.

"Pardon me," he said, suppressing a sly grin—proof enough that he had heard the devastating story about how I missed my wedding and got the air. "Faulty alarm clock, wasn't it? Too bad, Crackdown. And you always ragged *me* about being tardy!"

With this jibe Broscoe exploded into laughter. Some people have the damnedest notions about what constitutes humour. I backed into the entrance of the space ship uncomfortably. Broscoe followed.

Zzzzippp!

The automatic door cut past me. I jerked Broscoe through barely in time to keep him from being bisected.

"Tardy as usual, my friend," I hooted. "You've missed your gangplank! That makes you the first castaway in space."

We took off like a shooting star, and the last I saw of Bill Broscoe, he stood at a rear window cursing as he watched the Earth and the moon fall away into the velvety black heavens. And the more I laughed at him, the madder he got. No sense of humour.

Was that the last time I ever saw him? Well, no, to be strictly honest I had one more unhappy glimpse of him.

It happened just before I packed myself away for my first one hundred years' sleep.

I had checked over the "Who's Who Aboard the *Flashaway*"— the official register—to make sure that I was thoroughly acquainted with everyone on board; for these sixteen couples were to be the great-grandparents of the next generation I would meet. Then I had promptly taken my leave of Captain Sperry and his wife, and gone directly to my refrigeration plant, where I was to suspend my life by instantaneous freezing.

I clicked the switches, and one of the two huge horizontal wheels—one in reserve, in the event of a breakdown—opened up for me like a door opening in the side of a gigantic doughnut, or better, a tubular merry-go-round. There was my nook waiting for me to crawl in.

Before I did so I took a backward glance toward the ballroom. The one-way glass partition, through which I could see but not be seen, gave me a clear view of the scene of merriment. The couples were dancing. The journey was off to a good start.

"A grand gang," I said to myself. No one doubted that the ship was equal to the six-hundred-year journey. The success would depend upon the people. Living and dying in this closely cir-cumscribed world would put them to a severe test. All credit, I reflected, was due the planning committee for choosing such a congenial group.

"They're equal to it," I said optimistically. If their children would only prove as sturdy and adaptable as their parents, my job as Keeper of the Traditions would be simple.

*

But how, I asked myself, as I stepped into my life-suspension merry-go-round, would Bill Broscoe fit into this picture? Not a half bad guy. Still—

My final glance through the one-way glass partition slew me. Out of the throng I saw Bill Broscoe dancing past with a beautiful girl in his arms. The girl was Louise—*my* Louise—the girl I had been engaged to marry!

In a flash it came to me—but not about Bill. I forgot him on the spot. About Louise.

Bless her heart, she'd come to find me. She must have heard that I had signed up for the *Flashaway*, and she had come aboard, a stowaway, to forgive me for missing the wedding—to marry me! Now—

A warning click sounded, a lid closed over me, my refrigerator-merry-go-round whirled— Blackness!

CHAPTER II

BABIES, JUST BABIES

In a moment—or so it seemed—I was again gazing into the light of the refrigerating room. The lid stood open.

A stimulating warmth circulated through my limbs. Perhaps the machine, I half consciously concluded, had made no more than a preliminary revolution.

I bounded out with a single thought. I must find Louise. We could still be married. For the present I would postpone my entrance into the ice. And since the machine had been equipped with *two* merry-go-round freezers as an emergency safeguard — ah!

Happy thought—perhaps Louise would be willing to undergo life suspension with me!

I stopped at the one-way glass partition, astonished to see no signs of dancing in the ballroom. I could scarcely see the ballroom, for it had been darkened.

Upon unlocking the door (the refrigerator room was my own private retreat) I was bewildered. An unaccountable change had come over everything. What it was, I couldn't determine at the moment. But the very air of the ballroom was different.

A few dim green light bulbs burned along the walls—enough to show me that the dancers had vanished. Had time enough elapsed for night to come on? My thoughts spun dizzily. Night, I reflected, would consist simply of turning off the lights and going to bed. It had been agreed in our plan that our twenty-four-hour Earth day would be maintained for the sake of regularity.

But there was something more intangible that struck me. The furniture had been changed about, and the very walls seemed *older*. Something more than minutes had passed since I left this room.

Strangest of all, the windows were darkened.

In a groggy state of mind I approached one of the windows in hopes of catching a glimpse of the solar system. I was still puzzling over how much time might have elapsed. Here, at least, was a sign of very recent activity.

"Wet Paint" read the sign pinned to the window. The paint was still sticky. What the devil—

The ship, of course, was fully equipped for blind flying. But aside from the problems of navigation, the crew had anticipated enjoying a wonderland of stellar beauty through the portholes. Now, for some strange reason, every window had been painted opaque.

I listened. Slow measured steps were pacing in an adjacent hallway. Nearing the entrance, I stopped, halted by a shrill sound from somewhere overhead. It came from one of the residential quarters that gave on the ballroom balcony.

It was the unmistakable wail of a baby.

Then another baby's cry struck up; and a third, from somewhere across the balcony, joined the chorus. Time, indeed, must have passed since I left this roomful of dancers.

Now some irate voices of disturbed sleepers added rumbling basses to the symphony of wailings. Grumbles of "Shut that little devil up!" and poundings of fists on walls thundered through the empty ballroom. In a burst of inspiration I ran to the records room, where the ship's "Who's Who" was kept.

The door to the records room was locked, but the footsteps of some sleepless person I had heard now pounded down the dimly lighted hallway. I looked upon the aged man. I had never seen him before. He stopped at the sight of me; then snapping on a brighter light, came on confidently.

"Mr. Grimstone?" he said, extending his hand. "We've been expecting you. My name is William Broscoe—"

"Broscoe!"

"William Broscoe, the second. You knew my father, I believe."

I groaned and choked.

"And my mother," the old man continued, "always spoke very highly of you. I'm proud to be the first to greet you."

He politely overlooked the flush of purple that leaped into my face. For a moment nothing that I could say was intelligible.

He turned a key and we entered the records room. There I faced the inescapable fact. My full century had passed. The original crew of the *Flashaway* were long gone. A completely new generation was on the register.

Or, more accurately, three new generations: the children, the grandchildren, and the great-grandchildren of the generation I had known.

One hundred years had passed—and I had lain so completely suspended, owing to the freezing, that only a moment of my own life had been absorbed.

Eventually I was to get used to this; but on this first occasion I found it utterly shocking — even embarrassing. Only a few minutes ago, as my experience went, I was madly in love with Louise and had hopes of yet marrying her.

But now—well, the leather-bound "Who's Who" told all. Louise had been dead twenty years. Nearly thirty children now alive aboard the S.S. *Flashaway* could claim her as their great-grandmother. These carefully recorded pedigrees proved it.

And the patriarch of that fruitful tribe had been none other than Bill Broscoe, the fresh young athlete who had always been tardy for my history class. I gulped as if I were swallowing a baseball.

Broscoe—tardy! And I had missed my second chance to marry Louise—by a full century!

My fingers turned the pages of the register numbly. William Broscoe II misinterpreted my silence.

"I see you are quick to detect our trouble," he said, and the same deep conscientious concern showed in his expression that I had remembered in the face of his mother, upon our grim meeting after my alarm clock had failed and I had missed my own wedding.

Trouble? Trouble aboard the S.S. *Flashaway*, after all the careful advance planning we had done, and after all our array of budgeting and scheduling and vowing to stamp our systematic ways upon the oncoming generations? This, we had agreed, would be the world's most unique colonizing expedition; for every last trouble that might crop up on the six-hundred-year voyage had already been met and conquered by advance planning.

"They've tried to put off doing anything about it until your arrival," Broscoe said, observing respectfully that the charter invested in me the authority of passing upon all important policies. "But this very week three new babies arrived, which brings the trouble to a crisis. So the captain ordered a blackout of the heavens as an emergency measure."

"Heavens?" I grunted. "What have the heavens got to do with babies?"

"There's a difference of opinion on that. Maybe it depends upon how susceptible you are."

"Susceptible—to what?"

"The romantic malady."

I looked at the old man, much puzzled. He took me by the arm and led me toward the pilots' control room. Here were unpainted windows that revealed celestial glories beyond anything I had ever dreamed. Brilliant planets of varied hues gleamed through the blackness, while close at hand—almost close enough to touch —were numerous large moons, floating slowly past as we shot along our course.

"Some little show," the pilot grinned, "and it keeps getting better."

He proceeded to tell me just where we were and how few adjustments in the original time schedules he had had to make, and why this non-stop flight to Robinello would stand unequalled for centuries to come.

And I heard virtually nothing of what he said. I simply stood there, gazing at the unbelievable beauty of the skies. I was hypnotized, enthralled, shaken to the very roots. One emotion, one thought dominated me. I longed for Louise.

"The romantic malady, as I was saying," William Broscoe resumed, "may or may not be a factor in producing our large population. Personally, I think it's pure buncombe."

"Pure buncombe," I echoed, still thinking of Louise. If she and I had had moons like these—

"But nobody can tell Captain Dickinson anything..."

There was considerable clamour and wrangling that morning as the inhabitants awakened to find their heavens blacked out. Captain Dickinson was none too popular anyway. Fortunately for him, many of the people took their grouches out on the babies who had caused the disturbance in the night.

Families with babies were supposed to occupy the rear staterooms—but there weren't enough rear staterooms. Or rather, there were too many babies.

Soon the word went the rounds that the Keeper of the Traditions had returned to life. I was duly banqueted and toasted and treated to lengthy accounts of the events of the past hundred years. And during the next few days many of the older men and women would take me aside for private conferences and spill their worries into my ears.

CHAPTER III

BOREDOM

"What's the world coming to?" these granddaddies and grand-mothers would ask. And before I could scratch my head for an answer, they would assure me that this expedition was headed straight for the rocks.

"It's all up with us. We've lost our grip on our original

purposes. The Six-Hundred-Year Plan is nothing but a dead scrap of paper."

I'll admit things looked plenty black. And the more parlour conversations I was invited in on, the blacker things looked. I couldn't sleep nights.

"If our population keeps on increasing, we'll run out of food before we're halfway there," William Broscoe II repeatedly declared. "We've got to have a compulsory programme of birth control. That's the only thing that will save us."

A delicate subject for parlour conversations, you think? This older generation didn't think so. I was astonished, and I'll admit I was a bit proud as well, to discover how deeply imbued these old greybeards were with *Flashaway* determination and patriotism. They had missed life in America by only one generation, and they were unquestionably the staunchest of flag wavers on board.

The younger generations were less outspoken, and for the first week I began to deplore their comparative lack of vision. They, the possessors of families, seemed to avoid these discussions about the oversupply of children.

"So you've come to check up on our American traditions, Professor Grimstone," they would say casually. "We've heard all about this great purpose of our forefathers, and I guess it's up to us to put it across. But gee whiz, Grimstone, we wish we could have seen the Earth! What's it like, anyhow?"

"Tell us some more about the Earth…"

"All we know is what we get second hand…"

I told them about the Earth. Yes, they had books galore, and movies and phonograph records, pictures and maps; but these things only excited their curiosity. They asked me questions by the thousands. Only after I had poured out several encyclopedia-loads of Earth memories did I begin to break through their masks.

Back of this constant questioning, I discovered, they were watching me. Perhaps they were wondering whether they were not being subjected to more rigid discipline here on shipboard than their cousins back on Earth. I tried to impress upon them that they were a chosen group, but this had little effect. It stuck in their minds that *they* had had no choice in the matter.

Moreover, they were watching to see what I was going to do about the population problem, for they were no less aware of it than their elders.

Two weeks after my "return" we got down to business.

Captain Dickinson preferred to engineer the matter himself. He called an assembly in the movie auditorium. Almost everyone was present.

The programme began with the picture of the Six-Hundred-Year Plan. Everyone knew the reels by heart. They had seen and heard them dozens of times, and were ready to snicker at the proper moments—such as when the stern old committee chairman, charging the unborn generations with their solemn obligations, was interrupted by a friendly fly on his nose.

When the films were run through, Captain Dickinson took the rostrum, and with considerable bluster he called upon the Clerk of the Council to review the situation. The clerk read a report which went about as follows:

> To maintain a stable population, it was agreed in the original Plan that families should average two children each. Hence, the original 16 families would bring forth approximately 32 children; and assuming that they were fairly evenly divided

as to sex, they would eventually form 16 new families. These 16 families would, in turn, have an average of two children each—another generation of approximately 32.

By maintaining these averages, we were to have a total population, at any given time, of 32 children, 32 parents and 32 grandparents. The great-grandparents may be left out of account, for owing to the natural span of life they ordinarily die off before they accumulate in any great numbers.

The three living generations, then, of 32 each would give the *Flashaway* a constant active population of 96, or roughly, 100 persons.

The Six-Hundred-Year Plan has allowed for some flexibility in these figures. It has established the safe maximum at 150 and the safe minimum at 75.

If our population shrinks below 75, it is dangerously small. If it shrinks to 50, a crisis is at hand.

But if it grows above 150, it is dangerously large; and if it reaches the 200 mark, as we all know, a crisis may be said to exist.

The clerk stopped for an impressive pause, marred only by the crying of a baby from some distant room.

"Now, coming down to the present-day facts, we are well aware that the population has been dangerously large for the past seven years—"

"Since we entered this section of the heavens," Captain Dickinson interspersed with a scowl.

"From the first year in space, the population plan has encountered some irregularities," the clerk continued. "To begin with, there were not sixteen couples, but seventeen. The seventeenth couple—" here the clerk shot a glance at William Broscoe—"did not belong to the original compact, and after their marriage they were not bound by the sacred traditions—"

"I object!" I shouted, challenging the eyes of the clerk and the captain squarely. Dickinson had written that report with a touch of malice. The clerk skipped over a sentence or two.

"But however the Broscoe family may have prospered and multiplied, our records show that nearly all the families of the present generation have exceeded the per-family quota."

At this point there was a slight disturbance in the rear of the auditorium. An anxious-looking young man entered and signalled to the doctor. The two went out together.

"*All* the families," the clerk amended. "Our population this week passed the two hundred mark. This concludes the report."

The captain opened the meeting for discussion, and the forum lasted far into the night. The demand for me to assist the Council with some legislation was general. There was also hearty sentiment against the captain's blacked-out heavens from young and old alike.

This, I considered, was a good sign. The children craved the fun of watching the stars and planets; their elders desired to keep up their serious astronomical studies.

"Nothing is so important to the welfare of this expedition," I said to the Council on the following day, as we settled down to the job of thrashing out some legislation, "as to maintain our interests in the outside world. Population or no population, we must not become ingrown!"

I talked of new responsibilities, new challenges in the form of contests and campaigns, new leisure-time activities. The discussion went on for days.

"Back in my times—" I said for the hundredth time; but the captain laughed me down. My times and these times were as unlike as black and white, he declared.

"But the principle is the same!" I shouted. "We had population troubles, too."

They smiled as I referred to twenty-first century relief families who were overrun with children. I cited the fact that some industrialists who paid heavy taxes had considered giving every relief family an automobile as a measure to save themselves money in the long run; for they had discovered that relief families with cars had fewer children than those without.

"That's no help," Dickinson muttered. "You can't have cars on a space ship."

"You can play bridge," I retorted. "Bridge is an enemy of the birthrate too. Bridge, cars, movies, checkers—they all add up to the same thing. They lift you out of your animal natures—"

The Councilmen threw up their hands. They had bridged and chequered themselves to death.

"Then try other things," I persisted. "You could produce your own movies and plays—organize a little theatre—create some new drama—"

"What have we got to dramatize?" the captain replied sourly. "All the dramatic things happen on the Earth."

This shocked me. Somehow it took all the starch out of this colossal adventure to hear the captain give up so easily.

"All our drama is second hand," he grumbled. "Our ship's course is cut and dried. Our world is bounded by walls. The only dramatic things that happen here are births and deaths."

A doctor broke in on our conference and seized the captain by the hand.

"Congratulations, Captain Dickinson, on the prize crop of the season! Your wife has just presented you with a fine set of triplets—three boys!"

That broke up the meeting. Captain Dickinson was so busy for the rest of the week that he forgot all about his official obligations. The problem of population limitation faded from his mind.

I wrote out my recommendations and gave them all the weight of my dictatorial authority. I stressed the need for more birth control forums, and recommended that the heavens be made visible for further studies in astronomy and mathematics.

I was tempted to warn Captain Dickinson that the *Flashaway* might incur some serious dramas of its own—poverty, disease and the like—unless he got back on the track of the Six-Hundred-Year Plan in a hurry. But Dickinson was preoccupied with some family washings when I took my leave of him, and he seemed to have as much drama on his hands as he cared for.

I paid a final visit to each of the twenty-eight great-grandchildren of Louise, and returned to my ice.

CHAPTER IV

REVOLT!

My chief complaint against my merry-go-round freezer was that it didn't give me any rest. One whirl into blackness, and the next thing I knew I popped out of the open lid again with not so much as a minute's time to reorganize my thoughts.

Well, here it was, 2266—two hundred years since the takeoff.

A glance through the one-way glass told me it was daytime in the ballroom.

As I turned the key in the lock I felt like a prize fighter on a vaudeville tour who, having just trounced the tough local strong man, steps back in the ring to take on his cousin.

A touch of a headache caught me as I reflected that there should be four more returns after this one—if all went according to plan. *Plan!* That word was destined to be trampled underfoot!

Oh, well (I took a deep optimistic breath) the *Flashaway* troubles would all be cleared up by now. Three generations would have passed. The population should be back to normal.

I swung the door open, stepped through, locked it after me.

For an instant I thought I had stepped in on a big movie "take"—a scene of a stricken multitude. The big ballroom was literally strewn with people—if creatures in such a deplorable state could be called people.

There was no movie camera. This was the real thing.

"Grimstone's come!" a hoarse voice cried out.

"Grimstone! Grimstone!" Others caught up the cry. Then — "Food! Give us food! We're starving! For God's sake—"

The weird chorus gathered volume. I stood dazed, and for an instant I couldn't realize that I was looking upon the population of the *Flashaway*.

Men, women and children of all ages and all states of desperation joined in the clamour. Some of them stumbled to their feet and came toward me, waving their arms weakly. But most of them hadn't the strength to rise.

In that stunning moment an icy sweat came over me.

"Food! Food! We've been waiting for you, Grimstone. We've been holding on—"

The responsibility that was strapped to my shoulders suddenly weighed down like a locomotive. You see, I had originally taken my job more or less as a lark. That Six-Hundred-Year Plan had looked so airtight. I, the Keeper of the Traditions, would have a snap.

I had anticipated many a pleasant hour acquainting the oncoming generations with noble sentiments about George Washington; I had pictured myself filling the souls of my listeners by reciting the Gettysburg address and lecturing upon the mysteries of science.

But now those pretty bubbles burst on the spot, nor did they ever re-form in the centuries to follow.

And as they burst, my vision cleared. My job had nothing to do with theories or textbooks or speeches. My job was simply to get to Robinello—to get there with enough living, able-bodied, sane human beings to start a colony.

Dull blue starlight sifted through the windows to highlight the big roomful of starved figures. The mass of pale blue faces stared at me. There were hundreds of them. Instinctively I shrank as the throng clustered around me, calling and pleading.

"One at a time!" I cried. "First I've got to find out what this is all about. Who's your spokesman?"

They designated a handsomely built, if undernourished, young man. I inquired his name and learned that he was Bob Sperry, a descendant of the original Captain Sperry.

"There are eight hundred of us now," Sperry said.

"Don't tell me the food has run out!"

"No, not that—but six hundred of us are not entitled to regular meals."

"Why not?"

Before the young spokesman could answer, the others burst out with an unintelligible clamour. Angry cries of "That damned Dickinson!" and "Guns!" and "They'll shoot us!" were all I could distinguish.

I quieted them and made Bob Sperry go on with his story. He calmly asserted that there was a very good reason that they shouldn't be fed, all sentiment aside; namely, because they had been born outside the quota.

Here I began to catch a gleam of light.

"By Captain Dickinson's interpretation of the Plan," Sperry explained, "there shouldn't be more than two hundred of us altogether."

This Captain Dickinson, I learned, was a grandson of the one I had known.

Sperry continued, "Since there are eight hundred, he and his brother—his brother being Food Superintendent—launched an emergency measure a few months ago to save food. They divided the population into the two hundred, who had a right to be born, and the six hundred who had not."

So the six hundred starving persons before me were theoretically the excess population. The vigorous ancestry of the sixteen — no, seventeen — original couples, together with the excellent medical care that had reduced infant mortality and disease to the minimum, had wrecked the original population plan completely.

"What do you do for food? You must have *some* food!"

"We live on charity."

The throng again broke in with hostile words. Young Sperry's version was too gentle to do justice to their outraged stomachs. In fairness to the two hundred, however, Sperry explained that they shared whatever food they could spare with these, their less fortunate brothers, sisters and offspring.

Uncertain what should or could be done, I gave the impatient crowd my promise to investigate at once. Bob Sperry and nine other men accompanied me.   .

The minute we were out of hearing of the ballroom, I gasped,

"Good heavens, men, how is it that you and your six hundred haven't mobbed the storerooms long before this?"

"Dickinson and his brother have got the drop on us."

"Drop? What kind of drop?"

"Guns!"

I couldn't understand this. I had believed these new generations of the *Flashaway* to be relatively innocent of any knowledge of firearms.

"What kind of guns?"

"The same kind they use in our Earth-made movies—that make a loud noise and kill people by the hundreds."

"But there aren't any guns aboard! That is—"

I knew perfectly well that the only firearms the ship carried had been stored in my own refrigerator room, which no one could enter but myself. Before the voyage, one of the planning committee had jestingly suggested that if any serious trouble ever arose, I should be master of the situation by virtue of one hundred revolvers.

"They made their own guns," Sperry explained, "just like the ones in our movies and books."

Inquiring whether any persons had been shot, I learned that three of their number, attempting a raid on the storerooms, had been killed.

"We heard three loud bangs, and found our men dead with bloody skulls."

Reaching the upper end of the central corridor, we arrived at the captain's headquarters.

The name of Captain Dickinson carried a bad flavour for me. A century before I had developed a distaste for a certain other Captain Dickinson, his grandfather. I resolved to swallow my prejudice.

Then the door opened, and my resolve stuck in my throat. The former Captain Dickinson had merely annoyed me; but this one I hated on sight.

"Well?" the captain roared at the eleven of us.

Well-uniformed and neatly groomed, he filled the doorway with an impressive bulk. In his right hand he gripped a revolver. The gleam of that weapon had a magical effect upon the men. They shrank back respectfully. Then the captain's cold eye lighted on me.

"Who are *you*?"

"Gregory Grimstone, Keeper of the Traditions."

The captain sent a quick glance toward his gun and repeated his "Well?"

For a moment I was fascinated by that intricately shaped piece of metal in his grip.

"Well!" I echoed. "If 'well' is the only reception you have to offer, I'll proceed with my official business. Call your Food Superintendent."

"Why?"

"Order him out! Have him feed the entire population without further delay!"

"We can't afford the food," the captain growled.

"We'll talk that over later, but we won't talk on empty stomachs. Order out your Food Superintendent!"

"Crawl back in your hole!" Dickinson snarled.

At that instant another bulky man stepped into view. He was almost the identical counterpart of the captain, but his uniform was that of the Food Superintendent. Showing his teeth with a sinister snarl, he took his place beside his brother. He too jerked his right hand up to flash a gleaming revolver.

I caught one glimpse—and laughed in his face! I couldn't help it.

"You fellows are good!" I roared. "You're damned good actors! If you've held off the starving six hundred with nothing but those two dumb imitations of revolvers, you deserve an Academy award!"

The two Dickinson brothers went white.

Back of me came low mutterings from ten starving men.

"Imitations—dumb imitations—what the hell?"

Sperry and his nine comrades plunged with one accord. For the next ten minutes the captain's headquarters was simply a whirlpool of flying fists and hurtling bodies.

I have mentioned that these ten men were weak from lack of food. That fact was all that saved the Dickinson brothers; for ten minutes of lively exercise was all the ten men could endure, in spite of the circumstances.

But ten minutes left an impression. The Dickinsons were the worst beaten-up men I have ever seen, and I have seen some bad ones in my time. When the news echoed through the ship, no one questioned the ethics of ten starved men attacking two overfed ones.

Needless to say, before two hours passed, every hungry man, woman and child ate to his gizzard's content. And before another hour passed, some new officers were installed. The S.S. *Flashaway's* trouble was far from solved; but for the present the whole eight hundred were one big family picnic. Hope was restored, and the rejoicing lasted through many thousand miles of space.

There was considerable mystery about the guns. Surprisingly, the people had developed an awe of the movie guns as if they were instruments of magic.

Upon investigating, I was convinced that the captain and his brother had simply capitalized on this superstition. They had a sound enough motive for wanting to save food. But once their gun bluff had been established, they had become uncompromising oppressors. And when the occasion arose that their guns were challenged, they had simply crushed the skulls of their three attackers and faked the noises of explosions.

But now the firearms were dead. And so was the Dickinson regime.

But the menacing problem of too many mouths to feed still clung to the S.S. *Flashaway* like a hungry ghost determined to ride the ship to death.

Six full months passed before the needed reform was forged.

During that time everyone was allowed full rations. The famine had already taken its toll in weakened bodies, and seventeen persons—most of them young children—died. The doctors, released from the Dickinson regime, worked like Trojans to bring the rest back to health.

The reform measure that went into effect six months after my arrival consisted of outright sterilization.

The compulsory rule was sterilization for everyone except those born "within the quota"—and that quota, let me add, was narrowed down one half from Captain Dickinson's two hundred to the most eligible one hundred. The disqualified one hundred now joined the ranks of the six hundred.

And that was not all. By their own agreement, every within-the-quota family, responsible for bearing the *Flashaway's* future children, would undergo sterilization operations after the second child was born.

The seven hundred out-of-quota citizens, let it be said, were only too glad to submit to the simple sterilization measures in exchange for a right to live their normal lives. Yes, they were to have three squares a day. With an assured population decline in prospect for the coming century, this generous measure of food would not give out. Our surveys of the existing food supplies showed that these seven hundred could safely live their four-score years and die with full stomachs.

Looking back on that six months' work, I was fairly well satisfied that the doctors and the Council and I had done the fair, if drastic, thing. If I had planted seeds for further trouble with the Dickinson tribe, I was little concerned about it at the time.

My conscience was, in fact, clear—except for one small matter. I was guilty of one slight act of partiality.

I incurred this guilt shortly before I returned to the ice. The doctors and I, looking down from the balcony into the ballroom, chanced to notice a young couple who were obviously very much in love.

The young man was Bob Sperry, the handsome, clear-eyed descendant of the *Flashaway's* first and finest captain, the lad who had been the spokesman when I first came upon the starving mob.

The girl's name—and how it had clung in my mind!—was Louise Broscoe. Refreshingly beautiful, she reminded me for all the world of my own Louise (mine and Bill Broscoe's).

"It's a shame," one of the doctors commented, "that fine young blood like that has to fall outside the quota. But rules are rules."

With a shrug of the shoulders he had already dismissed the matter from his mind—until I handed him something I had scribbled on a piece of paper.

"We'll make this one exception," I said perfunctorily. "If any question ever arises, this statement relieves you doctors of all responsibility. This is my own special request."

CHAPTER V

WEDDING BELLS

One hundred years later my rash act came back to haunt me—and how! Bob Sperry had married Louise Broscoe, and the births of their two children had raised the unholy cry of "Favouritism!"

By the year 2366, Bob Sperry and Louise Broscoe were gone and almost forgotten. But the enmity against me, the Keeper of the Traditions who played favourites, had grown up into a monster of bitter hatred waiting to devour me.

It didn't take me long to discover this. My first contact after I emerged from the ice set the pace.

"Go tell your parents," I said to the gang of brats that were playing ball in the spacious ballroom, "that Grimstone has arrived."

Their evil little faces stared at me a moment, then they snorted.

"Faw! Faw! Faw!" and away they ran.

I stood in the big bleak room wondering what to make of their insults. On the balcony some of the parents craned over the railings at me.

"Greetings!" I cried. "I'm Grimstone, Keeper of the Traditions. I've just come—"

"Faw!" the men and women shouted at me. "Faw! Faw!"

No one could have made anything friendly out of those snarls. "Faw," to them, was simply a vocal manner of spitting poison.

Uncertain what this surly reception might lead to, I returned to my refrigerator room to procure one of the guns. Then I returned to the volley of catcalls and insults, determined to carry out my duties, come what might.

When I reached the forequarter of the ship, however, I found some less hostile citizens who gave me a civil welcome. Here I established myself for the extent of my 2366–67 sojourn, an honoured guest of the Sperry family.

This, I told myself, was my reward for my favour to Bob Sperry and Louise Broscoe a century ago. For here was their grandson, a fine upstanding grey-haired man of fifty, a splendid pilot and the father of a beautiful twenty-one-year-old daughter.

"Your name wouldn't be Louise by any chance?" I asked the girl as she showed me into the Sperry living room.

"Lora-Louise," the girl smiled. It was remarkable how she brought back memories of one of her ancestors of three centuries previous.

Her dark eyes flashed over me curiously.

"So you are the man that we Sperrys have to thank for being here!"

"You've heard about the quotas?" I asked.

"Of course. You're almost a god to our family."

"I must be a devil to some of the others," I said, recalling my reception of catcalls.

"Rogues!" the girl's father snorted, and he thereupon launched into a breezy account of the past century.

The sterilization programme, he assured me, had worked—if anything, too well. The population was the lowest in *Flashaway* history. It stood at the dangerously low mark of *fifty!*

Besides the sterilization programme, a disease epidemic had taken its toll. In addition three ugly murders, prompted by jealousies, had spotted the record. And there had been one suicide.

As to the character of the population, Pilot Sperry declared gravely that there had been a turn for the worse.

"They fight each other like damned anarchists," he snorted.

★

The Dickinsons had made trouble for several generations. Now it was the Dickinsons against the Smiths; and these two factions included four-fifths of all the people. They were about evenly divided—twenty on each side—and when they weren't actually fighting each other, they were "fawing" at each other.

These bellicose factions had one sentiment in common: they both despised the Sperry faction. And—here my guilt cropped up again—their hatred stemmed from my special favour of a century ago, without which there would be no Sperrys now. In view of the fact that the Sperry faction lived in the forequarter of the ship and held all the important offices, it was no wonder that the remaining forty citizens were jealous.

All of which gave me enough to worry about. On top of that, Lora-Louise's mother gave me one other angle of the set-up.

"The trouble between the Dickinsons and the Smiths has grown worse since Lora-Louise has become a young lady," Mrs. Sperry confided to me.

We were sitting in a breakfast nook. Amber starlight shone softly through the porthole, lighting the mother's steady imperturbable grey eyes.

"Most girls have married at eighteen or nineteen," her mother went on. "So far, Lora-Louise has refused to marry."

The worry in Mrs. Sperry's face was almost imperceptible, but I understood. I had checked over the "Who's Who" and I knew the seriousness of this population crisis. I also knew that there were four young unmarried men with no other prospects of wives except Lora-Louise.

"Have you any choice for her?" I asked.

"Since she must marry—and I know she *must*—I have urged her to make her own choice."

I could see that the ordeal of choosing had been postponed until my coming, in hopes that I might modify the rules. But I had no intention of doing so. The *Flashaway* needed Lora-Louise. It needed the sort of children she would bear.

That week I saw the two husky Dickinson boys. Both were in their twenties. They stayed close together and bore an air of treachery and scheming. Rumour had it that they carried weapons made from table knives.

Everyone knew that my coming would bring the conflict to a head. Many thought I would try to force the girl to marry the older Smith—"Batch", as he was called in view of his bachelor-hood. He was past thirty-five, the oldest of the four unmarried men.

But some argued otherwise. For Batch, though a splendid specimen physically, was slow of wit and speech. It was common knowledge that he was weak-minded.

For that reason, I might choose his younger cousin, "Smithy," a roly-poly overgrown boy of nineteen who spent his time bullying the younger children.

But if the Smiths and the Dickinsons could have their way about it, the Keeper of the Traditions should have no voice in the matter. Let me insist that Lora-Louise marry, said they; but whom she should marry was none of my business.

They preferred a fight as a means of settlement. A free-for-all between the two factions would be fine. A showdown of fists among the four contenders would be even better.

Best of all would be a battle of knives that would eliminate all but one of the suitors. Not that either the Dickinsons or the Smiths needed to admit that was what they preferred; but their barbaric tastes were plain to see.

Barbarians! That's what they had become. They had sprung too far from their native civilization. Only the Sperry faction, isolated in their monasteries of control boards, physicians' laboratories and record rooms, kept alive the spark of civilization.

The Sperrys and their associates were human beings out of the twenty-first century. The Smiths and the Dickinsons had slipped. They might have come out of the Dark Ages.

What burned me up more than anything else was that obviously both the Smiths and the Dickinsons looked forward with sinister glee toward dragging Lora-Louise down from her height to their own barbaric levels.

One night I was awakened by the sharp ringing of the pilot's telephone. I heard the snap of a switch. An *emergency* signal flashed on throughout the ship.

Footsteps were pounding toward the ballroom. I slipped into a robe, seized my gun, made for the door.

"The Dickinsons are murdering up on them!" Pilot Sperry shouted to me from the door of the control room.

"I'll see about it," I snapped.

I bounded down the corridor. Sperry didn't follow. Whatever violence might occur from year to year within the hull of the *Flashaway*, the pilot's code demanded that he lock himself up at the controls and tend to his own business.

It was a free-for-all! Under the bright lights they were going to it, tooth and toenail.

Children screamed and clawed, women hurled dishes, old tottering granddaddies edged into the fracas to crack at each other with canes.

The appalling reason for it all showed in the centre of the room—the roly-poly form of young "Smithy" Smith. Hacked and stabbed, his nightclothes ripped, he was a veritable mess of carnage.

I shouted for order. No one heard me, for in that instant a chase thundered on the balcony. Everything else stopped. All eyes turned on the three racing figures.

Batch Smith, fleeing in his white nightclothes, had less than five yards' lead on the two Dickinsons. Batch was just smart enough to run when he was chased, not smart enough to know he couldn't possibly outrun the younger Dickinsons.

As they shot past blazing lights the Dickinsons' knives flashed. I could see that their hands were red with Smithy's blood.

"*Stop!*" I cried. "Stop or I'll *shoot!*"

If they heard, the words must have been meaningless. The younger Dickinson gained ground. His brother darted back in the opposite direction, crouched, waited for his prey to come around the circular balcony.

"Dickinson! Stop or I'll shoot you dead!" I bellowed.

Batch Smith came on, his eyes white with terror. Crouched and waiting, the older Dickinson lifted his knife for the killing stroke.

I shot.

The crouched Dickinson fell in a heap. Over him tripped the racing form of Batch Smith, to sprawl headlong. The other Dickinson leaped over his brother and pounced down upon the fallen prey, knife upraised.

Another shot went home.

Young Dickinson writhed and came toppling down over the balcony rail. He lay where he fell, his bloody knife sticking up through the side of his neck.

It was ugly business trying to restore order. However, the magic power of firearms, which had become only a dusty legend, now put teeth into every word I uttered.

The doctors were surprisingly efficient. After many hours of work behind closed doors, they released their verdicts to the waiting groups. The elder Dickinson, shot through the shoulder, would live. The younger Dickinson was dead. So was Smithy. But his cousin, Batch Smith, although too scared to walk back to his stateroom, was unhurt.

The rest of the day the doctors devoted to patching up the minor damages done in the free fight. Four-fifths of the *Flashaway* population were burdened with bandages, it seemed. For some time to come both the warring parties were considerably sobered over their losses. But most of all they were disgruntled because the fight had settled nothing.

The prize was still unclaimed. The two remaining contenders, backed by their respective factions, were at a bitter deadlock.

Nor had Lora-Louise's hatred for either the surviving Dickinson or Smith lessened in the slightest.

Never had a duty been more oppressive to me. I postponed my talk with Lora-Louise for several days, but I was determined that there should be no more fighting. She must choose.

We sat in an alcove next to the pilot's control room, looking out into the vast sky. Our ship, bounding at a terrific speed though it was, seemed to be hanging motionless in the tranquil star-dotted heavens.

"I must speak frankly," I said to the girl. "I hope you will do the same."

She looked at me steadily. Her dark eyes were perfectly frank, her full lips smiled with child-like simplicity.

"How old are you?" she asked.

"Twenty-eight," I answered. I'd been the youngest professor on the college faculty. "Or you might say three hundred and twenty-eight. Why?"

"How soon must you go back to your sleep?"

"Just as soon as you are happily married. That's why I must insist that you—"

Something very penetrating about her gaze made my words go weak. To think of forcing this lovely girl—so much like the Louise of my own century—to marry either the brutal Dickinson or the moronic Smith—

"Do you really want me to be *happily* married?" she asked.

I don't remember that any more words passed between us at the time.

A few days later she and I were married—and most happily!

The ceremony was brief. The entire Sperry faction and one representative from each of the two hostile factions were present. The aged captain of the ship, who had been too ineffectual in recent years to apply any discipline to the fighting factions, was still able with vigorous voice to pronounce us man and wife.

A year and a half later I took my leave.

I bid fond good-bye to the "future captain of the *Flashaway*," who lay on a pillow kicking and squirming. He gurgled back at me. If the boasts and promises of the Sperry grandparents and their associates were to be taken at full value, this young prodigy of mine would in time become an accomplished pilot and a skilled doctor as well as a stern but wise captain.

Judging from his talents at the age of six months, I was convinced he showed promise of becoming Food Superintendent as well.

I left reluctantly but happily.

CHAPTER VI

THE FINAL CRISIS

The year 2466 was one of the darkest in my life. I shall pass over it briefly.

The situation I found was all but hopeless.

The captain met me personally and conveyed me to his quarters without allowing the people to see me.

"Safer for everyone concerned," he muttered. I caught glimpses as we passed through the shadows. I seemed to be looking upon ruins.

Not until the captain had disclosed the events of the century did I understand how things could have come to such a deplorable state. And before he finished his story, I saw that I was helpless to right the wrongs.

"They've destroyed 'most everything," the hard-bitten old captain rasped. "And they haven't overlooked *you*. They've destroyed you completely. *You are an ogre.*"

I wasn't clear on his meaning. Dimly in the back of my mind the hilarious farewell of four centuries ago still echoed.

"The *Flashaway* will go through!" I insisted.

"They destroyed all the books, phonograph records, movie films. They broke up clocks and bells and furniture—"

And I was supposed to carry this interspatial outpost of American civilization through *unblemished!* That was what I had promised so gayly four centuries ago.

"They even tried to break out the windows," the captain went on. " 'Oxygen be damned!' they'd shout. They were mad. You couldn't tell them anything. If they could have got into this end of the ship, they'd have murdered us and smashed the control boards to hell."

I listened with bowed head.

"Your son tried like the devil to turn the tide. But God, what chance did he have? The dam had busted loose. They wanted to kill each other. They wanted to destroy each other's property and starve each other out. No captain in the world could have stopped either faction. They had to get it out of their systems…"

He shrugged helplessly. "Your son went down fighting…" For a time I could hear no more. It seemed but minutes ago that I had taken leave of the little tot.

The war—if a mania of destruction and murder between two feuding factions could be called a war—had done one good thing, according to the captain. It had wiped the name of Dickinson from the records.

Later I turned through the musty pages to make sure. There were Smiths and Sperrys and a few other names still in the running, but no Dickinsons. Nor were there any Grimstones. My son had left no living descendants.

To return to the captain's story, the war (he said) had degraded the bulk of the population almost to the level of savages. Perhaps the comparison is an insult to the savage. The instruments of knowledge and learning having been destroyed, beliefs gave way to superstitions, memories of past events degenerated into fanciful legends.

The rebound from the war brought a terrific superstitious terror concerning death. The survivors crawled into their shells, almost literally; the brutalities and treacheries of the past hung like storm clouds over their imaginations.

As year after year dropped away, the people told and retold the stories of destruction to their children. Gradually the legend twisted into a strange form in which all the guilt for the carnage *was placed upon me!*

★

I was the one who had started all the killing! *I, the ogre*, who slept in a cave somewhere in the rear of the ship, came out once upon a time and started all the trouble!

I, the Traditions Man, dealt death with a magic weapon; I cast the spell of killing upon the Smiths and the Dickinsons that kept them fighting until there was nothing left to fight for!

"But that was years ago," I protested to the captain. "Am I still an ogre?" I shuddered at the very thought.

"More than ever. Stories like that don't die out in a century. They grow bigger. You've become the symbol of evil. I've tried to talk the silly notion down, but it has been impossible. My own family is afraid of you."

I listened with sickening amazement. I was the Traditions Man; or rather, the "Traddy Man"—the bane of every child's life.

Parents, I was told, would warn them, "If you don't be good, the Traddy Man will come out of his cave and get you!"

And the Traddy Man, as every grown-up knew, could storm out of his cave without warning. He would come with a strange gleam in his eye. That was his evil will. When the bravest, strongest men would cross his path, he would hurl instant death at them. Then he would seize the most beautiful woman and marry her.

"Enough!" I said. "Call your people together. I'll dispel their false ideas—"

The captain shook his head wisely. He glanced at my gun.

"Don't force me to disobey your orders," he said. "I can believe you're not an ogre—but they won't. I know this generation. You don't. Frankly, I refuse to disturb the peace of this ship by telling the people you have come. Nor am I willing to terrorize my family by letting them see you."

For a long while I stared silently into space.

The captain dismissed a pilot from the control room and had me come in.

"You can see for yourself that we are straight on our course. You have already seen that all the supplies are holding up. You have seen that the population problem is well cared for. What more do you want?"

What more did I want! With the whole population of the *Flashaway* steeped in ignorance—immorality—superstition—savagery!*

Again the captain shook his head. "You want us to be like your friends of the twenty-first century. *We can't be.*"

He reached in his pocket and pulled out some bits of crumpled papers.

"Look. I save every scrap of reading matter. I learned to read from the primers and charts that your son's grandparents made. Before the destruction, I tried to read about the Earth-life. I still piece together these torn bits and study them. But I can't piece together

---

* Professor Grimstone is obviously astounded that his charges, with all the necessities of life on board their space ship, should have degenerated so completely. It must be remembered, however, that no other outside influence ever entered the *Flashaway* in all its long voyage through space. In the space of centuries, the colonists progressed not one whit.

On a very much reduced scale, the *Flashaway* colonists are a more or less accurate mirror of a nation in transition. Sad but true it is that nations, like human beings, are born, wax into bright maturity, grow into comfortable middle age and ofttimes linger on until old age has impaired their usefulness.

In the relatively short time that man has been a thinking, building animal, many great empires—many great nations—have sprung from humble beginnings to grow powerful and then wane into oblivion, sometimes slowly, sometimes with tragic suddenness.

Grimstone, however, has failed to take the lessons of history into account through the mistaken conception that because the colonists' physical wants were taken care of, that was all they required to keep them healthy and contented.—Ed.

the Earth-life that they tell about. All I really know is what I've seen and felt and breathed right here in my native *Flashaway* world.

"That's how it's bound to be with all of us. We can't get back to your notions about things. Your notions haven't any real truth for us. You don't belong to our world," the captain said with honest frankness.

"So I'm an outcast on my own ship!"

"That's putting it mildly. You're a menace and a trouble-maker—*an ogre!* It's in their minds as tight as the bones in their skulls."

The most I could do was secure some promises from him before I went back to the ice. He promised to keep the ship on its course. He promised to do his utmost to fasten the necessary obligations upon those who would take over the helm.

"Straight relentless navigation!" We drank a toast to it. He didn't pretend to appreciate the purpose or the mission of the *Flashaway*, but he took my word for it that it would come to some good.

"To Robinello in 2666!" Another toast. Then he conducted me back, in utmost secrecy, to my refrigerator room.

I awoke to the year of 2566, keenly aware that I was not Gregory Grimstone, the respected Keeper of the Traditions. If I was anyone at all, I was the Traddy Man—the ogre.

But perhaps by this time—and I took hope with the thought—I had been completely forgotten.

I tried to get through the length of the ship without being seen. I had watched through the one-way glass for several hours for a favourable opportunity, but the ship seemed to be in a continual state of daylight, and shabby-looking people roamed about as aimlessly as sheep in a meadow.

The few persons who saw me as I darted toward the captain's quarters shrieked as if they had been knifed. In their world there was no such thing as a strange person. I was the impossible, the unbelievable. My name, obviously, had been forgotten.

I found three men in the control room. After minutes of tension, during which they adjusted themselves to the shock of my coming, I succeeded in establishing speaking terms. Two of the men were Sperrys.

But at the very moment I should have been concerned with solidifying my friendship, I broke the calm with an excited outburst. My eye caught the position of the instruments and I leaped from my seat.

"How long have you been going *that way?*"

"Eight years!"

"Eight—" I glanced at the huge automatic chart overhead. It showed the long straight line of our centuries of flight with a tiny shepherd's crook at the end. Eight years ago we had turned back sharply.

"That's sixteen years lost, gentlemen!"

I tried to regain my poise. The three men before me were perfectly calm, to my astonishment. The two Sperry brothers glanced at each other. The third man, who had introduced himself as Smith, glared at me darkly.

"It's all right," I said. "We won't lose another minute. I know how to operate—"

"No, you don't!" Smith's voice was harsh and cold. I had started to reach for the controls. I hesitated. Three pairs of eyes were fixed on me.

"We know where we're going," one of the Sperrys said stubbornly. "We've got our own destination."

"This ship is bound for Robinello!" I snapped. "We've got to colonize. The Robinello planets are ours—America's. It's our job to clinch the claim and establish the initial settlement—"

"Who said so?"

"America!"

"*When?*" Smith's cold eyes tightened.

"Five hundred years ago."

"That doesn't mean a thing. Those people are all dead."

"I'm one of those people!" I growled. "And I'm not dead by a damned sight!"

"Then you're out on a limb."

"Limb or no limb, the plan goes through!" I clutched my gun. "We haven't come five hundred years in a straight line for nothing!"

"The plan is dead," one of the Sperrys snarled. "We've killed it."

His brother chimed in, "This is our ship and we're running it. We've studied the heavens and we're out on our own. We're through with this straight-line stuff. We're going to see the universe."

"You can't! You're bound for Robinello!"

Smith stepped toward me, and his big teeth showed savagely.

"We had no part in that agreement. We're taking orders from no one. I've heard about you. You're the Traddy Man. Go back in your hole—and stay there!"

I brought my gun up slowly. "You've heard of me? Have you heard of my gun? Do you know that this weapon shoots men dead?"

Three pairs of eyes caught on the gleaming weapon. But three men stood their ground staunchly.

"I've heard about guns," Smith hissed. "Enough to know that you don't dare shoot in the control room—"

"I don't dare *miss!*"

I didn't want to kill the men. But I saw no other way out. Was there any other way? Three lives weren't going to stand between the *Flashaway* and her destination.

Seconds passed, with the four of us breathing hard. Eternity was about to descend on someone. Any of the three might have been splendid pioneers if they had been confronted with the job of building a colony. But in this moment, their lack of vision was as deadly as any deliberate sabotage. I focused my attack on the most troublesome man of the three.

"Smith, I'm giving you an order. Turn back before I count to ten or I'll kill you. One... two... three..."

Not the slightest move from anyone.

"Seven... eight... nine..."

Smith leaped at me—and fell dead at my feet.

The two Sperrys looked at the faint wisp of smoke from the weapon. I barked another sharp command, and one of the Sperrys marched to the controls and turned the ship back toward Robinello.

CHAPTER VII

TIME MARCHES ON

For a year I was with the Sperry brothers constantly, doing my utmost to bring them around to my way of thinking. At first I watched them like hawks. But they were not treacherous. Neither did they show any inclination to avenge Smith's death. Probably this was due to a suppressed hatred they had held toward him.

The Sperrys were the sort of men, being true children of space, who bided their time. That's what they were doing now. That was why I couldn't leave them and go back to my ice.

As sure as the *Flashaway* could cut through the heavens, those two men were counting the hours until I returned to my nest. The minute I was gone, they would turn back toward their own goal.

And so I continued to stay with them for a full year. If they contemplated killing me, they gave no indication. I presume I would have killed them with little hesitation, had I had no pilots whatsoever that I could entrust with the job of carrying on.

There were no other pilots, nor were there any youngsters old enough to break into service.

Night after night I fought the matter over in my mind. There was a full century to go. Perhaps one hundred and fifteen or twenty years. And no one except the two Sperrys and I had any serious conception of a destination!

These two pilots and I—*and one other*, whom I had never for a minute forgotten. If the *Flashaway* was to go through, it was up to me and *that one other*—

I marched back to the refrigerator room, people fleeing my path in terror. Inside the retreat I touched the switches that operated the auxiliary merry-go-round freezer. After a space of time the operation was complete.

Someone very beautiful stood smiling before me, looking not a minute older than when I had packed her away for safe-keeping two centuries before.

"Gregory," she breathed ecstatically. "Are my three centuries up already?"

"Only two of them, Lora-Louise." I took her in my arms. She looked up at me sharply and must have read the trouble in my eyes.

"They've all played out on us," I said quietly. "It's up to us now."

I discussed my plan with her and she approved.

One at a time we forced the Sperry brothers into the icy retreat, with repeated promises that they would emerge within a century. By that time Lora-Louise and I would be gone—but it was our expectation that our children and grandchildren would carry on.

And so the two of us, plus firearms, plus Lora-Louise's sense of humour, took over the running of the *Flashaway* for its final century.

As the years passed the native population grew to be less afraid of us. Little by little a foggy glimmer of our vision filtered into their numbed minds.

The year is now 2600. Thirty-three years have passed since Lora-Louise and I took over. I am now sixty-two, she is fifty-six. Or if you prefer, I am 562, she is 256. Our four children have grown up and married.

We have realized down through these long years that we would not live to see the journey completed. The Robinello planets have been visible for some time; but at our speed they are still sixty or eighty years away.

But something strange happened nine or ten months ago. It has changed the outlook for all of us—even me, the crusty old Keeper of the Traditions.

A message reached us through our radio receiver!

It was a human voice speaking in our own language. It had a fresh vibrant hum to it and a clear-cut enunciation. It shocked me to realize how sluggish our own brand of the King's English had become in the past five-and-a-half centuries.

"Calling the *S.S. Flashaway!*" it said. "Calling the *S.S. Flashaway!* We are trying to locate you, *S.S. Flashaway.* Our instruments indicate that you are approaching. If you can hear us, will you give us your exact location?"

I snapped on the transmitter. "This is the *Flashaway.* Can you hear us?"

"Dimly. Where are you?"

"On our course. Who's calling?"

"This is the American colony on Robinello," came the answer. "American colony, Robinello, established in 2550—fifty years ago. We're waiting for you, *Flashaway*."

"How the devil did you get there?" I may have sounded a bit crusty but I was too excited to know what I was saying.

"Modern space ships," came the answer. "We've cut the time from the Earth to Robinello down to six years. Give us your location. We'll send a fast ship out to pick you up."

I gave them our location. That, as I said, was several months ago. Today we are receiving a radio call every five minutes as their ship approaches.

One of my sons, supervising the preparations, has just reported that all persons aboard are ready to transfer—including the Sperry brothers, who have emerged successfully from the ice. The eighty-five *Flashaway* natives are scared half to death and at the same time as eager as children going to a circus.

Lora-Louise has finished packing our boxes, bless her heart. That teasing smile she just gave me was because she noticed the "Who's Who Aboard the *Flashaway*" tucked snugly under my arm.

SURVIVAL SHIP

Judith Merril

Judith Merril (1923–97) was one of the early post-war women writers of science fiction, and she also became one of the field's leading editors, compiling twelve volumes of her S-F: The Year's Greatest Science Fiction and Fantasy *between 1956 and 1968. She was one of the first American authors to champion the New Wave in science fiction which was emerging in Britain in the mid-1960s. She relocated to Canada in 1968 and in 1970 she donated her collection of books to the Toronto Public Library. Initially called the Spaced-Out Library it became The Merril Collection of Science Fiction, Speculation and Fantasy in 1990. Her first published story, "That Only a Mother" proved something of a shock when it appeared in* Astounding SF *in 1948, and her first novel,* Shadow on the Hearth *(1950) likewise packed a punch in describing a post-nuclear holocaust.*

She wrote only one further novel, The Tomorrow People *(1960), plus two others in collaboration with Cyril Kornbluth as Cyril Judd, but she wrote many short stories, which are often overlooked. They were collected as* Homecoming and Other Stories *in 2005, a volume which is already becoming difficult to find.*

HALF A MILLION PEOPLE ACTUALLY MADE THE ROUND TRIP to Space Station One that day, to watch the takeoff in person. And back on Earth a hundred million video screens flashed the picture of Captain Melnick's gloved hand waving a dramatic farewell at the port, while the other hand slowly pressed down the lever that would fire the ship out beyond the orbit of the artificial satellite, past the Moon and the planets, into unknown space.

From Station, Earth and Moon, a hundred million winged wishes added their power to the surge of the jets, as a rising spiral of fire inside the greatest rocket tower ever built marked the departure of the thrice-blessed ship, *Survival*. In the great churches, from pole to pole, services were held all day, speeding the giant vessel on its way, calling on the aid of the Lord for the Twenty and Four who manned the ship.

At mountain-top telescopes a dozen cameras faithfully transmitted the messages of great unblinking glass eyes. Small home sets and massive pulpit screens alike looked to the sky to follow the flare dimming in the distance, to watch the man-made star falling away.

Inside the great ship, Melnick's hand left the firing lever, then began adjusting the chin-rest and the earphones of the acceleration couch. The indicator dashboard, designed for prone eye-level, leaped into focus. Securing the couch straps with the swift competence of habit, the Captain intently watched the sweep of the big secondhand around the takeoff-timer, aware at the same time that green lights were beginning to glow at the other end of the board. The indicator reached the first red mark.

"The show's over, everybody. We're in business!" The mike built into the chin-rest carried the Captain's taut voice all over the ship. "Report, all stations!"

"Number One, all secure!" Melnick mentally ticked off the first green light, glowing to prove the astrogator's couch was in use.

"Number two, all secure!"

"Number three"... "four"... "five." The rhythmic sing-song of pinpoint timing in takeoff was second nature by now to the whole crew. One after another, the green lights glowed for safety, punctuating the litany, and the gong from the timer put a period neatly in place after the final "All secure!"

"Eight seconds to blackout," the Captain's voice warned. "Seven... six... stand by." The first wave of acceleration shock reeled into twenty-four helmet-sheathed heads on twenty-four individually designed headrests. "Five..." *It's got to work*, Melnick was thinking, fighting off unconsciousness with fierce intensity. "Four..." *It's got to... got to...* "Three..." *got to... go to...* "Two..." *got to...*

At the Space Station, a half-million watchers were slowly cleared from the giant takeoff platform. They filed in long orderly lines down the ramps to the interior, and waited there for the smaller Earth-rockets that would take them home. Waiting, they were at once elated and disappointed. They had seen no more than could be seen at the same place on any other day. The entire rocket area had been fenced off, with a double cordon of guards to make sure that too-curious visitors stayed out of range. Official explanations mentioned the new engine, the new fuel, the danger of escaping gases—but nobody believed it. Every one of the half-million visitors knew what the mystery was: the crew, and nothing else. Giant video screens all over the platform gave the crowd details and closeups, the same that they would have seen had they stayed comfortably at home. They saw the Captain's gloved hand, at the last, but not the Captain's face.

There was muttering and complaining... but there was something else, too. Each man, woman, and child who went to the Station that day would be able to say, years later, "I was there when the *Survival* took off. You never saw anything so big in your life."

Because it wasn't just another planet hop. It wasn't just like the hundreds of other takeoffs. It was the *Survival*, the greatest spaceship ever engineered. People didn't think of the *Survival* in terms of miles-per-second; they said, "Sirius in fifteen years!"

From Sunday supplements to dignified periodicals, nearly every medium of communication on Earth had carried the story. Brightly coloured graphs made visibly simple the natural balance of life forces in which plants and animals could maintain a permanently fresh atmosphere, as well as a self-perpetuating food supply. Lecture-demonstrations and videocasts showed how centrifugal force would replace gravity.

For months before takeoff, the press and video followed the preparations with daily intimate accounts. The world over, people knew the nicknames of pigs, calves, chickens, and crew members—and even the proper botanical name of the latest minor masterpiece of the biochemists, a hybrid plant whose root, stems, leaves, buds, blossoms, and fruit were all edible, nourishing and delicious, and which had the added advantage of being the thirstiest CO_2 drinker ever found.

The public knew the nicknames of the crew, and the proper name of the plant. But they never found out, not even the half-million who went to the field to see for themselves, the real identity of the Twenty and Four who comprised the crew. They knew that thousands had applied; that it was necessary to be single, under twenty-five, and a graduate engineer in order to get as far as the physical exam; that the crew was mixed in sex, with the object of filling the specially-equipped nursery, and raising a second generation for the return trip, if, as was hoped, a lengthy stay on Sirius' planet proved possible. They knew, for that matter, all the small characteristics and personal idiosyncrasies of the crew members—what they ate, how they dressed, their favourite games, theatres, music, books, cigarettes, preachers, and political parties. There were only two things the public didn't know, and couldn't find out: the real names of the mysterious Twenty and Four; and the reason why those names were kept secret.

There were as many rumours as there were newsmen or radio-reporters, of course. Hundreds of explanations were offered at one time or another. But still nobody knew—nobody except the half-hundred Very Important Persons who had planned the project, and the Twenty and Four themselves.

And now, as the pinpoint of light faded out of the screens of televisors all over Earth, the linear and rotary acceleration of the great ship began to adjust to the needs of the human body. "Gravity" in the living quarters gradually approached Earth-normal. Tortured bodies relaxed in the acceleration couches, where the straps had held them securely positioned through the initial stage, so as to keep the blood and guts where they belonged, and to prevent the stomach from following its natural tendency to emerge through the backbone. Finally, stunned brain cells awoke to the recognition that danger signals were no longer coming through from shocked, excited tissues.

Captain Melnick was the first to awake. The row of lights on the board still glowed green. Fumbling a little with the straps, Melnick watched tensely to see if the indicator lights were functioning properly, sighing with relief as the one at the head of the board went dead, operated automatically by the removal of body weight from the couch.

It was right—it was essential—for the Captain to wake up first. If any of the men had showed superior recuperative powers, it could be bad. Melnick thought wearily of the years and years ahead during which this artificial dominance had to be maintained in defiance of all Earth conditioning. But of course it would not be that bad, really. The crew had been picked for ability to conform to the unusual circumstances; they were all without strong family ties or prejudices. Habit would establish the new castes soon enough, but the beginning was crucial. Survival was more than a matter of plant-animal balance and automatic gravity.

While the Captain watched, another light went out, and then another. Officers, both of them: good. Three more lights died out together. Then men were beginning to awaken, and it was reassuring to know that their own couch panels would show them that the officers had revived first. In any case, there was no more time for worrying. There were things to be done.

A detail was sent off immediately to attend to the animals, release them from the confinement of the specially prepared acceleration pens, and check them for any possible damage incurred in spite of precautions. The proportions of human, animal and plant life had been worked out carefully beforehand for maximum efficiency, and for comfort. Now that the trip had started, the miniature world had to maintain its status quo or perish.

As soon as enough of the crew were awake, Lieutenant Johnson, the third officer, took a group of eight out to make an inspection of the hydroponic tanks that lined the hull. Nobody expected much trouble here. Being at the outermost part of the ship, the plants were exposed to high "gravity." The outward pull exerted on them by rotation should have held their roots in place, even through the tearing backward thrust of the acceleration. But there was certain to be a large amount of minor damage, to stems and leaves and buds, and whatever there was would need immediate repair. In the ship's economy, the plants had the most vital function of all—absorbing carbon dioxide from dead air already used by humans and animals, and deriving from it the nourishment that enabled their chlorophyl systems to release fresh oxygen for re-use in breathing.

There was a vast area to inspect. Row upon row of tanks marched solidly from stem to stern of the giant ship, all around the inner circumference of the hull. Johnson split the group of eight into four teams, each with a biochemist in charge to locate and make notes of the extent of the damage, and an unclassified man as helper, to do the actual dirty work, crawling out along the catwalks to mend each broken stalk.

Other squads were assigned to check the engines and control mechanisms, and the last two women to awake got stuck with the booby prize—first shift in the galley. Melnick squashed their immediate protests with a stern reminder that they had hardly earned the right to complain; but privately the Captain was pleased at the way it had worked out. This first meal on board was going to have to be something of an occasion. A bit of ceremony always helped; and above all, social procedures would have to be established immediately. A speech was indicated—a speech Melnick did not want to have to make in the presence of all twenty-four crew members. As it worked out, the Four would almost certainly be kept busy longer than the others. If these women had not happened to wake up last...

The buzzing of the intercom broke into the Captain's speculations. "Lieutenant Johnson reporting, sir." Behind the proper, crisp manner, the young lieutenant's voice was frightened. Johnson was third in command, supervising the inspection of the tanks.

"Having trouble down there?" Melnick was deliberately informal, knowing the men could hear over the intercom, and anxious to set up an immediate feeling of unity among the officers.

"One of the men complaining, sir." The young lieutenant sounded more confident already. "There seems to be some objection to the division of the work."

Melnick thought it over quickly and decided against any more public discussion on the intercom. "Stand by. I'll be right down."

All over the ship airducts and companionways led from the inner-level living quarters "down" to the outer level of tanks; Melnick took the steps three at a time and reached the trouble zone within seconds after the conversation ended.

"Who's the trouble-maker here?"

"Kennedy—on assignment with Petty Officer Giorgio for plant maintenance."

"You have a complaint?" Melnick asked the swarthy, dungareed man whose face bore a look of sullen dissatisfaction.

"Yeah." The man's voice was deliberately insolent. The others had never heard him speak that way before, and he seemed to gain confidence from the shocked surprise they displayed. "I thought I was supposed to be a pampered darling this trip. How come I do all the dirty work here, and Georgie gets to keep so clean?"

His humour was too heavy to be effective. "Captain's orders, that's why," Melnick snapped. "Everybody has to work double time till things are squared away. If you don't like the job here, I can fix you up fine in the brig. Don't worry about your soft quarters. You'll get 'em later and plenty of 'em. It's going to be a long trip, and don't forget it." The Captain pointed significantly to the chronometer built into the overhead. "But it's not much longer to dinner. You'd better get back to work if you want to hit the chow while it's hot. Mess call in thirty minutes."

Melnick took a chance and turned abruptly away, terminating the interview. It worked. Sullen but defeated, Kennedy hoisted himself back up on the catwalk, and then began crawling out to the spot Giorgio pointed out. Not daring to express their relief, lieutenant and captain exchanged one swift look of triumph, before Melnick walked wordlessly off.

In the big control room that would be mess hall, social hall, and general meeting place for all of them for fifteen years to come—or twice that time if Sirius' planet turned out to be uninhabitable— the Captain waited for the crew members to finish their checkup assignments. Slowly they gathered in the lounge, ignoring the upholstered benches around the sides and the waiting table in the centre, standing instead in small awkward groups. An undercurrent of excitement ran through them all, evoking deadly silences and erupting in bursts of too-noisy conversation, destroying the joint attempt at an illusion of nonchalance. They all knew—or hoped they knew—what the subject of the Captain's first speech would be, and behind the façade of bronzed faces and trimly-muscled bodies they were all curious, even a little afraid.

Finally there were twenty of them in the room, and the Captain rose and rapped for order.

"I suppose," Melnick began, "you will all want to know our present position, and the results of the checkup." Nineteen heads turned as one, startled and disappointed at the opening. "However," the Captain continued, smiling at the change of expressions the single word brought, "I imagine you're all as hungry and... er... impatient as I am, so I shall put off the more routine portions of my report until our other comrades have joined us. There is only one matter which should properly be discussed immediately."

Everyone in the room was acutely conscious of the Four. They had all known, of course, how it would be. But on Earth there had always been other, ordinary men around to make them less aware of it. Now the general effort to maintain an air of artificial ease and disinterest was entirely abandoned, as the Captain plunged into the subject most on everyone's mind.

"Our ship is called the *Survival*. You all know why. Back on Earth, people think they know why, too; they think it's because of our plants and artificial gravity, and the hundreds of other engineering miracles that keep us going. Of course, they also know that our crew is mixed, and that our population is therefore..." The Captain paused, letting an anticipatory titter circle the room. "... is therefore by no means fixed. What they don't know, naturally, is the division of sexes in the crew.

"You're all aware of the reason for the secrecy. You know that our organization is in direct opposition to the Ethical Principles on which the Peace was established after World War IV. And you know how the planners of this trip had to struggle with the authorities to get this project approved. When consent was granted, finally, it was only because the highest prelates clearly understood that the conditions of our small universe were in every way different from those on Earth... and that the division proposed was *necessary for survival*."

The Captain paused, waiting for the last words to sink in, and studying the attitudes of the group. Even now, after a year's conditioning to counteract Earthly mores, there were some present who listened to this public discussion of dangerous and intimate matters with flushed faces and embarrassed smiles.

"You all realize, of course, that this consent was based, finally, on the Basic Principle itself." Automatically, out of long habit unbroken by that year's intensive training, the Captain made the sign of the Olive Branch. *"Survival of the race is the first duty of every Ethical man and woman."* The command was intoned meaningfully, almost pontifically, and brought its reward as confusion cleared from some of the flushed faces. "What we are doing, our way of life now, has the full approval of the authorities. We must never forget that.

"On Earth, survival of the race is best served by the increasing strength of family ties. It was not thought wise to endanger those ties by letting the general public become aware of our—unortho-dox—system here on board. A general understanding, on Earth, of the true meaning of the phrase, 'The Twenty and the Four,' could only have aroused a furore of discussion and argument that would, in the end, have impeded survival both there and here.

"The knowledge that there are twenty of one sex on board, and only four of the other—that children will be born outside of normal family groups, and raised jointly—I need not tell you how disastrous that would have been." Melnick paused, raising a hand to dispel the muttering in the room.

"I wanted to let you know, before the Four arrive, that I have made some plans which I hope will carry us through the initial period in which difficulties might well arise. Later, when the groups of six—five of us, and one of them in each—have been assigned their permanent quarters, I think it will be possible, in fact necessary, to allow a greater amount of autonomy within those groups. But for the time being, I have arranged a—shall we call it a dating schedule?" Again, the Captain paused, waiting for tension to relieve itself in laughter. "I have arranged dates for all of you with each of them during convenient free periods over the next month. Perhaps at the end of that time, we will be able to choose groups; perhaps it will take longer. Maternity schedules, of course, will not be started until I am certain that the grouping is satisfactory to all. For the time being, remember this—

"We are not only more numerous than they, but we are stronger and, in our social placement here, more fortunate. We must become accustomed to the fact that they are our responsibility. It is because we are hardier, longer-lived, less susceptible to pain and illness, better able to withstand, mentally, the difficulties of a life of monotony, that we were placed as we are—and not alone because we are the bearers of children."

Over the sober silence of the crew, the Captain's voice rang out. "Lieutenant Johnson," Melnick called to the golden-haired, suntanned woman near the door, "will you call the men in from the tank-rooms now? They can finish their work after dinner."

LUNGFISH

John Brunner

For over forty years John Brunner (1934–1995) was one of Britain's leading writers of science fiction, and one of the most prolific. During the 1950s he produced a vibrant series of space operas and temporal adventures which included his series set in an alternate Britain where the Spanish Armada was victorious. This was recently reprinted by the British Library as The Society of Time. *By the 1960s he had developed a more cynical view of mankind as incapable of looking after itself and likely to become a "nonviable species". Out of this came some of his best work, notably the award-winning* Stand on Zanzibar *(1968), a bleak view of an overpopulated Earth and the machinations of government in population control and genetic engineering. Other major works include* The Jagged Orbit *(1969) with its even bleaker vision of the year 2014 where drugs and weapons are taking over;* The Sheep Look Up *(1972) where the deterioration of the environment leads to famine, civil unrest and war; and* The Shockwave Rider *(1975), a proto-cyberpunk novel portraying a world where hackers can control and manipulate computer networks. This cynical attitude is very evident in the following story where, as you can imagine, Brunner is of the view that putting people in a generation starship could be a recipe for disaster.*

Once upon a time there was a sea. It was full of life. But the sea grew smaller and the life-forms more numerous. There was the problem of overcrowding. Perhaps, if any of the inhabitants had been capable of wonder, they would have turned their flat eyes upwards and asked themselves what it was like above the sky, beyond the shining barrier of the surface. There was plenty of room there.

Eventually, some of them found out the hard way what it was like. Stranded by the tide, they gasped their lives away along the shore; dying, they left their outline in the mud, which dried, and was compressed, and became rock.

A BILLION YEARS LATER, AND MANY MORE THAN A BILLION miles away—a man was studying the fossil shapes of some of those remote ancestors.

The reflection seemed suddenly to telescope time, and Franz Yerring gasped. He put out a shaking hand to turn off the projector which cast microfilm images on the wall before him.

For a long time after that he sat at the desk and listened to the sounds of the ship, identifying every one of those that seeped through the thick insulating walls of the office with an ease born of thirty-seven years of hearing them. He did not move except to breathe deep shuddering sighs, until the buzzer on the door sounded. Then he roused himself to say, "Come in."

Tessa Lubova, his senior aide, slid the panel aside and stepped through with her habitual lithe grace. She carried the daily productivity reports, which she put on the desk before him.

On the verge of going out again, she paused and stared at him curiously. "What's the matter?" she demanded. "You look as white as paper!"

"It's nothing," said Yerring, getting stiffly to his feet. His voice had an irritable edge on it which he tried to disguise—it was not good to be sharp with the tripborn.

Tessa shrugged with one shoulder, hesitated a moment, and left the room. *Nice girl*, thought Yerring absently. Nicer than most of the tripborn, anyway—most of them would never have noticed, and if they had, they wouldn't have given a damn.

But then, she was one of the eldest.

He tripped the switch of the multipanel on the wall. It could be a picture, or an observation screen, or a mirror, according to the whim of the user. He selected the mirror setting and examined himself critically.

Yes, no wonder Tessa had been startled.

He forced himself consciously to relax, and went back to the desk, glad of the work which she had just brought him. He had been trying to throw away time by studying the text-film, and had been unable to lose himself in it. No one in the ship now could get away from the tension which hung in the air like smoke. It had not been publicly announced that Trip's End was near—if anyone did know the exact time, it would be Sivachandra and possibly one or two of his navigation aides—but there were rumours.

And how reliable is a rumour? he asked himself wryly. He knew as well as any of the earthborn aboard that the trip was estimated to take not less than thirty-six and not more than forty years, but he had been there when the estimate was made, and he knew how much of it depended on guesswork, as well.

*

He glanced through the summary on top of the sheaf of reports, and frowned. Taking up a red write-stick, he entered the day's returns on the master ecological chart which occupied one full wall of the office. On it, population was plotted against productivity: two curves, opposing and balancing each other, averaged out from dozens of daily entries relating to air supply, vegetation, water reclamation.

Sometimes he wondered how he kept track of it all.

His frown remained as he mentally extended the current downward sweep of the productivity line. Either Trip's End was close—

"Or we," he said to the air, "are going to be on short rations in less than a month."

That would be the sterile mutation in Culture B, he knew; it had been weighing the whole output down for days now. All the staff he had available was busy tracking down the mutated plasm, but it would take some time to eliminate it, and if one found more after that one could never tell if it was descended from a previously altered strain, or if it was a new series altogether.

"Hear this!" said the voice of George Hattus, the ship administration officer, from the public address speaker under the multipanel. "There will be a Captain's Conference at fourteen."

Yerring took the information in automatically, his eyes still fixed on the down-trending curve. It was bad—it really was. The cultures not only served to provide food for the crew; they were a main element in the oxygen recycling system. Perhaps he had recommended too optimistic an increase in population on the strength of having got away without a major incidence of sterility. He should have allowed for an increase in mutation with the rising radiation level as they homed on the sun of their goal...

Just as well Magda's called this conference, he thought.

The chronometer showed it lacked only eight minutes of fourteen hours. He gave a glance round the room by force of habit and went out, down the long green corridor towards the administration section.

Outside his main charge—the hydroponics section—he found a crew from maintenance taking up the plates to get at a gravity coil which had been on the blink, and called to the man directing operations.

"Captain's conference, Hatcher! Did you hear the announcement?"

Quentin Hatcher turned burning eyes on him. He seemed on the brink of saying something acid, but contented himself with a weary nod. He gestured to the workers round him, and they stood back to let Yerring pass, which he did with a word of thanks. He could almost feel those eyes on the back of his neck as he walked on.

I wonder when it first began, he thought. Of course, like the rest of the earthborn, he wouldn't have noticed it. Only the education staff, probably, had the chance. His life was shared with his friends, whom he had known for over forty years—since they came together to work on a ship which was no more than drawings on a board, stress equations in a computer, and a dream burning in their minds.

But the slow antagonism had arisen all about them, until now they faced it as a fact.

What made it that way? The tripborn's knowledge that it was with them that the future lay? That the earthborn in the ship were condemned to spend their lives in space, perhaps living long enough to see Earth again before they died—and perhaps not—while they, the tripborn, would go on to plant the first human colony under an alien sun?

Somehow, though that explanation was pleasing, he could not be satisfied with it.

Aside from the technicians checking the recording equipment, there was only one person ahead of him in the conference room, and that was Tsien, the senior psychologist. He sat in the chair on the right of the captain's place, bald head bent low over a stack of psychometric data sheets.

He glanced up as Yerring entered and nodded to him. On the point of looking down again, he checked himself. "What's with you, Franz?" he inquired. "You look as if you've seen a ghost."

Hadn't he got over it yet? Yerring restrained an impulse to reach up and feel for the betraying expression on his face. "In a way, I have," he said wryly, taking his place one chair away from Tsien. "Don't let me interrupt you."

"You aren't interrupting," said Tsien promptly. "I've read all these papers already, and going through them again won't alter the facts in them. What's the trouble?"

Yerring shrugged. "I was thinking about the size and duration of the universe. It was as if—well, as if I'd had a vision of the full extent of it. It was disturbing."

"I can imagine it would be." Tsien settled back in his chair, big-shouldered, pot-bellied, reassuring of tone. "What did you find so particularly uncomfortable about it, though?"

"The sheer naked size of it!" Yerring was astonished at his own vehemence, and tried to continue in a lighter tone. "I mean, I was thinking in terms of millions of years, and we ourselves only live a hundred and twenty or so. That's the twinkle of an eye—"

"To whom?" Tsien shot back. "Not to us, Franz. To us it's a lifetime, and can't be otherwise."

"Yes, I suppose so. But we do quite cheerfully talk about millions of years, and yet we never stop and think just how long that is. We can speak of an age, an eon, but we can't appreciate them."

"Why should we?" Tsien spread his hands, palms upward; the movement made his chest and shoulders heave like a mountain in an earthquake. "No one ever experienced a million years, any more than anyone ever paced out the miles from here to M-39 in Andromeda. They just measured them. Think of yourself as one of Sivachandra's astronomy boys, trying to find the parallax of a star—only you're sighting on a fossil and using radio-carbon dating instead of a telescope."

"How did you know I was thinking of archaeology?" Yerring was startled.

"A guess," said Tsien frankly. "Probably because I've been re-reading the basics of my job—Freud, and Hal Jenning's work on space neuroses. It's symbolic. We're here to make a new beginning, so we look at what we know of other, earlier beginnings which we know to have had successful results. We may recognize intellectually that each beginning is unique, but it comforts us to see resemblances and convince ourselves that we aren't walking into unknown darkness."

"And are we?"

Tsien grinned. "All the time! But on your argument, Franz—to go back to what you were saying—a man is unable to appreciate any period longer than his own lifetime. I disagree. This whole trip of ours has been a contradiction of that. Do you honestly think that Garmisch, who designed the ship, and Yoseida, who devoted his whole life to financing it and finding a crew for it, were incapable of appreciating a longer period than a hundred-odd years? Would you yourself have volunteered to come if you hadn't been thinking in terms of millennia? Because it may be that long before the results are in, and neither you nor I will be around to see it."

Almost reluctantly, Yerring nodded. "I guess you're right," he said.

Towards the end of Tsien's speech, Tessa Lubova had come into the room and taken her place as usual low down on the left-hand side of the table, where the tripborn members of the conference always sat in a tight, exclusive knot.

This sort of thing is going to have to stop, thought Yerring. With the toughest part of the job still ahead, they couldn't have petty jealousies and discriminations.

He raised his voice. "Tessa, I'd like you up here next to me," he said, trying not to make the words sound like an order.

She turned her sullen face, very striking under its crown of dark hair, towards him. "What's the point?" she said sharply. "We"—the word conjured up a sudden vision of Quentin Hatcher, Vera Hassan and Fatima Shan, the other tripborn members of the conference in their places beside her—"never have anything to say, anyway."

The atmosphere seemed to become ten degrees chillier.

"So you've noticed it, have you?" said Tsien softly, as soon as Tessa turned away, and Yerring nodded.

"That's something we weren't bargaining for, isn't it?" he said.

II

The techs finished checking the recorders and went out, and one by one the remainder of the twenty members of Captain's Conference took their places about the table. Lola Kathodos of engineering sat opposite Yerring; Philippa Vautry of Medical came between him and Tsien; Sivachandra of navigation next to Lola—Yerring greeted each in turn.

There was a slight stir as George Hattus of ship admin took his place on the left of the captain's chair; he was the most—unknown?—man in the ship. *Like a policeman*, Yerring thought, and remembered back to the days when there had been such people in his daily life; whenever the familiar blue uniform appeared round the corner, even the most law-abiding searched their consciences.

Last of all, precisely on time, Magda Gomez took her place at the top of the table, and they all fell silent, looking towards her.

"Captain's conference, Magda Gomez presiding, declared open at fourteen hundred hours, day ninety-one, year thirty-seven," she said for the benefit of the record. "All right. Now I suppose you want to know why I've called this conference so soon on top of the last one. It's because there have been too many sanitation rumours going round about the approach of Trip's End. People are starting to get sloppy and careless. I want it to be borne in mind that when we reach Tau Ceti II, our job will be *beginning*—not over! We came here for a purpose, and we're going to carry it through."

Her gimlet eyes fixed on Sivachandra, and he looked uncomfortable; it was plain she had her own ideas as to who let the rumours get started.

"All right," she said finally. "Let's kill the false reports once for all. Siv, tell 'em when we make Trip's End."

There was a rustle of excitement all round the table, and Yerring sat up in surprise. The first time that question had ever been asked in conference! Whispered comment spread and was swiftly killed among the tripborn.

Sivachandra looked around impressively and waited for complete silence. "We will be in orbit around Tau Ceti II," he said, "in less than fifteen days."

This time the talk was loud and assured; only Tsien sat silent among the exchange of congratulations.

"Quiet!" said Magda at length, and there was quiet. To Lola Kathodos: "Yes?"

"Is that for official circulation?" the engineering officer asked. "My staff have been particularly full of 'inside information' and I'd like to crush it."

"Yes! Yes, by all means!" Magda looked down at a note in front of her. "All sections will have four hours' celebration time this evening, by the way, but I don't want anyone reporting tomorrow morning with a hangover. We're getting down to real work then. We can put some real meaning into boat drill and things like that from now on. Hatcher!"

Quentin Hatcher looked up.

"The flight simulator comes under you, doesn't it? I'd like you to pick your half-dozen best trainees and run them through final tests. Then Siv can decide who gets the chance at the first touchdown."

Hatcher nodded and made a note.

"I'll ask Siv to give us an idea of his first plans in a moment, but before that, has anyone anything they want to say? Engineering? Medical? Admin? Psychology?"

The representatives shook their heads.

"Ecology, what about you?"

Yerring spread his hands. "I was going to have to give some bad news, but the nearness of Trip's End solves the problem."

"Better tell us what it is, anyway."

"Well, we had a major attack of sterility in one of our important cultures; with the drop in productivity, consumption would have been due to exceed output in a month or so. But by that time we'll have raw materials from the planet to tide us over, so it's okay."

★

Magda glanced to her left. "George, what's the population right now?"

"Uh—two thousand, one hundred forty-nine," said Hattus. "It's one below schedule, but there's a late birth coming up in Franz's section somewhere—hydroponics, I think."

"That's right," confirmed Philippa Vautry. "Edna Barsavitza's having a long pregnancy—she's five days past due. I think I'd better stimulate labour artificially; we won't want advanced pregnancies to cope with when we actually hit orbit." She scribbled a memorandum, and Magda waited for her to finish before speaking again.

"Siv, give them a rundown of the immediate programme, will you?"

The navigation chief put up a pale brown hand and sleeked back his silver hair. "Fifteen days distant may not seem like a lot compared with thirty-seven years," he began. "But we're making for a small planet rather close to its primary, and it's been on the opposite side of its star for the past several weeks. So far, we haven't done much more than confirm that it's where it ought to be."

Someone down the table sniggered; Magda glared at the offender, but Sivachandra continued with unruffled dignity. "We've confirmed the composition of the air by checking the absorption lines, and that's about all. Of course, this is duplication of effort, since the survey teams did a very thorough job when they were here a century ago, but a remote chance does remain, I suppose, that they overlooked something because they weren't thinking of staying.

"So tomorrow we'll be launching some TV-eye missiles. With them, we'll carry out a complete survey of the planet, during our approach run. As soon as they start sending in good pictures, by the way, I'll have them plugged into the multipanel circuit so everyone gets a chance to see them. By the time we go into orbit, we should know what site will suit us best—"

"Are you landing party?" said Vera Hassan loudly and rudely from the lower end of the table. There was dead silence for a minute.

"What was the point of that, Vera?" said Magda at length, in a voice like an arctic wind.

Vera leaned back in her chair, a defiant expression on her face. "He said which site will suit *us* best. I just want to know if he's one of the people it's going to *have* to suit whether they like it or not."

There were murmurs of agreement from the other tripborn present, and Yerring saw Tessa give a nod of encouragement. Magda slammed her open palm down on the table.

"Vera, we have a job to do, and it's the responsibility of all the crew—not just of part of it. You know as well as I do that Siv isn't landing party. Nor am I; nor is Franz, or any of the earthborn. But it isn't from choice, believe me—we'd change places with you straight off. We're just too old."

Too old: the words echoed in Yerring's mind. Too old at seventy-seven, even if that was scarcely two-thirds of his lifetime gone, because the remaining third was due to be spent in this same ship, with nothing but the knowledge of having achieved a historic aim as compensation…

He felt a sudden shiver go down his spine as he thought: what would it be like to have *nothing* to show for it? What if we fail?

Magda was still speaking in a persuasive tone. "We—all of us, Vera!—have given our lives to an ideal. We aren't going to relax our efforts simply because the period of waiting is over. The greatest task in history lies ahead of us." She touched a switch set in the table-top. "It lies there!"

No one heard her last words clearly. They had all turned to face the multipanel on the wall, which had just sprung to life. It showed the disc of the reddish sun called Tau Ceti, set against a background of stars which were familiar to them all. But there was a new star among the rest: small, tinged with the same red as its parent.

Trip's End!

Yerring heaved a slow sigh, and stole a covert glance around the group. The earthborn were staring dreamy-eyed at their goal, except for Tsien, who was more interested in the reactions of his companions, but that was natural. The tripborn, however, were sitting stony and impassive, wearing expressions of—contempt? Nausea? Disappointment? He struggled to find a suitable word and rejected each of them in turn.

Finally Magda broke the spell. "That'll do for now. Remember what I said, won't you? Now go and inform your sections about the celebration time tonight. Conference adjourned at fourteen nineteen."

She slumped back in her chair, turning off the multipanel, and with a scraping of chairs and shuffling of feet the members started to leave the room. Yerring was rising stiffly to his feet when he felt Hattus's hand on his arm. The admin officer looked grave.

"Magda wants to see heads of departments for a moment," he said. "Won't keep you long."

The pose of efficient domination which Magda had worn at the conference table dropped off her like a cloak when she stepped through the connecting door into her own office. She indicated with a gesture that the others present should sit down, and looked at Tsien. "Well?" she said.

The psychologist nodded. "I'm afraid so."

"As you think best. What did everyone think of that little scene?"

Yerring leaned forward. "The trick with the multipanel, you mean?" he asked. "You hadn't by any chance primed Vera to explode like that and focus the tension, had you?" He tried to sound hopeful, but he knew as he spoke it was wishful thinking, and Magda shook her head with a weary smile.

"No, Tsien warned me something like that might happen. It was an idea he had."

"How can they be so wooden?" Philippa Vautry spoke with vehemence. "Damn it, Tsien, why didn't you foresee this?"

"You're wrong, Phil," the psychologist answered. "We did. At least, Yoseida did. George, get out the orders, will you? We have no choice but to use them now."

Hattus nodded and crossed to the safe set in the wall. Opening it, he took out a sheaf of envelopes with person-keyed destruction seals which would render the contents illegible if anyone but the addressee tried to open them, and handed the little bundle to Magda.

"I myself," the captain began, "don't know what's in these envelopes. I was told, though, during one of the final briefings George and I attended before we left Earth, that I might be called on to use certain emergency procedures at the request of the psychological section. Since Tsien first told me he was worried about the tripborns' attitude to landing, I've suspected one of the procedures might deal with that, and I was right.

"All of us here had the privilege of knowing Yoseida in person, and working under his guidance before the ship left. I think it's plain that only a man who was completely devoted to the high ideal of spreading mankind through the galaxy could have visualized so far in advance the need for plans to cover such an unlikely contingency."

She sounded a little self-conscious as she finished the speech; it was platitudinous to say such things to people who had also known and admired that fanatical old Asiatic, but Yerring knew it was only her respect and regard speaking for her, and nodded his approval. The others followed suit.

"We can't let him down now," said George Hattus, in his soft, agreeable voice. "A man like that deserves the memorial of success. I suspect what's in these orders may not be entirely pleasant to enforce, but we owe it to his memory to carry this thing through."

Taking the envelopes back from Magda, he distributed them; the recipients eyed them curiously but awaited permission to open them from the captain.

"Fifteen days isn't a long time to re-orient twenty-one hundred people," said Tsien thoughtfully. "It means this action will be pretty drastic."

"What do you mean?" said Philippa indignantly. "There are nearly two hundred and fifty earthborn, remember!"

Tsien nodded vigorously, but Yerring had the impression that he was cursing himself for making a slip. Magda interrupted before he was able to speak.

"Take these orders and read them in your own offices," she said. "On no account let them get anywhere where the tripborn can see them. All right, on your way. Good luck."

All except Hattus rose and went out. In the corridor, Yerring caught Tsien's eye and drew him aside for a moment.

"*Were* you making a mistake when you said twenty-one hundred?" he inquired doubtfully. "It seems ridiculous—but I got the idea you meant it!"

The psychologist looked him soberly in the eye. "Franz, when did you last use the picture setting of the multipanel in your office?"

Yerring paused, dumbfounded. "Why—it must have been all of three years ago!" he exclaimed. "I hardly use it at all now except as a mirror."

"Exactly," said Tsien heavily, and walked on.

III

Yerring returned to his own section with his mind in turmoil. Tsien's sudden question had taken him by surprise; it brought back with discomforting vividness the terror he had experienced when he wondered what it would be like to know he had wasted his life in vain.

He passed the envelope from hand to hand, impatient to gain the security of his own office and find out what it was that constituted their last defence against failure.

But before that he would have to announce the news given at the conference to his own staff. Tessa would already be back, and could quite well have done it, but he knew it had not entered her head; like all the tripborn, she insisted with almost childish obstinacy that he exercise the full authority to which his status entitled him.

He tucked the envelope securely and inconspicuously into a pocket and stepped through the sliding door into the warm, slightly steamy air of the hydroponics section. Sometimes he thought, looking down the lines of transparent culture tubes towards the blindingly bright focus of the light area, that it was odd how an ecological cycle which had begun as a planet-sized unit could be fined down to essentials and tucked into the comparatively tiny hull of this ship.

He followed the direction of the culture flow until he found Tessa studying a sample drawn from the mixture. He called to her, and she looked up slowly.

"I suppose you want to address the hands?" she said, putting down the testing phial. "I'll go and round them up for you." There was a faint sneer on her face, as if she were implying that Yerring could not be sure they would come at his order.

And in a way, Yerring was forced to admit, she was right. He had begun the trip with a staff of twenty-one, all earthborn—naturally—but since biology and ecology were two subjects the colonists would need to know backwards, they had gradually been transferred off to ship administration. Now he had a staff of a hundred and three, but he was the only remaining earthborn member of it.

Must remember to have some of my old assistants re-posted while we're in orbit, he reminded himself. *We'll need them on the way home.*

He felt for his dark glasses and put them on before walking out across the big open space between the tubes where dead cultures were slued for drying, lysis and recycling as organic intake materials. One by one, the hands came in—not talking, not excited, just coming in.

He tried to remember how he had pictured the enthusiasm which would greet the news of Trip's End, thirty-seven years ago. Very different from this; the passive concentration in their faces reminded him of what Tessa had said in the conference room—"We never have anything to say, anyway."

And it was true.

What had happened to all the talking and shouting? *When I go into the conference room, I start a conversation with Tsien or someone; Tessa sits alone, not speaking even when one of her own generation joins her.*

What did these taciturn people do off duty? *Shock; I have scarcely an idea. They eat and watch the shows on the panels, sometimes we*

*have dances they attend, some of them play music and some read books
from the microfilm library; that's not the point. For example: could they
fall in love?*

Are they really alive?

These had been children like any other children: noisy, inquisitive, foolhardy, disobedient. If they had been otherwise, Tsien as director of the education staff would have been alarmed.

And yet they had grown up into these frighteningly self-reliant people who could run the ship better than the earthborn any time they put their minds to it, and still refused to take the initiative.

"Everyone's here," said Tessa, just loudly enough to break through his musing, and he scrambled up on a breeding chest to make his announcement.

They took it as they took everything else, as if they were adding it to some store of information already prepared for use in some calculation Yerring could not guess at.

When he had delivered his message and got no response, his tension boiled over.

"If you knew how we envy you!" he exploded.

That startled them. He rushed on: "You have your whole lives to look forward to on a good world, a brand-new planet! We gave up ours to see you achieve that aim, and I for one don't regret it—but I wish I could be your age again and take your place!"

He got down blindly to the floor and walked hurriedly into the protection of an aisle between the banks of tubes.

Someone was standing there, immobile; with his dark glasses still on, Yerring could not tell who it was until he stirred and spoke. It was Quentin Hatcher.

"What are you doing here?" said Yerring gruffly, half-ashamed of his outburst.

"I came to see Tessa," said Hatcher placidly, and Yerring remembered that he had known in a vague way the two were having an affair; promiscuity had to be encouraged to ensure the mixing of all available genetic factors.

He wanted to pass on to his office and read the orders in his pocket, but Hatcher looked at him steadily, and he did not dare even feel to make certain they were still there. "Are you in a hurry?" the other asked.

With an effort Yerring controlled himself; it would be a mistake to admit he was in fact in haste, when Tessa knew quite well there was no urgent work on hand in the section. Someone might draw the right conclusion. He shook his head. "Did you want something?"

"Yes. You earthborn are very free with your description of this planet as a 'good' world"—Yerring could hear the quotation marks. "But I know nothing about it beyond the fact that it's said to be habitable. Why?"

"Tessa could tell you as well as I can."

"Tessa could not." The girl moved out of shadow, and he wondered how long she had stood there listening. "I do know more about the planet than Quentin does, but it's going to be my job, apparently."

Yerring gave ground reluctantly. "You've found the reason," he said, thinking fast. "You'd have to ask the psychological section for full details, but I know the rough idea. When we set up the colony—"

"We?" whispered Hatcher, with a glance at the girl; Yerring caught the word but pretended he hadn't, even to the extent of cancelling an impulse to frown at the echo of Vera Hassan's attack on Sivachandra.

He went on: "—we've got to have the best possible combination of experts to get the work done in minimum time. That's why, even though you know nothing about Cetian ecology, for example, you're three times as good a metallurgist and electronics engineer as someone your age on Earth. You're a specialist. So's Tessa. There's going to be so much to do at Trip's End that we can't afford to waste time teaching people knowledge they can't use. Of course, the data from the early survey is in the library for anyone to read who wants it—"

"I know," said Hatcher bitterly. "I've looked at it. But I haven't the time to teach myself the basics I need to follow it."

This time Yerring had to frown. He noticed that Tessa had stepped out of sight again.

"Give it to me in simple language," said Hatcher, managing to make it seem that Yerring would be in the wrong if he refused. "What kind of a planet *is* this?"

Yerring was tempted to snap that it was habitable and wasn't that good enough? Instead, he put it another way.

"Promising enough for us to have begun and carried through a project lasting all these years to colonize it, and that means very good indeed."

"If it's so habitable, why isn't it inhabited?"

"Because it hasn't got a moon." Yerring was falling automatically into the teaching style he used when taking trainee classes in the ship's school. "There's a lot of life in the sea—some of it eatable, by the way, which is useful—but the oxygen in the air is replenished only by colonies of free-floating algae which drift across the oceans. We'll probably supplement them with some of our own species.

"But on Earth, life was driven from the sea to the land largely by the effect of tides. Without a moon, the sea-level doesn't change significantly or frequently enough to produce land life."

Tessa had moved back into his range of vision during the last sentence. "That means," she put in sourly, "there's nothing to bind eroded rock into soil. It's all desert."

"So was Mars!" said Yerring sharply. "And it didn't even have good air. We took it over and re-made it until it was nearly as good as Earth. This world could well be made *better*." After a pause he added pleadingly, "Do you honestly think we'd have started on this trip if it wasn't worth it?"

"You started on this trip," said Hatcher softly. "We hadn't much choice, had we?"

Yerring was silent.

"Suppose it's changed since the survey teams were here?" Hatcher pursued. "After all, it was nearly a hundred years ago that they discovered this system—"

"But a hundred years is"—Yerring remembered the way he had put it to Tsien—"a twinkle of an eye when you're thinking of biological processes. No, there won't be any important change."

"So you say," insisted Hatcher doggedly. "But what will we do if it isn't the paradise you've promised us? Has anyone thought about that?"

Yerring had been thinking of it—entirely too recently for the remark to be pleasant. He turned on his heel.

"It will be!" he threw over his shoulder. And as he drew out of earshot, he muttered, "It's *got* to be!"

Alone in the privacy of his office, he sat down at the desk and put his hand in his pocket to take out the orders. He experienced a momentary surge of panic as his hand closed on nothing.

Then he felt in the other pocket, and breathed a sigh when he found the familiar oblong shape. *Odd; I could have sworn it was in the other—*

But when he examined the seal carefully, it showed no signs of tampering.

As he prepared to unfasten it, his eye fell on the multipanel, and he recalled Tsien's questions. Was it really three years since he had used it last as a picture?

He paused to think of the scenes he had liked most out of the enormous repertoire stored as electronic memory patterns in the master library. That flower garden, for instance—the play of colours was magnificent. But so was the sunset scene, and neither was as majestic as the view of Niagara, or as nostalgic as the riot of foliage under the dome of Copernicus Crater on the moon, where he had spent his first holiday off Earth as a small boy, stalking his younger brother through the "jungle"...

He took out the index of settings, which he had once had almost by heart, from a drawer, and chose one which had always been a particular favourite of his: a panorama of wheat fields in North America. Suddenly, yellow corn seemed to stretch into the distance through the wall when he tripped the switch; on the horizon, it melted into blue sky. Mile upon square mile of earth-surface, and every last inch of it bearing for the benefit of man!

And yet, somehow, it didn't provide the shiver of awe which it had once induced.

He dismissed the reflection with annoyance, and broke the seal of the envelope. There was only one sheet of paper inside; closely typed, it ran:

Deliver at the captain's discretion to the senior ecologist.

It is considered possible by the psychologists who have studied the likely mental development of the crew after so long in space, that some measure of unconscious resistance to the prospect of landing may arise when the time of planetfall draws near.

This is especially to be looked for in the case of those who, having been born on board, will not actually have set foot on terra firma.

As it has been explained to me, there is a close mental analogy between landing from a ship such as this, and the process of birth. A child objects to being born; it longs for the comfort and security of the womb to some extent for the rest of its life. The environment of the ship represents an extension of similar security into adulthood.

In the event of such a situation arising, action is to be taken as briefly outlined below WHEN THE SHIP IS CLOSE ENOUGH TO THE PLANET FOR CONDITIONS ON BOARD TO REMAIN BEARABLE UNTIL IT IS REACHED. An absolute maximum of two weeks is suggested; within that limit, time of commencement is left wholly to the psychological section.

(a) The medical officer is to prepare sufficient quantities of a suggestibility-heightening drug to render all affected members of the crew susceptible to influences designed for combating the subconscious compulsion against landing.

(b) The ecologist is to select a method of administering the drug. It will be essential to exclude those personnel who will be returning to Earth to report the success of the mission, and whose business on the planet is only temporary; aerosol administration is therefore inadvisable.

(c) The senior psychologist is to organize counter-compulsions, given in detail in an appendix to be delivered only to that officer, directed to instilling a distaste for shipside conditions in the crew.

This expedient is analogous to shock treatment, and is to be resorted to in cases of emergency only. The chance of permanent mental effects, however, is estimated at less than one per cent. Man is a planetary animal; any other environment is unnatural

to him, and re-adaptation will proceed much more smoothly than
did the original adaptation to spatial conditions.

Yerring read the document through carefully, a frown deepening
on his forehead, until he came to the signature. He looked at it
closely. It was Yoseida's own.

Instantly, a curtain seemed to roll back in his mind, and he
was once again a youth listening with adoration to the plans of
a thin, fanatical Asiatic who was set on sending men out among
the stars, and resolving that when the ship was built, he would be
one of the crew. Yoseida was that sort of a man; in another age he
would have conquered himself an empire at the head of an army
prepared to die on his casual command, or formed a business
concern and controlled the lives of millions, decreed whether they
would starve or surfeit.

The old idealism was still smouldering in Yerring's mind, like
a fire burning under a heap of ashes. He clenched his fists with
determination. In that moment he was more certain of one thing
than he had ever been; they were not going to fail!

He reached for the diet charts and studied them with care. The
drug would have to reach everyone it was intended for, yet those
who had to avoid it must be able to refuse the item containing it
without exciting suspicion. It was an interesting problem.

He made his choice and sat back in his chair. This was a job he
was going to have to do himself, obviously; he was the only earthborn left in the ecological section. None of the tripborn could be
expected to understand just what this journey meant to the race
of man, and to far-sighted geniuses like Yoseida, who had given
his life to this ideal...

He would have to add it to the diet when the section was
deserted, therefore, and during tonight's celebration was the

obvious moment. The question was whether Philippa would have enough of the drug ready by then.

He reached for the phone, and then changed his mind; a tripborn technician might be monitoring the wires, looking for a fault. He would have to go down to medical section.

At the door, he gave his habitual glance around, and saw with momentary surprise that the multipanel was blank. He did not remember turning off the picture.

IV

Sounds of singing from the mess rang the length of the empty corridors as he walked slowly through semi-darkness towards the dietary room. At least the tripborn were still human enough to enjoy themselves. He kept his mind blank and receptive to every stir of noise, acutely aware of the jar of reddish liquid in his hand. He hoped it might pass for a drink if anyone saw him.

He kept reminding himself that the section would be deserted; nonetheless, he found himself rehearsing the phrases of excuse he would have to use if anyone found him there. But as he stepped into the dietary room, he realized that the singing from the mess adjacent would drown any slight sound he made himself; if there was anyone in the sleeping quarters opposite, where his own staff slept, he would notice nothing.

The synthesizers which turned the raw material of the cultures into flavoursome, substantial and nourishing food were quietly humming; the air was warm, and had a pleasant rich smell. He knew the layout too well to bother turning on the lights; he crossed the floor swiftly, opened the additive cap on one of the synthesizers, and poured a careful half of the reddish liquid into the mixture. Then he moved to the next unit and repeated the process.

Closing the caps, he slipped the empty jar into a recycler for reduction to its elements and absorption into the resources of the ship. It was not until he was safely outside again in the corridor that he dared admit he had successfully completed his task.

In the humming warmth of the dietary room, Tessa Lubova came gracefully out of the cramped corner between two synthesizers where she had been hiding, and crossed to the door of the sleeping quarters. She made no attempt to discover what had been added to the food supply, nor did her face betray any hint of emotion whatsoever.

It was heartening to see the determination on the faces of his companions, thought Yerring, and knew that the same resolution inspired himself. Even when Magda passed a tired hand across her forehead, it was with impatience at her own inadequacy.

"Phil, how did the tests go?" she asked. "Maybe you'd better say what you actually did."

The doctor nodded. "Well, we took blood samples from random members of the crew, ostensibly to be included in the equipment of the TV-eyes to detect bacteria which can breed in them. We shall be doing that anyway, of course—can't have anyone getting suspicious. But the samples we took show a hundred per cent incidence of the drug in the tripborn."

"That's Franz's doing," said Magda, with a glance at Yerring. "You picked an excellent medium to give it in. Right. Siv, the missiles were launched this morning—when do you expect the first pictures in?"

"Assuming a minimum of solar activity, late this evening," said the navigation officer. "They won't be of good quality over this distance, but they'll be clear enough to give us a rough idea."

"Fine. Plug them into the panels as soon as you can. Tsien wants to see what their effect is before going ahead."

The psychologist grunted heavily. "I'm still hoping we may not have to do this," he admitted. "It'll be a foul job with only a few of my staff to help me out."

"How's that again?" said Lola Kathodos.

"Well, naturally," Tsien shrugged, "I can't ask the tripborn to work on this, and as it turns out I can't even rely on all the earthborn."

"That's bad," said Lola complacently. "Well, I'm glad to say I'm every bit as determined to see this job through as I was when we left Earth."

"Of course you are," said Tsien with an effort at reassurance. "All of us in this room are. Not everyone is affected by the tripborn's apathy."

But I am, thought Yerring, and found Tsien's eyes on him. *After all this time, the men must practically be able to read my mind.*

"I think it might be a good idea to tell us what you'll have to do," put in Hattus quietly. "Franz, for example, has no one but tripborn under him now, and he's worried about production as things are. Will he suffer any more for what you're doing?"

"Possibly." Tsien was dubious. "We'll be using verbal suggestion, of course—if any of you want hints on how to weight your orders to your staff, I'll be glad to advise you. But we ourselves are going through the book—subsonics, trigger smells, tactile suggestion. There's latent claustrophobia for the asking, too, of course; we'll have to touch off as much of that as possible."

"And what if it doesn't work?" Sivachandra voiced the idea which Yerring had not dared utter.

"Of course it'll work," said Tsien bluntly. "Believe me, I've looked after the psychological state of the crew long enough to be certain of that. My only reservation is that we shouldn't have had to use it." He hunched forward.

"Every mass entertainment we've put out during the voyage, every programme of tuition in the school, every talk and every briefing—they've all been slanted towards the resumption of planetside life. That's why we've refused to permit the germination of any culture with a shipside background; we've taken special note of people with originality and qualities of leadership and diverted their aims, in case they made too great an impression on their fellows. The authority and the power is vested in the earthborn; we insisted on holding the prospect of independence up as a carrot for a donkey, and tried to make Trip's End the focal point of all the tripborns' ambition. The entire crew should have a load of subconscious commands twice as strong as their inherent womb-retreat factor."

"*Should* have!" echoed Philippa. "We even carried it so far as to develop easy birthing methods, to reduce birth trauma to a minimum. And yet look what we've wound up with!"

"There's something wrong," said Yerring. He watched Tsien's face as he spoke. "Isn't there?"

"Yes," the psychologist admitted. "Somewhere along the line, this trip has altered our mental attitudes in a way no one could foresee. Why? Because this ship is the first completely closed subplanetary ecological unit, Franz?"

Yerring shook his head. "It's not that easy. The exploration ships of a century ago were completely closed, too; what's more, the crews—except those which visited this system, naturally—found nowhere to land, so they spent the period of the round trip on board. Yet they were only mildly maladjusted when they returned to Earth."

"Yes, I've pored over their psychological records long enough to be sure of that. What's the difference, then?"

"That we've bred in this environment?" suggested Hattus shrewdly.

Tsien shrugged. "Could be. But what else could we do? Load a cargo of babes-in-arms when we took off? Of course not! All the successful pioneering groups in history have included widely assorted age-ranges. By deciding to expand our population *en route*, we manage to arrive with not only a larger complement of capable workers than if we had kept to our original strength, but with about two hundred children who can be trained to take their places in the colony."

He looked around the room. "All of us here have grown children now; how many of us are grandparents besides myself?" Four people nodded—Magda, Hattus, Sivachandra and Lola. "And the rest of you will be soon; when we land, we can expand our population without foreseeable limit. No, if this revulsion against landing is an inescapable result of breeding in the ship, we're sunk, and human expansion to the stars is going to have to await the coming of a faster-than-light drive."

"Which is still impossible to the best of our knowledge," said Sivachandra flatly. "But—well, I don't know quite why, but somehow I'm *certain* this revulsion against landing is just a phase. We'll get around it."

The others echoed his confidence in assured voices, and Tsien said emphatically, "Of course we shan't admit defeat!"

There was silence for a while. Finally Magda stirred. "Siv, how about the landing itself?" she inquired.

"As soon as we hang up in orbit, we'll have a landing boat ready to go down. We're running the pilot tests all the time."

"Send your best man along to me before you tell him he's going," Tsien put in. "I'll need to make sure the conditioning has taken."

"Who is he—do you know yet?" asked Philippa.

Sivachandra shook his head, the lie was beautifully camouflaged, but Yerring was sure he could see through it. "We're down to a short list of half a dozen or so," he said. "I can't say yet which of them will actually go."

"Okay," Magda frowned. "Anything else before we go back to our jobs? Yes, Franz?"

"Suppose one of the tripborn *has* missed the drug," Yerring suggested. "Suppose he spots Tsien's 'influences'—what do we tell him?"

"A good point," the captain nodded. "George, any ideas?"

"Say we're slowing to turn into orbit," Hattus offered. "It's producing stress noises in the fabric of the hull. Does that sound convincing, Siv?"

"Not to anyone in my section, or Lola's," Sivachandra answered. "But to anyone else it might. It'll do, anyway."

There were no further comments; they rose and went out. In the passage, Yerring drew Sivachandra aside.

"You've already picked the man to make the first touchdown, haven't you?" he said flatly. "Why not admit it?"

Sivachandra's pale brown face remained enigmatic. "I had reasons for not mentioning his name in there," he said.

"Who is it?"

"Felipe Vautry. He's Philippa's son."

And then he realized, as Yerring's face went blank, he had made a slip after all. "And yours?" he said in a questioning tone.

"Yes," agreed Yerring. "And mine."

V

Does he know, himself? Yerring's mind wandered all round the question. There could be no such thing as a home in the ship; it was home, in itself, and therefore the ties of parenthood were not strong. He had three children—Felipe and two daughters—but they had gone into the creche under the efficient, understanding care of the nursing staff, and then through the ship's school; they were dropped, like pieces of a jigsaw puzzle, into places in the crew exactly the right shape to receive them.

After that, they were just—tripborn.

How old is Felipe now, anyway? Twenty-six? Twenty-eight?

"We have two courses of action to prepare for," he said doggedly to Tessa, who sat impassively on the far side of his desk. "Which we choose, depends on whether the TV-eyes find an ideal spot for the settlement soon, or not. We'll know in another day or two—you've heard that the first pictures are going to be relayed this evening on the panels?"

Silence.

"Tessa!"

The girl's sullen face turned towards him, and he demanded, "Were you listening?"

"Yes."

"Well, why not answer my question?"

"Oh, I wasn't listening to *you*," she said with a hint of contempt in her tone. "I was listening to the ship."

"What about it?" Yerring hoped that the sudden guarded alertness in his manner escaped her. "We're slowing down to fall into orbit, remember—it alters the stress noises of the hull. It was much the same while we were accelerating away from the solar system, I remember," he added glibly, thinking that if he was going to tell a lie it might as well be a good one. He had no way of knowing whether she accepted it or not, but ploughed on.

"Now pay attention, for goodness sake! Our position is getting damned near dangerous, and you're supposed to be director of ecology for the settlement, you know. As I was going to say: our margin for error is dropping like a stone. Our resources will take us barely two weeks past orbit as things stand. If we can land the advance party straight away, that'll lighten our burden enough to get us by; if not, we're going to have to import raw materials from the planet to tide us over."

He reached out and turned on the multipanel, choosing a view of some Martian plantations; it had just occurred to him that the surface of that world had been similar to that of Trip's End under its reddish sun, and the proof it had been made habitable was a useful semantic factor to work on the minds of the tripborn. He was surprised it hadn't struck Tsien.

He ran quickly through the arrangements which needed to be made for either contingency, and finished, "Pass on what I've said to the rest of the staff as they need it. Sivachandra will be asking for opinions on the site for the colony, by the way; you ought to make the decision rather than me, since after all you'll be living there." He had to avoid saying "have to live there" by a conscious effort.

"Thank you for thinking of that," said Tessa, and he glanced at her sharply, wondering if she was being sarcastic. "Is that all?"

"Yes, that's all."

She rose with her usual fluid grace and went out; Yerring waited till the door had closed and then brought in the observation circuit of the multipanel, anxious not to miss a moment of the pictures relayed from the planet. He had been staring at the blankly luminous surface of the screen for fully fifteen seconds before he realized it had previously been equally blank.

What happened to the picture of Mars? This absent-minded turning off of the panel—

He pulled the index of panel settings out of the drawer again and hastily thumbed through it. When he had checked twice to make absolutely sure, he sat back and drew a deep breath.

No wonder Tsien hadn't thought of using that picture of Mars as a tool to work on the tripborn.

There wasn't one.

Badly frightened, he got blindly to his feet and walked down the corridor the short distance to the mess. Just as he reached it, Hattus's voice echoed from the public address speakers warning that the relayed views from the missiles were about to be put on the panels.

Instantly, that drove his preoccupation away, and he ran into the mess-hall. It was already half-full of people arriving for the evening meal, but he ignored them and sat alone where he could get a good view of a panel.

The first pictures were blurred and indistinct, but as the operators got the feel of the circuit, and grew more practised at cutting in the one which was currently giving the best reception, they improved rapidly. Even the colour registration was good; Yerring could tell that from so often studying the photographs taken by the survey teams.

Good, thought Yerring, catching sight of one of the gigantic free-floating drifts of algae which kept the air oxygen-high; *if there are many more that size, we won't have to worry about force-breeding our own strains to help out.*

There was an ache in him at seeing the surface of their destination and knowing: *it's only a little way now!* It was like—well, like coming home.

Tripborn came and went around him; the earthborn, their eyes glued to the panels, let their food grow cold untasted, or—if they had to go elsewhere and thus lose sight of the pictures for even an instant—reminded themselves that anything important they missed would be on film with the rest of the records. He scarcely noticed when Tsien dropped into the chair next to him, except to glance and see who it was. It was several minutes later that he turned to face the other and breathe, "Isn't it wonderful?"

But the quizzical look on the psychologist's face cut through the warmth and excitement in him. Abruptly, he sobered.

"Is it bad?" he asked.

"Pretty bad," acknowledged Tsien. "I'd hoped the visual stimulus would touch off the drive we've tried to instil. It hasn't."

"But—you mean you haven't started your programme?"

"No!" Tsien stared. "Who told you we had?"

Yerring explained about Tessa listening to the ship, and Tsien looked relieved. "That's all right," he said. "I was thinking about something which happened this afternoon. To one of my own earthborn staff. He was convinced he was susceptible to the command to leave the ship, and tried to do it through an airlock right now."

The expression on Tsien's face scared Yerring; it was no longer that of his habitual self-assurance and confidence—he looked gravely disturbed.

"I wanted to ask you about something," he said slowly, and told Tsien of the Martian picture episode. When he had finished, the psychologist nodded.

"A consequence of stress release, Franz. All through this trip, we earthborn have been getting wound up like a violin string, tighter and tighter. Now we're being let down, we can expect some pretty funny results. Nothing to worry about, in your case—it was

autohypnosis from your seeing an identity between the conquest
of Mars and the work to be done at Trip's End. Go down to Philippa
before you go to bed and ask her for a sedative, will you?"

Yerring nodded; a comfortable amount of Tsien's assurance
had returned during his last speech, and he felt relieved.

"Well, I've been here long enough—can't keep putting off the
decision," said Tsien abruptly. "Excuse me. I've got to go kick us
off the ship."

Yerring nodded and watched him go. Somehow, he was no
longer so keen to watch the panels, and he finished his meal and
left the mess without reluctance.

The usual evening pastime had been suspended tonight; every
panel in the ship seemed to be glowing with the TV-eye transmission. Restlessly, he wandered through his own section to see the
night shift, passing through hydroponics, biolab, feedmix monitoring, air control, master water room, dietary room—all the space
which formed the lungs, heart and digestive organs of the ship.
The staff were going about their tasks as usual: adjusting controls,
setting up new programming, testing the cultures.

He paused beside a young worker as he took a sample and
studied it, seeming not to notice Yerring next to him. "What's
the incidence of sterility now?" he asked for want of anything
else to say.

The boy turned calm eyes on him. "Going down," he said.

Irritated—by what, he could not tell—Yerring went on, "How
do you think you're going to like working with soil when we land?"

"I won't," said the boy, and replaced the sample in the culture
tube; it mingled with the rest of the semi-liquid mass and joined
the slow flow towards the light-irradiation area. Then he passed
to the next tube and bent to repeat the process.

Baffled, Yerring did not try to stop him; there had been something so final about those two words. And they sounded not only final.

They sounded utterly honest.

Man had made the environment of the ship, and therefore it was as seemed good to him; the environment of a planet, on the other hand, had made man, and perhaps that was deflating to remember.

But we aren't going to fail!

They had planned for this time before the ship had even been half-built, and the procedure went into operation with oiled smoothness. That was one advantage of having everyone a part of a jigsaw, thought Yerring—of specializing. Ship admin: *who goes down when and with what cargo?* Ecology: *what can we use when we get there, what do we take?* Navigation: *at what height do we orbit exactly over the colony?* Psychological: *are we going to—?*

That was a question no one asked in full. There was always the subtle, nagging knowledge at the edge of consciousness: *we are having to force these people into something we gave up our lives for gladly.*

Somehow, it seemed—unworthy.

But the days passed in a flurry of work, until the ship was safely in its orbit, and they were ready to make the first landing.

Yerring walked slowly through the corridors towards a section of the ship he had almost forgotten existed. He had meant—somehow—to find time to get to know this pilot who was going to be remembered by the colonists all through their history. But the days had gone by, and there had been no time. Now, as he scanned the group around the boat lock, he had to think twice before he recognized this tall, black-haired young man with a set face and deep, unsmiling eyes.

Sivachandra and Lola Kathodos were directing final checks of the instruments and engines of the boat; a group of orderlies from Medical, and Tsien and some of his staff, surrounded the tall Felipe. He met Philippa's eye as he approached, and wondered if she was thinking the same thing: that perhaps they should have taken another few years to plan and find a way in which *father* and *mother* might remain more than biologically inevitable terms.

They had been in love, he remembered—but each, to the other, had inescapably been one of many, and now there was hardly more than a flicker of memory to share.

He dropped his eyes and found Tsien approaching, mopping his forehead. The psychologist looked cautiously optimistic.

"Is everything all right?" Yerring demanded.

"As far as we can tell. Medically, Phil says, he's as fit as possible, and we've done all in our power to make the landing easy for him."

There was a call from Sivachandra, who was studying his wrist chronometer. "Felipe!" he said. "Better go in now."

Yerring could stand back no longer; he pushed aside a couple of shipborn medical orderlies and grasped Felipe's hand. "Good luck!" he said with sudden fervency.

And then he turned slowly away, realizing that there was no sense of history in this son of his; he had been told to do a job, and that was all.

Perhaps we should have harped on the wonder of it all, he thought; perhaps we could have brought home to them how marvellous it is that beings spawned of the hot seas of a ball of rock enveloped by gas could have spread across the gap between the stars...

It was too late to think of that now.

And yet—a fierce pride burned in him—we've done it! Whether they realize it or not, we've done something without equal in the universe; we've planned and waited and carried it through until success is in our grasp.

"Let's go up to navigation section," said Tsien softly. "We can watch it all from there."

Yerring suffered himself to follow the psychologist, glancing back only once, to see the door of the little boat closing behind Felipe.

VI

It seemed like an age before the tell-tales on the hull of the boat reported the first whispers of atmosphere. In the navigation section, a tense, excited group faced the banks of screens and the instrument panels which kept them in contact with Felipe. At intervals he told them in a flat, monotonous voice that he was still all right.

Yerring heaved a sigh, and grew conscious that Philippa was standing next to him; in a gesture he was scarcely conscious of, so deep a need did it fulfil, he put an arm around her, and she gave him a quick, wan smile.

The red surface of Trip's End loomed up on the screens; rough-featured mountains gashed by narrow, swift-flowing rivers passed under the boat as it rushed towards the broad flat expanse of ground near the sea which was to be their first settlement.

"I can see the landing-place now," Felipe called at last. There was no hint of strain in his tone, and Yerring gave Tsien an inquiring hopeful look. The psychologist nodded and wiped away a fresh stream of sweat.

The rocket motors cut in to check the boat's progress; it tilted and settled on its tail, finding firm footing. "He's made it," reported

Sivachandra from his post at the instrument panel—and his companions went wild. They shouted congratulations to Felipe and Tsien, shook hands and kissed each other—even taciturn, sober Hattus seized Magda by the arm and tried to make her dance.

They recovered their calmness slowly, and Tsien shouldered his way through them towards the microphone. "How is it where you are, Felipe?"

"As I expected." The voice was still toneless, with a hint of enormous patience in it.

"How's the air?" called Magda, glancing at the repeater dials.

"Good," said Sivachandra. "A full twenty per cent oxygen."

"Well, open the door and go out!" Magda exclaimed.

The screen showing the view inside the boat revealed Felipe silently undoing his harness and getting to his feet. He started towards the door, slowly, as if walking under water.

"High gravity?" said Lola suddenly. "Look how he's moving!"

"Can't be," said Hattus flatly. "The gravity's barely a twentieth higher than aboard ship."

A chill of premonition seemed to go up Yerring's spine as he watched Felipe undoing the door. He wanted to shout, "Stop him! Stop him!"

But before he could utter the words, they could see over Felipe's shoulder the rolling landscape, dying into red hills on the skyline. The sky was not blue, but it was at least not black.

Still with the air of a man in a trance, Felipe stepped over the sill of the door and climbed down the ladder to the ground. A camera in an external housing tracked down with him until he was standing at the foot of the ladder, turning to look round. The tension was beyond bearing.

And then he screamed.

★

For an instant there was absolute stillness in the room, only the echoes of the cry dying into silence. Tsien was staring at the screen as if he did not believe his eyes.

"What's wrong?" demanded Magda, rounding on him. "Look at him!" She gestured; the pilot had fallen to the ground, knees drawn up to his chin, and his face was slack-jawed, staring-eyed.

The question was taken up, each person present trying to find refuge from despair in accusations against Tsien. The psychologist buried his head in his hands.

"What's happened is obvious," he muttered. "We didn't condition him properly."

"But you said you couldn't fail," Philippa insisted, starting forward. Her voice was angrily pleading.

"I thought we couldn't." Tsien dropped his hands. "No human being should have been able to resist our efforts. But somehow—"

Hattus stiffened, and they all turned and looked to see what had startled him.

The tripborn technicians in the room had quietly moved from their posts; now they stood about the officers—not speaking—their faces threatening, their attitude vigilant and alert.

Quentin Hatcher moved out from among them when the silence had stretched to breaking point; his face was peaceful, his manner assured and confident.

"I think now you should be convinced," he said. "You have seen for yourselves what we have known must happen for a long time. I assure you we regret the necessity to take over the ship from you, but you are no longer capable of facing facts."

"Mutiny..." breathed Magda as if she was blaspheming.

"Say rather that the real is supplanting the ideal." He paused as Sivachandra made a move towards him, only to be deterred by a

minute adjustment of position from one of the tripborn near him.
"We do not intend to harm you—in fact, you will be permitted to
go about your sections freely when you have accepted one thing.
There must be no more talk of landing."

"You're mad!" said Hattus huskily. "You're insane!"

Hatcher laughed shortly. "Ask the psychologist," he suggested.

"You knew!" Tsien declared. "You must have known about the
conditioning."

"Yes, we knew. Tessa Lubova watched Yerring putting the drug
into the synthesizers."

"But you ate the food," Yerring broke in. "I know you did,
because I saw you. How did you avoid the effects? What did you
do?"

"Nothing," Hatcher answered, with a lift of one shoulder.
"There was no need. You see, we knew it would not work."

They were breaking down now; Yerring felt Philippa collapse
against his arm, and Sivachandra had begun to sob, dry-eyed;
Magda was biting her nails, seeming not to dare take her gaze
from Hatcher's face.

He spoke in a voice whose steadiness surprised him. "But we
shall have to land, Hatcher. Or we will starve to death."

Hatcher lifted an eyebrow at him. He went on, "Our own
resources will provide food, air and water enough for only two
more weeks in orbit; our numbers are too great."

Hatcher shrugged. "Then we'll bring material up from the
surface. Since you earthborn are so determined to found your
colony, why should you not take our place?"

"That would only postpone the end." Yerring felt a desperate
fear growing in his mind; he had to convince this bland young man
of the truth in his arguments, or they had no chance left at all.
"The boats were designed for shipping cargo down, not up. Once

we start using forty tons of fuel to bring one ton of material up from the planet, we're finished. Ask Tessa," he finished pleadingly. "She'll tell you I'm speaking the truth."

"I didn't know it was that bad." Magda stared at him.

"It wouldn't have been. With our population cut to what it was when we started out, we could have imported enough materials to last us the whole voyage back." Yerring tried not to let the implications in his statements come home to him; he knew he would break down if they did.

"I thought this was a closed system," Lola said, staring.

"It is. Landing on the planet would open it, though."

"Then what are you talking about?" said Hatcher with exaggerated patience. "Didn't you hear what I said? We are not landing!"

Yerring mastered his growing terror and thought of the sharpest way to bring it home. "Then you'll nominate one thousand people to be killed," he said.

There was a pause. Hatcher broke it in quite a different voice. "What did you say?"

"That's better. Start listening with your mind instead of your muscles. This ship is a closed system, but it's overpopulated. You stand there and tie up water, calcium, carbon, oxygen, nitrogen, about eighty or a hundred pounds of valuable organic compounds—*now* do you see what I'm getting at? At half its present population, the ship could in theory continue indefinitely. Right now, we have too much of our resources bound up in our bodies."

He finished flatly, "We stay up here, and starve, or we stay up here and eat each other till the population drops, or we land. Which is it to be?"

We stay up here and go mad, he thought. *At least, I'll go mad if I stay here any longer.*

He paced restlessly up and down the office; there was nowhere else for him to go. All the earthborn had been confined to their quarters, efficiently, without fuss, but without mercy.

Three days' reserves wasted, he thought; he could almost taste the foulness starting to taint the air, feel the slow drain of their last resources—

The door opened, and he whirled to face it. Two stern-faced tripborn stood in the gap.

"Come with us," said the first, and he numbly obeyed.

They led him down the corridors, guessing about his destination. Not ship admin; not navigation—they passed the entrances to those. In the end there was only one possibility left.

They brought him into the psychological section, and a sunken-cheeked Tsien looked wearily up from his desk. The only other persons in the room were Hattus and Quentin Hatcher; the tripborn looked—frightened.

"So you're still sane, Franz," said Hattus with charnel humour, and Yerring stiffened.

"What's been going on?" he demanded. "I've been locked in my room these past three days—"

"George, and you, and I," said Tsien flatly, "are the only three sane earthborn left in the ship. Everyone else has gone into fugue—Magda, Siv, Lola, Phil, every last one."

"But—why?"

Tsien slammed his hand down on his desk. "Because they have been faced with an intolerable decision! They have to plant the colony, and they've been forbidden to, and there's nothing they can do about it!"

"Why can't they accept that it must be so?" Hatcher put in, and Tsien gave him a sour stare.

"That's what I want to find out. Franz, when you received the sealed orders detailing the compulsions we had to instil in the tripborn, how did you feel?"

Yerring remembered clearly. "I felt extra determination to see things through."

Tsien gestured to Hattus, and the admin officer thrust a piece of paper under Yerring's eyes; it was folded so that he could see only one line of it, but that line—

He had to see that the colony succeeded, but the tripborn refused to land. Consequence: failure. If they didn't land, they starved. Consequence: death—

It was suddenly overwhelming, terrifying. He cried out, feeling a weight of black despair loom up in his brain. The prick of the needle in his arm scarcely produced even a reflex withdrawal; his mind was running around a closed system. Closed system—starve—

Slowly, his eyes focused, and he was looking at Tsien's anxious face. "Are you all right?" the psychologist asked. Weakly, Yerring nodded.

"What—?"

"A shot of euphoric. It'll hold you for the time being, until we can cure you. This settles it, you know."

"Am I ill?" Yerring was confused. "What of?"

"A form of contagious madness." Hattus was grim, but seemed to gain melancholy pleasure from the words. "You caught it the same way I did. From Yoseida."

"You thought you volunteered for this trip, didn't you?" said Tsien. "Well, you didn't. None of us did. You reacted when I showed you Yoseida's signature just now, because it was the trigger of an ordinary post-hypnotic compulsion. Every earthborn in the crew had that compulsion."

★

Watching his face, Yerring believed the incredible. So Yoseida, the visionary, the dreamer, turned out to be a megalomaniac who wanted nothing less than a planet as tribute to his mania...

"Why have we three got away so far?" he demanded.

"You, I suspect, because you had a sane reason for demanding a landing," said Tsien. "The others hadn't. You were arguing from a viewpoint of simple self-preservation. George seems to have got away because his concern is shipside; the matter of the colony is incidental to him, and no major worry. And I"—he shrugged—"maybe I subconsciously diagnosed Yoseida's condition, and it led me to suspect the trouble could be put right."

So I gave my life for nothing, Yerring thought. He waited for despair, and oddly it did not come.

"We still"—Hattus broke the silence—"haven't solved anything."

The three earthborn turned slowly to look at Hatcher, who trembled under their gaze. "Yes," said Yerring, remembering. "Do we suffocate, or turn cannibal, or land?"

Hatcher's face wrinkled, and he burst quite unexpectedly into tears.

They sat in amazement and watched him. "Is this the way the greatest feat in history must end?" said Hattus in a hushed voice. "A shipload of catatonics to carry the race of man to the stars?"

"If our inescapable compulsion is hypnotic," Yerring demanded of Tsien, "what's theirs?"

Hatcher got blindly to his feet and ran from the room. "He'll recover without difficulty," Tsien said without sympathy. "They brought Felipe back, you know? By remote control. He got over a shock which would have scarred you or me mentally for life in less than a day. Oh, their compulsion?" He spread his hands. "Lifelong, Franz. Total."

"How long will it take to cure the rest of us?" George asked.

"Days, at least, maybe months. We shall have to dredge through their minds and find out where and when the compulsion was instituted, and then erase it. It'll be a long, slow process."

"Wouldn't it be quicker to cancel it with a new one?"

Tsien gazed at Yerring. "You have a reason for asking that, haven't you, Franz? What is it?"

"Would an earthborn be able to land on the planet?"

"Damn! Franz, you should have been the psychologist instead of me." Tsien's mind was a step ahead of his tongue—the words tumbled over one another. "Convince them the colony is founded?"

"Better. Land them. Land us all—"

"You said that was no answer," objected Hattus.

"But it will be! *If we build another ship.*"

Blank faces greeted his words, and he rushed on. "Look, the tripborn will never land. I've worked all this out in the past few days—how long they could last without the earthborn but the new ship just hit me. Cutting the population by two-fifty would give a margin of perhaps five years, supplemented by material shipped up to orbit. At the end of those five years, they have assembled, in orbit, a new ship—"

"Impossible," said Hattus. "It took ten years to build this one, with all the resources of Earth behind us."

"George, that was thirty-seven years ago," said Yerring soberly. "There has been progress. With the materials on hand—the tools we were going to use to build a modern town for ten thousand, remember!—we can build that ship."

The sincerity in his tone struck through Hattus's apathy, and the admin officer nodded, hope dawning on his face. "And we go back to Earth," he said softly.

Yes, that's one thing the tripborn have lost, Yerring thought. *The looking forward to going home. Because they are home already. Anywhere. Anywhere else.*

"It's a solution," frowned Tsien. "Yes, the earthborn can be cured if they're landed; the tripborn live in space and assemble the ship; when it's over—where do they go?"

"Anywhere."

"But why?" Hattus turned pleading eyes to Yerring. "Why does it have to end like this—in this untidy, empty way?"

"I don't know," said Yerring steadily. *Once there was a sea...* "But I can guess.

"Tsien said that any normal human being would have succumbed to his conditioning to planetside life. The tripborn didn't. And I think the answer is this: they aren't human.

"They didn't need to plan and plot to mutiny against us—they *did* it, by common decision. George, you had your finger on the pulse of the ship; conspiracy could never have escaped you. And you've noticed that they scarcely talk, except to us, but the ship has run smoothly nonetheless. They aren't human any more. They're—crew."

"So this is the end of humanity," said Hattus softly, and Yerring shook his head vigorously.

"Never! George, long ago on Earth the sea was the only habitat of life—as it is today on that world down there. But the sea grew crowded; certain species were forced into the shallows, and sometimes the shallows dried up. So some of the creatures learned to take the sea with them, as we brought the air of Earth in this ship. The blood in your body now is precisely as salty as was that long-ago sea. Of course, for a long time the animals had to come back to the water to breed.

"But—one day—an animal left the water and never came back.

"This isn't the end of man; there are still snakes and birds and dogs on Earth, still amphibians which have to return to the water. We're the amphibians, you and I. For a long time we've had to return to our rock pools, our planetary bases, at frequent intervals. But the ship we build here need never do so. We have found out how to breed now. And after that, there will be a snake, and a bird, and a dog—"

The certainty was growing; he could *feel* it.

"And in the end," said Yerring slowly, "there will be a man."

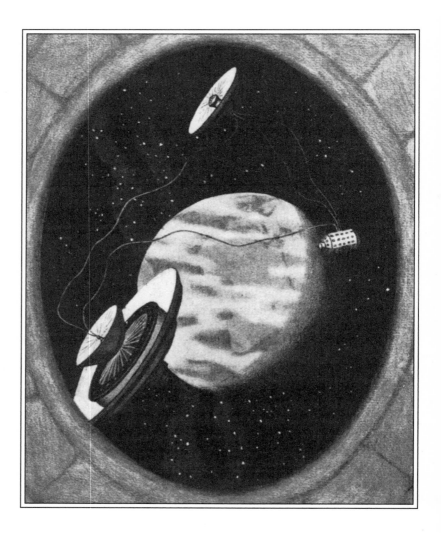

STORY SOURCES

"Lungfish" by John Brunner. First published in *Science Fantasy*, December 1957.

"The Ship Who Sang" by Anne McCaffrey. First published in *The Magazine of Fantasy & Science Fiction*, April 1961.

"The Longest Voyage" by Richard C. Meredith. First published in *Fantastic*, September 1967.

"Survival Ship" by Judith Merril. First published in *Worlds Beyond*, January 1951.

"Ultima Thule" by Eric Frank Russell. First published in *Astounding Science Fiction*, October 1951.

"Umbrella in the Sky" by E. C. Tubb. First published in *Science Fiction Adventures*, January 1961.

"Sail 25" by Jack Vance. First published as "Gateway to Strangeness" in *Amazing Stories*, August 1962.

"O'Mara's Orphan" by James White. First published in *New Worlds SF*, January 1960.

"The Voyage That Lasted 600 Years" by Don Wilcox. First published in *Amazing Stories*, October 1940.

ALSO AVAILABLE

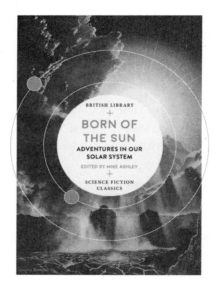

On Mercury: How do you outrun the dawn and its lethal sunrise?
On Jupiter: When humans transfer their minds into the local fauna
to explore the surface, why do they never return?
On Pluto: How long must an astronaut wait for rescue
at the furthest reaches of the system?

We have always been fascinated by the promise of space and the distant lure of our fellow planets orbiting the Sun. In this new collection of classic stories, Mike Ashley takes us on a journey from the harsh extremes of Mercury to the turbulent expanses of Saturn and beyond, exploring as we go the literary history of the planets, the influence of contemporary astronomy on the imagination of writers, and the impact of their storytelling on humanity's perception of these hitherto unreachable worlds.

Featuring the talents of Larry Niven, Robert Silverberg, Clare Winger Harris and more, this collection offers a kaleidoscope of innovative thought and timeless adventures.

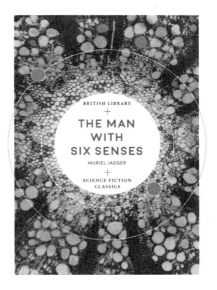

What I know... How can I tell you? You can't see it, or feel it...
You live in a universe with little hard limits... You know nothing...
You can't feel the sunset against the wall outside... or the people moving...
Lines of energy... the ocean of movement... the great waves...
It's all nothing to you.

Extra-sensory perception is a unique gift of nature—or is it an affliction? To Hilda, Michael Bristowe's power to perceive forces beyond the limits of the five basic senses offers the promise of some brighter future for humanity, and yet for the bearer himself—dizzied by the threat of sensory bombardment and social exile—the picture is not so clear.

First published in 1927, Muriel Jaeger's second pioneering foray into science fiction is a sensitive and thought-provoking portrait of the struggle for human connection and relationships tested and transformed under the pressures of supernatural influence.

BRITISH LIBRARY
SCIENCE FICTION CLASSICS

SHORT STORY ANTHOLOGIES
EDITED BY MIKE ASHLEY

Nature's Warnings
Classic Stories of Eco-Science Fiction

Lost Mars
The Golden Age of the Red Planet

Moonrise
The Golden Age of Lunar Adventures

Menace of the Machine
The Rise of AI in Classic Science Fiction

The End of the World
and Other Catastrophes

Menace of the Monster
Classic Tales of Creatures from Beyond

Beyond Time
Classic Tales of Time Unwound

Born of the Sun
Adventures in Our Solar System

Spaceworlds
Stories of Life in the Void

Future Crimes
*Mysteries and Detection through
Time and Space*

○────────○

CLASSIC SCIENCE FICTION NOVELS AND NOVELLAS

By John Brunner

The Society of Time

By William F. Temple

Shoot at the Moon
Four-Sided Triangle

By Ian Macpherson

Wild Harbour

By Charles Eric Maine

The Tide Went Out
The Darkest of Nights

By Muriel Jaeger

The Question Mark
The Man with Six Senses

○────────○

We welcome any suggestions, corrections or feedback you may have, and will aim
to respond to all items addressed to the following:

The Editor (Science Fiction Classics)
British Library Publishing
The British Library
96 Euston Road
London, NW1 2DB

We also welcome enquiries through our Twitter account,
@BL_Publishing